CLAMHUNGER ROW

M. K. Jones

A Case for
Maze Investigations

Book 8

This story is a work of fiction. Names and characters are the product of the author's imagination and any resemblance to actual persons, living or dead, is entirely co-incidental. Where real historical persons, places and events are featured, they appear only as the author imagined them to be.

First paperback edition: 2023
Published by: Mary Kathryn Jones
Cover Picture Mary Evans Picture Library
Cover Design: Alison Morgan at Ali-Cat Design

ISBN: 9781739228477

Category: Historical Thrillers/Private Investigator Mysteries

The Main Characters

The Maze Investigations Team

Maggie Gilbert One of the two founders of the team, she is the owner of Garthwood House, the team's HQ. She is a widow, and mother of two children, Jack and Alice. She is practical, has become an accomplished researcher with a particular interest in brick wall cases. She is the front person for the team.

Zelah Trevear Zelah is the co-founder of Maze, having met Maggie Gilbert during Maggie's first search for her ancestors. They hit it off and set up the Company. Zelah is the widow of Martin Fitzgerald, and internationally renowned artist. Zelah can be difficult with people and therefore keeps in the background. She is the most experienced researcher.

Nick Howell Nick joined in the first investigation and was subsequently invited to join the company. He is quiet and shy, but is a dogged investigator, and especially good at thinking 'outside the box'.

Close Connections

Bob Pugh Bob is Maggie's partner. He is a Detective Chief Inspector in South Wales Police and advises the team on how to proceed when any of their cases bring them close to legal limits.

Rick Matheson	Rick is Zelah's closest friend. He is quiet and appears grumpy, but this is due to his shy personality. He lives in Canada. He and Zelah meet up around four times a year, sometimes in the UK and Ireland, sometimes in Canada.
Stella Bell	Stella is Nick's wife. They met on a case. She is the Manager of Llanyrafon Manor, a beautiful, haunted Tudor former farmhouse, where one of Maze's early cases took place.
Mischa Quinn	Mischa is the daughter of the deceased Kennet Quinn, head of a criminal family, who beat her and deserted her. Zelah took on the role of surrogate mother, and sent Mischa to stay in Ireland, where Zelah has an estate run by her nephews Niall and Stephen McCarthy Miller. Mischa is now engaged to Niall.
Max Howell	Max is Nick's son from a previous marriage. His mother took him away when Max was young. He returned to the UK to find Nick. At first they were enemies but are now reconciled.

Part One

The Great Famine, Ireland: 1845 – 1851

Chapter 1

'This one's for you, Maggie. Another brick wall case, an international one.'

Maggie Gilbert spun around in her office chair so fast she knocked pens, notepad and a – fortunately empty – coffee mug off the table.

'Oops.' She grabbed the items, put them beyond reach, then spun back to Nick Howell. 'My favourite. Tell me the good tidings.'

Since completing their last case and – hopefully – having witnessed the humiliation and removal from their lives of Sir Henry Camberwell, the people trafficker posing as an art expert, life had been quiet. There were always cases coming in but for Maggie, who loved to get stuck into a big fat brick wall problem and hadn't had one for months, this was excellent news.

The three Maze Investigators had each taken time out at the end of the case of the Chinese vase. The encounter with Camberwell, three months earlier, had left each of them with mixed feelings: Nick Howell, furtive and not wanting to discuss the case at all. Zelah Trevear: tired and, for her, emotional. She had taken herself off to her estate in Ireland, to stay with her family for an undefined period. Maggie had unanswered questions about her colleagues' actions and behaviour, but was ignoring them, on the basis that knowing the answers wouldn't make any difference to the outcome and she wouldn't gain anything from that knowledge. The three months had passed, and they each believed they had moved on.

He smiled at her. 'This sounds right up your street.'

'Tell me more.'

'The client is American, from New York. His name is Michael Walker. He retired a year ago and began tracing his family tree, something he says he's always wanted to do. He's been successful on his paternal Walker family. The Walkers were from Yorkshire so, good records. His grandfather was James Walker, but it's his grandmother, James's wife, Mary Donald, with whom he's hit the wall. He had always believed her family came originally from Scotland. Then, he spoke to a relative, an elderly aunt, who told him the family name was originally O'Donald, which became just Donald. She told him that the O'Donalds, or Donalds might, in fact, have originated, not in Scotland but in…' He grinned as his hands made a drumroll on the table.

'Don't tell me. Ireland.'

'Yep. Great-grandparents arrived in New York in the 1890s, and now he's stuck. So, over to you. I'm putting the file on the shared drive. I've entered up as much as I can.'

Maggie spun her chair back around to face her laptop. 'Ireland,' she muttered. 'Let's hope it's a county with decent records.'

Nick had already allocated the case a number, with Maggie as the lead investigator, under the name of Michael Walker, Client.'

She waited a few seconds, viewed it quickly and printed it out, as Nick rolled his eyes.

'What? You know I prefer paper.'

'But it's all in the electronic file.'

'I prefer paper.'

He turned his chair back to his laptop.

As soon as the printer finished churning out half a dozen pages, Maggie picked them up and took them to the kitchen.

So far, it was a brief file. Just the email from Michael Walker, a little about his background, what he had learned about his grandfather Walker's family origins in Yorkshire. More relevant to the case, Michael had included a rough tree of what little he had found out about his family, which he had thought came originally, on his grandmother's side, from Scotland.

His personal details were included. He, Michael, aged sixty-seven and retired from the role of a high-level executive in banking, now lived in Manhattan, New York. He and his wife Jane had four children, all spread around the USA, with two in California, one in Ohio and one in Florida, and six grandchildren. Michael himself had two younger sisters, Deborah and Ellen.

Michael's father was Tim Walker, born in 1932, died in 2001. Tim was the eldest child of three, with a younger brother Henry and a younger sister, Ellen. This must be the aunt who had told Michael about the two versions of the family name. Uncle Henry Walker had died in 1997, but Aunt Ellen Walker was still alive, at eighty-three years old and living close by Michael in New York. Maggie marked her down as someone she could potentially speak to, to see if there was more to be gleaned.

Tim Walker's mother, Michael's grandmother, had been Mary Donald before she married the Yorkshireman James Walker in New York in 1930.

After speaking to his aunt, Michael obtained one of the documents pertaining to his grandparents' marriage: the "State of New York Affidavit for License to Marry". This showed that James Walker was twenty-five when he married Mary Donald, also twenty-five. His stated occupation was "Laborer" and hers was "Servant". They were both born in New York. The document also confirmed the names of their parents and their places of birth. James Walker's father was Henry Walker, born in Whitby, Yorkshire, as was his wife, Anne Sheridan. Mary's father Timothy Donald was born in Ireland and his wife, Mary's mother, was Mary Reilly, also born in Ireland. The emigration from Ireland to the USA must have been in the 1890s, or possibly the early 1900s, as Mary had been born in 1905. There was no indication where Mary sat in the births of Timothy and Mary's children, assuming Mary wasn't the only one, which was unlikely in a

Catholic family of that period. That was something Maggie would have to work on if the client agreed.

Michael noted also that he remembered a little about his grandmother, Mary Donald Walker, who had died when he was in his early twenties.

When he searched for her on the 1930 census he discovered not a Mary, but an Ellen M Walker, married to James Walker, who had declared her parents to be from Ireland, not Scotland, confirming the information on the marriage license. He wasn't entirely sure if this was the right woman, but as James Walker and Mary Donald had only married in 1930, a month or so before the census was taken, he had nothing else to go on. A check of previous census returns, in 1910 and 1900, had not yielded a Mary or an Ellen M Donald or O'Donald.

Maggie's first act was to draw up a more detailed family tree for herself with the information Michael had provided, in which she saw evidence of family naming traditions; first son: father's father; second son: mother's father and so on; something else to explore. At the top of the tree were currently Timothy Donald/O'Donald and Mary Reilly. Michael hadn't provided any information for possible siblings at this generation level, just for his later direct ancestors. Aunt Ellen, from whom he had gained his key piece of information, lived in a retirement home. Her everyday memory was poor but retained memories from the past and growing up, the most important of which was that her own grandmother, whose name she thought was Mary, might have come from Ireland, not from Scotland. This was where Michael had hit his brick wall. At the beginning of his search of Scottish records he had not been able to find any mention of O'Donalds or Donalds with the few names he had to go on; not in emigration, birth, marriage nor death records but which now made sense. As soon as he had seen the marriage license, he turned to Irish records, but again found nothing. It was at this point, after weeks of fruitless searching, that he had turned to Maze for help.

To Maggie, it seemed on the surface a fairly straightforward case with many avenues to explore, but, still, a brick wall – her favourite. She already had four generations – basic information only but a good start. The email asking for help contained nothing further of interest. Michael had mentioned USA census records for both the USA nationally and New York City, from 1900 onwards and described his search both in the UK and on ScotlandsPeople, plus the Irish national genealogical sites.

She walked back into the office, with a coffee for herself and one for Nick. She put his down on the table.

'He probably thinks he's done loads, but it's a small amount. I'm sure we can help. I'll set up a call with him, to make sure he knows what the costs and likely timelines will be.'

'Fair enough. Do you want me to sit in?' She was about to refuse, but something prompted her otherwise.

'Yes, if you wouldn't mind Nick. Something nagging in my gut is saying this could turn out to be interesting.'

'We can't ignore that. What time?'

'There's a five-hour time difference, so I'll send back an email to ask him what he prefers. Do you have any times you can't do tomorrow?'

'No. First thing, Stella and I have a quick meet with the health visitor, but Flora's developing so well it should be quick. So any time after ten-ish for me.'

'I expect it'll be mid-afternoon for us, but I'll let you know.'

Maggie sent the email, to which she received an immediate response. Michael Walker would be delighted to speak to them. He suggested 10am New York time, which would be 3pm for her and Nick. She accepted, set up the call, and sent the details and login to Michael.

'I'll start taking a quick look, see if I can find more dates on some of Mary's or Ellen M's siblings,' she said, wiping sweat from her brow. The weather had been particularly good and today the temperature had climbed again.

'Nothing from the boys yet?' Nick asked. 'They should have arrived by now.'

'I hope they manage to see something. There'll be thousands of people, all waiting.'

'It's spectacular.'

'You've been?'

'Yes. Haven't you?'

'No, not for midsummer sunrise,' Maggie replied, 'but I have been as close as you can get. When I was in school, we had a geography field trip, in the days when Stonehenge wasn't fenced off. We could walk right in, wander around the circles, touch the stones. That was magical.'

Tonight, would be the eve of the summer solstice. Maggie's son Jack and his friend Max Howell, Nick's son, had decided to travel to Salisbury Plain to view the spectacle of sunrise over the 5000-year-old lintelled stone monument, Stonehenge, where, at sunrise on the summer solstice, the sun would rise between two pillars, firing its first rays into the heart of the monument. The weather was co-operating. It was going to be a warm evening and night. This event had been on Maggie's bucket list for as long as she could remember. Her partner, Bob Pugh, had offered to take her there, but somehow, yet again, she had turned down the opportunity. She pondered for a few moments on ageing, and lack of energy and enthusiasm for things that once mattered. The thought of a night with no sleep, surrounded by thousands of excited, chattering people, just didn't appeal.

Nick's phone rang. 'Talk of the devils. It's Max.'

He took the call, listening, smiling and nodding as he turned to Maggie. 'They've arrived. There's thousands of people and they're all having a great time. Jack says hi.'

'Hi, Jack,' she yelled. 'Hope it works out OK. Weather forecast looks good.'

'He says they're not going to sleep tonight, to try to get themselves as close as possible.'

Maggie could hear the excited chatter in the background. Nick ended the call. 'Can you imagine the state they'll be in when they get back tomorrow night?'

'Filthy, exhausted and happy, hopefully. Then, back to work. They only have a couple of months now before they go to University.'

Jack, having taken a gap year, would be starting his degree course in Archaeology in late September at Cardiff University. In early September Max would be off to Birmingham City University School of Health Sciences, to begin a two-year course towards becoming a paramedic.

'When are the AS results out for Alice and friend Matthew?' Nick asked.

'Late August. They'll both be fine. They're predicted 'A's in all of their subjects and goodness knows, they've worked hard enough.'

'Have they decided what they want to go on to do?'

'Matthew is set on medicine. Alice – no idea. She's still thinking about something environmental. She's not interested in medicine. But they want to stay together. I think that's developing into a permanent relationship.'

'Do you mind?' Nick asked.

'Not at all. He's a lovely boy. The only thing is, they're both so young. They've seen nothing of the world,' Maggie mused.

'They have the option to take a gap year, after next year, when their exams are done, or they could just take the four months between the end of school and the start of university to go to work on a project somewhere. There are enough environmental projects and schemes around the world that would welcome a couple of committed volunteers.'

'We'll see. There's plenty of time yet. Have you heard from Zelah?'

Nick grinned. 'No. There's another friendship that might develop into something more permanent.'

Zelah had now travelled on from Ireland to Canada for three weeks to stay with her friend Rick Matheson, in Nova Scotia. She was due back in a couple of days.

'You think that might be?' Maggie said. 'I'm not so sure. They both like their space. Perhaps this time he'll come back with her. He likes it here and he likes her place in Ireland.'

Nick looked at his watch. 'I'm off. It's almost five. Stella wants to go out this evening so I'm looking after Flora.'

'Dad duties,' Maggie said. 'Lucky you have a good baby.'

'I can't believe our luck. She's already sleeping through the night.' He shut down his computer and packed his briefcase, as the front door opened and Maggie's partner, Detective Chief Inspector Bob Pugh walked into the office.

'You're early,' she said.

'The criminal empires of South Wales must be on holiday. Probably on the Costa del Sol, having a lovely time. So I'm getting a quiet life, for the moment. You leaving, Nick?'

'He's on baby duties tonight. Stella's having a night off.'

'Good for her. Are you still working?'

'I was going to,' Maggie replied, 'but now you're home, and the sun's still shining, let's make the most of this weather and have a chilled-out barbeque, just the two of us. Bye Nick,' she called out as the front door slammed.

**

Over dinner in the garden, she told him about her new case.

'Any immediate thoughts?' Bob asked.

'Loads. First, I have to make sure the client's in for the long ride. This case is going to take some time to sort out. Look, the sun's going down over the mountain.'

'Heard from the boys?' Bob asked as the red sun slowly disappeared.

'Yes, Max called Nick earlier and Jack said hello. They're both excited.'

'When are they back?'

'Tomorrow evening. I expect we'll have to pick them up from the station.'

'Yeh. Filthy and exhausted.'

'That's exactly what Nick and I said,' Maggie replied. 'Anyway, I have a call tomorrow afternoon with this new guy in New York. That's what I'll be focussing on tomorrow morning.'

He stroked her face. 'You're looking forward to this one.'

'How well you know me,' she replied. 'It sounds simple enough, but I have a gut feeling …'

Bob chuckled. 'I know what that means. Good luck. I'm working tomorrow, but probably home early again. I'll look forward to hearing what you've found out.'

Chapter 2

When Bob left at eight the following morning – late for him – Maggie was already at her computer. He leaned his head around the office door. 'See you later,' he said, receiving a wave in response. He smiled and left the house.

Maggie had already planned where to start, hoping she could have some information for Michael Walker later. She had emailed him a contract and had let Zelah know about the case. Surprisingly, Zelah was intrigued. She replied at once, asking Maggie to keep her informed and confirmed she and Rick were on their way to Ireland. They would spend a couple of weeks there and were then going to visit the west coast, which was a new part of Ireland for Rick to explore, before they came back to Wales.

Maggie mused for a minute on the unlikely friendship between these two grumpy people. They had met on a case when Zelah had been looking for a family member of a client, in Nova Scotia. The person, who was Nick's DNA cousin, wasn't at home, but her next-door neighbour was Rick. He and Zelah had become firm friends, both grieving the loss of their partner, each socially inept. They had found so much common ground, with shared interests, that they now visited each other at least twice a year and this year would be the longest time they had spent together. Maggie liked Rick, who was quiet and could appear miserable, but she knew that he was shy, a deep thinker who found it difficult to converse with people he knew, never mind strangers. She was glad that he and Zelah had found each other.

Back to the case.

Her immediate thought was that she had to confirm one hundred percent the name of the client's ancestors – either

O'Donald or Donald. If it had been a Scottish name, MacDonald, or McDonald were known varieties, but O'Donald didn't sit as well. Ten minutes research told her she was right. Donald was a Gaelic surname, but it had variants including Donnell and O'Donnell. In the USA, most were O'donald with a lower case "d". Could it have been that one of Mary's parents had been of Scottish origin, although Mary had stated twice, when officially required to do so, that both her parents came from Ireland? Worth checking. She searched on Irish Records and on ScotlandsPeople

but found nothing to confirm any possible Scottish ancestry. Scotland was out.

There was also the anomaly of the name on the 1930 census – Ellen M. Walker. She'd have to explore that, but first, siblings.

She was sure that Mary Donald Walker would have had siblings. She had been born in New York. The client's Aunt Ellen had been certain of that. So, birth records. The most likely places to search were Ancestry, Family Search, and Cyndi's List, which between them had the best collection of records for the USA. However, she couldn't find a Mary O'Donald or a Mary Donald. She did find the death record for Mary under her married name, Walker. She had died in 1975, with her age given as seventy, so Mary had been born in 1905, confirming the information on the marriage license. Yet, there was still no Mary O'Donald/Donald. She widened the search to areas outside New York, using just the surname. Still nothing. What next?

A gut feeling told her to check the marriage license again. She had noted something that didn't seem important at first glance, but worth another check, just in case. And when she looked closely, she found the "something" that had made a fleeting impression the first time round. It was just a mark, but now, looking with a magnifying glass, it could be a letter, which meant Mary might have had another name. Checking the document carefully, comparing it against others on similar pages, she concluded it was a letter, an "E", followed by a dot, in a scripted handwriting. The ink had spread, which was why at first she hadn't recognised it. And, better still, it came before "Mary", and the surname was Donald. Was it possible that Michael's grandmother was E. Mary Donald? What could the "E" stand for? If she were of Irish descent, Maggie's first guess was "Ellen", which would match the name on the 1930 census.

Back in the birth records, she entered Ellen Mary Donald, then O'Donald, in 1905. Nothing. On certain New York online records, some Catholic churches had retained their baptismal records. She tried again. Success! There she was: Ellen Mary Donald, born 16 July 1905, baptised 18 July 1905. Parents: Timothy M Donald and Mary B Donald. There was no maiden name for Mary B, but there was a good chance this was the Mary Reilly named as Mary's mother on the marriage license. Now she could look for the birth of other children to this couple.

This opened up other possible lines of exploration, but Maggie had to contain herself, not go too far. The temptation was exquisite, but Michael Walker hadn't yet signed the contract. She had to wait. It was now ten o'clock. Five hours to go.

**

Jack texted at eleven to say they were just packing up and at the start of their journey home. They had made great friends, most of whom Maggie suspected would fade away within a couple of weeks. They expected to be back at Newport station at five and would someone please give them a lift home? All as expected, and it gave her enough time to hold the call with Michael Walker to find out how far he wanted to proceed.

Bob arrived home at two. 'What, no crime whatsoever?' Maggie asked.

'Too hot,' he replied, rubbing his closely shaved head. 'There was always the paperwork to catch up on, so I came home. What time is your call?'

'Three. I'm ready.'

'I'm guessing you'll have done just a little work, a small starter, something to move him onto the main course?'

'Of course I have. But I haven't gone too far. Just enough to – hopefully – persuade him to let me take it from here.'

'Come on you, let's go have a cup of tea in the garden. I can see you chomping at the bit. We need to have a talk about a holiday this year.'

Nick arrived at two thirty. He joined them in the garden to discuss what Maggie would tell Michael, to give him a taster of what they could accomplish. She decided she would take the risk of telling him about Timothy and Mary Reilly and offer to research their marriage, their arrival in the US and everything else pertaining to them, in both the US and Ireland.

'I did some checking at home this morning,' Nick said. 'There's also a good spread of O'donalds in the US, although mostly in Ohio and Pennsylvania, but it was just a quick check. What would you plan to do next, if he agrees?'

'I can't find the marriage of Ellen Mary's parents in the US, so I thought I'd look at Ireland, but with name variations. Then, there's immigration records under the variable names, and there's the siblings. There's plenty I can do. It will depend on how much he wants from us.'

'You'd better both get going then,' Bob said, looking up from his newspaper.

Maggie and Nick went into the office, opening up the window as the heat had built up to a stifling level, and set up the white screen to make sure they were in a position behind the office table where Michael would have a good view of them. Behind them was a wall of bookshelves and files, split by the long window. To the side, their desks and computers were in view. Zelah had re-organised the room back when they had installed the white board, to ensure clients saw a professional set up,.

At three exactly, Maggie began the call. Michael was ready and waiting.

He was accompanied by his wife Jane, who looked as enthusiastic and excited as Michael. Maggie could see that he was a man of middling size, both in height and girth, with a head of thick grey hair, and dark eyes. He had a wide, eager smile.

After the introductions, Maggie began by asking Michael to tell as much as he could about what he had discovered. It didn't differ much from the written version.

'He's been so frustrated by not being able to find out more about his grandmother and his great-grandparents beyond their names,' Jane said. 'Do you think you'll be able to do anything? It feels like a hopeless case to us.'

Maggie shook her head. 'Far from it, Mr and Mrs Walker.'

'Mike and Jay, please.'

'OK, Mike and Jay. We haven't made a formal arrangement yet, but I did do a small amount of research yesterday afternoon, once we'd agreed to meet and here's what I've found.' She described in detail her discoveries about E. Mary Donald, Mike's grandmother. 'Mike, your grandmother's birth name was Ellen Mary Donald, although she was known in the family as just "Mary". I've verified the records you gave us and discovered your grandmother's actual date of birth.' She then took a deep breath, crossed her fingers beneath the table and added as calmly as she could, 'and, I may have a start on Ellen Mary's parents, Timothy and Mary Reilly. They may have married in Dublin.'

Mike's response was instant. 'No! That's amazing. If you've been able to find that much in a couple of hours, I can't imagine what else you can get to. I'd very much like you to continue.'

Nick raised his eyebrows at Maggie but didn't say anything.

'That's so he can get onto my family,' Jay added. 'They were from a village in Devonshire. I think that search will be the easier one for him.' She gave Mike's arm a squeeze. 'He's becoming quite fanatical.'

Maggie jumped in. 'Yes, I've recently done a huge project based in Devon and the online records are excellent. There are gaps, depending on how far back you go. For instance, they had an amazing collection of wills and inventories, but, disastrously, the building in which they were kept in Exeter was bombed in World War II and they were mostly destroyed, no more than a few fragments remaining. What's the name of the village?'

'It's Uffculme.'

'Wow, well that's amazing. And wonderful for you. That village came under a different ecclesiastical precept, and all of the wills and inventories from the 16th to the 18th century are in a book. What was your family name, Jay?'

'It was Pook, and spelled sometimes with an extra "e", plus a few others, Poke and Pouke,' she replied.

'I'll give you the name and the ISBN. You can get it online. There are a couple of books about Uffculme.'

'That's just wonderful, thank you so much,' Mike beamed.

'You're happy to agree that we explore the potential Irish connection then, Mike?'

'Please go ahead. Everything I've read and heard about Ireland says the records are notoriously tough to find and have significant gaps.'

That's true enough, Maggie thought. 'I'm happy to make a start, in that case. Now, have you read the contract?'

For the next ten minutes they went through the contract, discussed exactly what Mike wanted, which was, if Maze could find his ancestry in Ireland, Maggie should go as far back as possible. He had no issue with the cost, even if it involved a research trip to Ireland.

'That's great, Mike. Should a trip become necessary, I'll let you know the location and the potential cost, and you can decide if you want to cover it. In the meantime, I'll send you a weekly update, and anything of particular interest I find in between, if it's significant.'

'Deal,' he replied.

'Thanks, Mike. Enjoy researching Devon. It's a beautiful County. Maybe you'll decide to take a trip over.'

The call ended and Maggie sat back, punching the air.

'How come you know so much about that village – what was it called?' Nick asked.

'Uffculme. It's a peculiar parish.'

'What's peculiar about it?' Bob had heard the call finish and wandered in.

'Not that kind of peculiar, meaning "odd", like the modern use of the word. In Tudor times, a "peculiar" was a parish out of its local boundaries. Uffculme is in Devon, but belonged to the jurisdiction of Salisbury, not Exeter, like the rest of Devon. Don't ask me why.'

'I wasn't going to,' he replied, shaking his head. 'The stuff you come out with …'

'Well, what I happened to know about peculiar Uffculme has given us the job of finding Mike Walker's Irish connection. Which reminds me, I must send him the details of the books. And I hope he'll send through the signed contract this evening.'

They went back to the garden, Maggie with a notebook to begin writing down what she'd start on.

At five, Bob went to the station to collect Jack and Max who were, as expected; tired and mud splattered, but full of wonder.

Nick waited to hear Max's account of the sunrise over the ancient monument and the Druid ceremony that took place as the sun hit the centre of the monument, then took him back to his flat in Newport.

Before he left with Max, Nick said, 'What was that about Timothy Donald and Mary Reilly marrying in Dublin?'

Maggie blushed. 'I've taken a flier on that one. I found a marriage for Bridget Mary Reilly to Timothy Michael O'Donnell. It was in Dublin, and it was in 1892.'

'But it's the wrong name, Maggie. And that's not what we do. Our reputation is for finding the truth and I know you have good hunches, but if you're wrong…' He shook his head.

'I know,' she replied, baring her teeth in a grimace of a smile. 'But it's a really good hunch. I'm thinking they were amongst those people whose name was changed at immigration on arrival. I'm just praying I can find the record.' She paused and gave him a keen look. 'I just know there's something more to this story, Nick. I can feel it.'

'You'd better be right,' he said. 'Because if you've picked up the wrong people, Zelah is going to eat you alive.'

Maggie had prepared a meal, which Jack just managed to eat before staggering off to bed. 'No doubt to dream about Druids and archaeology,' Maggie said to Bob as the sun went down over the mountain. 'The signed contract has arrived already.'

'You can begin your latest quest tomorrow,' Bob added.

'Can't wait,' she replied. 'Something interesting always comes out of a brick wall case. I can feel it, it's on its way.'

Chapter 3

Knowing she had to work backwards as quickly as possible, Maggie's first act of the morning was to email Mike Walker, to ask if his Aunt Ellen had mentioned any of her own aunts and uncles. She was sure she'd find them, probably on census records, but any information that Ellen might be able to provide about her relatives would be useful. Finding grandmother Ellen Mary's siblings would be her first search.

It took most of the morning to find the first three, two boys and a girl. The eldest was Bridget, born in 1894 in New York, followed by Michael in 1897, then Timothy in 1902. Ellen Mary appeared to be the final child, in 1905. She suspected there might have been another one, between Michael and Timothy, as five years was a long gap for a Catholic couple but found nothing in New York. She also found that the recording of surnames at birth varied between O'Donald – for Bridget and Ellen Mary – and Donald for Michael and Timothy.

She also checked the marriage in Ireland again. It was for a Timothy O'Donnell and a Bridget Mary Reilly, in 1892. She wondered fleetingly why – if this were the right couple, and she was certain it was but would need proof – Timothy hadn't corrected his name at any point. The cases she knew of where the family name was changed at immigration were usually for people for whom English was not their first language and couldn't understand enough to correct the mistake. That wouldn't have been the case for this Irish couple. That could wait. Confirming it was the right couple was her first priority.

Nick arrived at nine.

'How was your evening?' Maggie asked.

'Uneventful,' he replied, yawning. 'But Flora woke up twice in the night. She's teething.'

'Poor thing,' Maggie replied. 'Let's hope it doesn't go too hard for her. Or for you, at your age.'

'Very funny. How's Jack?'

'I doubt we'll see anything of him until lunchtime at least. He practically fell asleep in his dinner last night.'

'Max probably did the same, if he ate at all. They're both working tonight.'

Jack and Max had jobs in a Newport nightclub, tending the bar, so sleeping through the morning was nothing new.

'How's it going?' Nick asked.

'I'm starting on siblings for Ellen Mary Donald. You still on your Australia project?'

'Yes. The family thought their relative, who was Irish, went out around 1848 or 1849, as a voluntary passenger not as a convict but I haven't found anything yet. I'll keep trying. It would have been during the worst years of the Irish famine, so I'm planning to research background this morning. If it's OK with you, I'll take the books into the garden.'

He left her, carrying a precariously balanced pile of books, on many aspects of the famine years, plus his laptop.

Maggie had just joined Nick in the garden for a lunch break when Bob returned and sat with them. 'How's it going? Any progress?'

'Help yourself to a sandwich and coffee. Yes, it's good so far. I've confirmed that Mike's grandmother was baptised Ellen Mary Donald, and her parents definitely came from Ireland, but I don't know when. I've found four siblings for Ellen Mary, but I suspect there's at least one more. I'm wondering if the family moved away from New York for a short time. But I do now know for certain that we're looking at Ireland for the next generation. The four children I've found so far were born in New York, but the parents listed their place of birth on the US census records as Ireland, for themselves and their own parents. I'm also thinking that

Irish naming conventions come into play in the naming of their children. The parents, who'd be Mike's great grandparents, were Timothy and Bridget Mary O'Donald or Donald. It varies from child to child. I also suspect their name changed when they arrived in the US. It became O'Donald but was originally O'Donnell.

'Does it say where in Ireland?' Bob asked.

'No. The later UK census records give a county as well as country for people of Irish origin, but I've not found that in the US records. If I'm right and they are the O'Donnell couple, I'll try again after lunch. What time do you have to be back?'

'I've taken the afternoon off. There's something about the paperwork that made me think about sitting here.'

'Make the most of it,' Maggie said. 'This is Wales. It won't last.'

'No,' he sighed, leaning forward and picking up a sandwich. 'It's probably the eye of the storm. How are you getting on Nick?'

'Quite well, actually. I've found another route to check out.'

Maggie was about to ask but he had put his head back in the book. She had enough of her own to do so left him to it.

A couple of hours later, to her delight, Maggie found another child, or at least she was almost sure this was the same family. The discovery had come from a census record of 1900, in Harrisburg, Pennsylvania. All of the names and dates of birth, ages etc., were the same, except for the name of the mother, which was B. Mary O'Donald. There were three children, Bridget aged 6, Michael aged 3, both born in New York and Timothy, aged 0, born in Harrisburg. For whatever reason, maybe work, Timothy O'Donald had moved his family out of New York. In New York his work had been recorded as a "Laborer". In Harrisburg he was recorded as a "Laborer, Steel Mill". Better prospects? Whatever, it hadn't worked out and they were back in New York by 1905. She noted that the birth of baby Timothy didn't tally with later census returns up to 1930, all of which recorded his birth being in New York, in 1902.

Expecting that they would have been of the Catholic faith and knowing also of the high death rate of young children, Maggie began to search for records of Catholic baptisms in Harrisburg. She found the name of the Catholic church but was disappointed to discover that there were no online records of baptisms. There was an email address for the parish office, so she sent off a message, explaining who she was and asking if the records existed and if so, how could she access them.

To her surprise, an hour later she received a response. It was from an enthusiastic parish clerk, a family history 'nut' as he described himself, who said he had access to the historic records and would be pleased to assist, if he could. Maggie immediately sent him back the details of Timothy O'Donald's birth. An hour later, the clerk, Larry Marino, came back to her with the information. Timothy Michael O'Donald had been born in Harrisburg on 4th June 1900 and baptised on 9th June 1900. He had also discovered that this Tim had died ten days later. Perhaps, Maggie thought, that was why they left Pennsylvania and went back to New York. It also explained the difference in the dates and places of birth of two boys both named Timothy.

There was one particular gem of information – fundamental, a real case changer that would alter the course of her research from hereon in. The names of the parents were written out in detail. The father Tim O'Donald was also written in brackets as O'Donnell. And the mother was Bridget Mary Reilly. This was gold.

It must have been that, when they reached New York and presented themselves to the immigration officer, their family name had been incorrectly recorded. They were indeed O'Donnell, not O'Donald. Now she could look at the available records for passengers arriving from Liverpool and Queenstown, who would have been from Ireland.

She went back out to the garden, where Bob and Nick were engaged in an animated chat.

'I have news,' she said.

'Me too,' Nick replied. 'You go first.'

'I can confirm my suspicion was right, that the O'Donalds were originally the O'Donnells when they first arrived in New York. It changed when they arrived at immigration. It was in the baptismal record of one of their children born in Pennsylvania, a Timothy Michael O'Donald.'

'What does that tell you?' Bob asked.

'Three things,' she replied. 'First, the names "Timothy" and "Michael" might be significant in the family. Second, that the name Timothy was used again, given that Tim, our client's great-uncle, appears in later census records as being born in New York in 1902, explaining the small anomaly of his age and place of birth in the records. I don't know if it matters, but I'll check him out, just in case. And the third thing, the most important, is that Ellen Mary's mother was indeed Bridget Mary Reilly. I presumed the reason the first daughter was named Bridget was because she was named after her mother's mother. That could still be the case, but again I'll check it out. However, it gives me potentially the start of a further generation – another Bridget and a Michael. It will all need checking, of course, it's very tentative, but—'

'Just a minute,' Bob said. 'Going back to the two Timothys, are you saying that, after a child died, they had another one and gave him the same name? That's creepy, isn't it?'

'Not at all. It fits with the family naming conventions and does prove there was significance to the name. It happened often in Ireland. I'll find out.'

'And what about the change of name?' Bob asked. 'Sounds suspicious to me. He understood the language. Why didn't he object and make sure it was right?'

'Something I've already thought of,' Maggie replied. 'Your "copper's nose" has made me more alert to issues like this. Maybe there was something that happened in the family in Ireland that made him decide to leave it as O'Donald. But, I have more immediate searches to do. I will try to find out, though, Mr Policeman.' Bob gave her a sarcastic grin.

'Where will you go next?' Nick asked.

'A couple of places,' Maggie replied. 'Immigration records, first and foremost, for Timothy and Bridget Mary – who must have been known in the family as Mary, which also explains why Aunt Ellen thought her own grandmother was called Mary – to find out where and when they arrived, whether it was Castle Garden or Ellis Island. Then, passenger lists. As it was supposed to have been in the 1890s and given that their first child, Bridget, was born in New York, there's a better chance of their journey having been recorded.'

"'Why?' Bob asked.

'Because before 1855 there was no official immigration. People just turned up, were examined by a health official and if they weren't sick, off they went. Official immigration started with Castle Garden in 1855, then moved to Ellis Island in the 1890s. So once I have a date – if I get one – I can start on Irish records. My guess for now is that they are the couple who married in Dublin as Timothy O'Donnell and Bridget Mary Reilly, which is a huge relief, as I won't have Zelah attempting to decapitate me. That's me for now. What about you, Nick?'

'I've found something of great interest in my search. The ancestor, a girl named Susan Aherne, from Cork, was married in Australia in 1849 to a convict called Sidney Grove, who'd been transported for theft. He'd stolen food and money, not much money, but enough to be transported. As far as the family can tell, Susan was about seventeen or eighteen when she married Sidney. He eventually gained his grant of freedom, and they had four children. She died when she was sixty-five.'

'Why did you find that of great interest, Nick?'

'The family didn't know how Susan had come to be in Sydney in 1849 when she married. There were assisted passages, but the only Aherne family they've been able to find came from Suffolk, and although they had a daughter called Susan, who would have been the right age, she married at 21, not at fifteen.'

'Mistake on the register?' Bob asked.

'I don't think so. The girl who married at twenty-one became Susan Whittaker. She's traced already and ruled out. What I found is the story of the Irish potato famine orphan girls. I'm now wondering if the Susan Aherne I'm looking for was one of them.'

'The who?' Maggie asked.

'It was a scheme, thought up and organised by Earl Grey in 1847. The famine had caused devastation with the failure of the potato crop for the second year running and the Workhouses had filled up, well beyond capacity. Thousands in the Workhouses were young children who'd been orphaned. Australia had a surplus of men many of them former convicts. His idea was to send girls from the Workhouses between the ages of 14 and 18, and therefore of marriageable age, to Australia, to help rebalance the population and to get rid of the girls from the Workhouses.'

'Were they forced to go?' Maggie asked.

'Technically, no. But let's say, the encouragement was great. The historic accounts say many were forced, being "chosen" by the local Workhouse Guardians, who sold a lovely story. It turned out to be not so great when they arrived.'

'How many went under this scheme?'

'Four and a half thousand.'

Maggie was dumbstruck for a moment. 'That's horrendous. I'd like to hear more about this Nick, but for now I must get on with Mike's research. Can we talk again later?'

'Of course. The more I read about the famine in Ireland and the British government's response, the more horrified I become.'

Maggie leaned over and kissed Bob. 'Back to work for me.' As she walked back to the office, her head was filled with pictures of desperate, malnourished young girls – they were girls, not yet women – being shipped off in such a callous way. She wanted to know more.

Chapter 4
Dublin 1849

Ellen had cried until she could barely open her eyes for the soreness of them. She watched Dublin disappear until it was no more than a thin, dark line on the horizon. When it was gone, she turned around and began to look for England. In her heart, she knew she would never see Ireland again.

The Workhouse master had chosen her. Some said she shouldn't have to go, especially with her baby brother not being allowed to travel with her. She had begged, pleaded, cried, and shouted. All in vain. She was of age, and she was going. If she didn't agree she'd be thrown out, left to fend for herself with the "brat". What kind of a choice was that?

The master had hand-picked twenty girls. They were to travel across from Kilrush to Dublin, where they would board a ship that would take them to Liverpool in England. From there another ship would take them to a city called Portsmouth. The final part of the journey would then begin, to Australia, to a place called Melbourne.

Ellen was terrified. Her village had been small, by the sea. They hadn't much, but they caught fish to supplement the potatoes. The thought of a city, even bigger than Dublin, teeming with thousands of people, was monstrous.

There were more than a hundred girls packed onto the ship. She hadn't yet had the courage to speak to any of them, apart from her friends. She thanked God for the company of Margaret and Norrie. They were close to the same age, related as cousins – their mothers were the Corcoran sisters from Kilrush: Johanna, Margaret and Kitty – and had grown up together, had suffered together when the potato crop had failed in '46, lived through the small improvement in '47, then survived the horror of '48 and even worse conditions in

'49. Together they had become living skeletons, no flesh on their bones, hair falling out, sunken, hollow cheeks and caved-in bellies. They had watched the old and the young wither and die, either from pure starvation or from the diseases that rabid hunger allowed in: Typhus, yellow fever, dysentery, diarrhoea.

Margaret, or Peg as she had been known in the family, and Norrie had been in the Workhouse like her, but they, unlike her, were glad to be out. Neither had family. All three had watched their families starve to death. Not one living parent and just one sibling remained between the three of them. And their cabins all gone, demolished by the landlord's agent in one swoop, unexpected, and devastating. They had had no choice but to enter the Workhouse.

Peg Dillon's mother, who had become too weak to stand, had already died from starvation fever. Peg, with the four little ones and her father, who was showing signs of famine fever himself, had taken shelter in a ditch. It had rained that night, and the following day and night.

Peg, the only one capable of walking despite her weakness from hunger, had gone begging for food. She returned after two days with some bread, to find them gone. The two babies had died in the cold overnight. Her father had taken the remaining two little ones to the Workhouse, leaving a message she should join them there. When she arrived, he had died already. Her remaining two siblings, John aged six and Darby aged four, lasted two weeks. They had both developed typhus and had been removed to the room for the sick. She never learned where they were buried. Peg rarely spoke these days. When she was selected, she didn't object. Her condition had improved a little, due to the Indian cornmeal given once a day, but Ellen knew that Peg had begun to cough.

Norrie spoke for all of them. She had improved fastest. Norrie's parents had died, and Ellen had expected Norrie, who was barely able to stand, to follow them soon. Her sisters and her mother had died the day before their cabin had been pulled down. Their father had buried them, but without a box, just a shroud. He had become angry and sullen, cursing the callous English government, calling them murderers. He had not died of hunger, although he was starving. When the notice of eviction came he refused to leave but did so when the Agent threatened violence on his family, which now only consisted of Norrie, her father and her grandfather. Norrie's grandfather, who lived with them and was already at death's door, was unable to stand. He lay curled up in a corner of the cabin. As the soldiers stood by and watched, the Agent's thugs dragged him out and beat him to death before pulling down their cabin. The families all stood in motionless horror, knowing what would happen if they tried to intervene.

Norrie left later that day, telling her father she was going to look for work. By the time she came back with two shillings, three days later, her father had also left to look for work. She never saw him again.

Ellen hadn't expected to see Norrie again either and was amazed when she stumbled into the Workhouse, looking stronger in body, but with vacant eyes. She hadn't objected when she was chosen for Australia. Since they had left Clare, Norrie had spent much of her time muttering about what she'd like to do to the agent who had organised the destruction of her home and the death of her family, especially the murder of her helpless aged, already dying grandfather.

Norrie Madigan wanted revenge for the death and horrors of Clamhunger Row.

Chapter 5

When Nick arrived the following morning at nine, Maggie was well into work.

She had sent off a report to Mike Walker about the breakthrough in her research: the discovery of the siblings of his grandmother, Mary Ellen Donald, the subsequent discovery of the name of his family originally being O'Donnell, which she would confirm later once she had checked ship and immigration records, and her focus now moving to Ireland.

'He won't read it for a few hours yet,' she explained to Nick. 'I've also asked him if he's willing to submit a DNA kit, to see if he can find any closer relatives. He has a great-aunt Bridget, and two great-uncles, Michael and Tim, his great-grandmother's brothers and sister. They'll all be dead now, but assuming they married and had children, he should have some of their descendants come up on a list of DNA cousins.'

'That'll take about four to six weeks,' Nick replied. 'Why haven't you tried finding them in family trees? If their descendants have put their trees on Ancestry or one of the other sites, you may find something out about their shared ancestry with Mike.'

'It's on my list for this morning,' she replied. 'But for now, I want to concentrate on the direct line, which is what the client asked for. If I can't find anything about Tim and Bridget Reilly O'Donnell, that will be my next move. I have a feeling I'll get through this quickly enough. How about you?'

Nick spun around, and Maggie was surprised to see that he looked glum. 'No progress?'

'The opposite. Too much information. I read again at home, last night, and I've ordered a couple more books to come here this morning. Plus, somewhere around midnight, I found a list of the girls who went to Australia under the Earl Grey scheme. There was a Susan Aherne on it.'

'Oh. The right one this time?'

'I think so.'

'Unusual for you to feel emotional about a case, Nick.'

'Like I said yesterday, the more I read, the more disgusted I become.' He shook his head. 'I'm going to try to trace the story of this Susan Aherne and what happened to her after she arrived in Australia. The list I found gives the names of the girls: their status, orphaned, abandoned, or whatever, and which ship they sailed with its port and date of arrival.' He paused again and licked his lips. 'Some of the early ones were found to be pregnant on arrival. They were viewed as fair game by the sailors.' He closed his eyes.

'Did Earl Grey ever admit it was a mistake?'

'Not that I can find, yet. But after two years the newly arriving girls weren't well received by the Australians. They called them "Workhouse sweepings". A lot of them ended up in prostitution. Others were made servants, treated more as slaves, and some were forced into marriage to convicts.'

Neither of them spoke for a moment, contemplating the fate of girls who set off with so much sorrow behind them and so much hope for the future.

Nick went on, 'And as a million people were starving to death, in their own homes, or on roadsides and in ditches, or in the dreadful Workhouses, the British Government continued to allow the export of food being produced on their own Irish land that was denied to the Irish people.'

'Did any of the girls do well out of the scheme, Nick?'

'Yes. Some did. They found work as servants to decent people, or on farms. They married good men and lived out long lives. But they were the minority.'

'I hope your Susan Aherne turns out to be one of the lucky ones.'

'If the one I've found is the right one, then she was. The family in Dublin has done a DNA test, to see who might turn up in Australia. It will only be a small amount of DNA, after six or seven generations, but you never know.'

'Back to work for me. I'm starting with Irish marriage records.'

Half an hour later, she said, 'I have a result. There were three marriages of a Timothy M O'Donnell: one in Cork and two in Dublin. The Cork marriage and one of the Dublin marriages, in the early 1890s, were to a Mary. The third, in Dublin, was the one I think is the correct one, of a Timothy O'Donnell to a Bridget Mary Reilly. Both were "of full age", which doesn't help establish their dates of birth, but the record does give the name of Timothy's father, which was Michael, who was a "Labourer". It fits with the B. Mary O'Donald. And in terms of the naming conventions, her mother may also have been called Bridget.'

'The first daughter of the marriage, the one born in New York in 1894, was also called Bridget?' Nick asked, not turning around.

"Yep. So next, Michael O'Donnell and Bridget something. That's another one I'll have to check up on.'

'When would they have married?'

'That would depend on Timothy's age and, like I said, the record only says, "of full age", but if I start with an assumption that he was somewhere between twenty and twenty-five and would therefore have been born somewhere between 1867 and 1872, then his father Michael, making the same assumption, would have been born between 1842 to 1849.'

'Right in the middle of the famine years,' Nick replied.

Maggie paused. 'That would mean he survived the famine as a child. Maybe that's the feeling I have in my gut about this case. My unconscious brain somehow made that calculation.'

'That's quite a stretch,' Nick said with a grin. 'Unconscious it may be, but right from the beginning? Really?'

'Well, perhaps not right from the beginning,' Maggie conceded. 'But you know I had a gut feeling.'

'No need to be defensive, your gut is rarely incorrect in its assumptions,' Nick said.

'Hmm. Anyway, back to solid ground. The marriage of Tim O'Donnell and Bridget Reilly was in 1892. They must have emigrated soon afterwards, because the first child, Bridget, was born in New York in January 1894.'

'Pins the date down for you in emigration records.'

Maggie didn't reply, but turned back to her search, muttering to herself. She needed an approximate date of birth for Timothy O'Donnell. Back in the family tree, she checked his death. He had died in 1942, at the age of seventy. So, he would have been born around 1872 allowing a couple of years either side, as people often weren't sure about their year of birth and rounded up or down to the closest decade or five years. At least this birth was after the introduction of civil registration in Ireland in 1865. Mentally crossing her fingers, she entered the name Timothy O'Donnell in the Irish national database of births, with a range of 2 years around 1872, and parents called Michael and Bridget. Only one record appeared. It was for 1872, in May of that year. The parents were Michael O'Donnell and Bridget Cusack. Michael was a farm labourer.

'Got it, first time, too. Another generation confirmed, Nick. With a bit of luck, I can find the parents' marriage after 1865. Fingers crossed, again.'

She went back to the national database of marriages, and again found it immediately. Michael O'Donnell had married Bridget Cusack in Dublin in 1869. And his father's name was also Michael. This time, an age was given for both parties. Michael O'Donnell was twenty-four, Bridget Cusack nineteen. So Michael had been born in 1845 or 1846, the two years of the serious rise of the famine. Maggie felt a lump in her stomach. She wanted to know more about this man. She began to look in Dublin for other children born to the couple.

She began with national records, then checked these against church records, for baptisms. The first were twins, Michael Cornelius and Ellen Anne, born in 1870, six months after the marriage. Not unusual. Then came Timothy Michael, the direct ancestor born in 1872, followed by Bridget in 1878 and finally Mary in 1880. Each record was confirmed by a baptism, all with parents listed as Michael O'Donnell and Bridget Cusack.

Another hour of searching for Michael O'Donnell, born 1845 or 1846, yielded nothing in Dublin. Yet this was a man who had survived the famine as a small child. She speculated on how this could be. He could not have survived alone. Someone must have cared for him. She had read of how families left their homes, ragged and penniless, heading for somewhere to find work, shelter and, maybe, food. Dublin had been such a magnet. Therefore, perhaps his origins were not in the capital city. She widened the search out to the whole country and was flooded with results. After another hour she stopped in frustration. There was nothing that gave her any clue as to which Michael O'Donnell he might be. She knew that his father's name was Michael and had made a few guesses at his mother's name, based on naming conventions. The twins would have been named after his father and his wife's mother, which meant that she should have been Ellen. Another website for a possible concentration of names gave her nothing useful. O'Donnells were spread across the province of Munster, mostly in the centre and some on the west coast. Over a thousand of them.

What about Michael's wife, Bridget Cusack, who was nineteen when they married in Dublin? She would have been born around 1850. But at least, from the names of her children, Maggie worked out that Bridget's parents would have probably been Timothy and Ellen.

She couldn't find a marriage, but did find a birth, just one, Bridget Cusack born to Timothy Cusack and Ellen Fitzpatrick, baptised on 4th December 1849. But not in Dublin. This Bridget had been born in County Clare, in the south, in the village of Cappa, in the Kilrush Union. Her baptismal sponsors were Michael and Mary O'Donnell. She felt the rush of excitement that always came when she knew she was onto something.

For whatever reason, Bridget Cusack had moved from Clare to Dublin. With or without family, she wasn't sure, yet. She was certain that in Dublin she had met and married Michael O'Donnell. Was it possible that he was also from Clare? Changing her focus to births in County Clare she began to search the church records again.

An hour later, when Nick joined her, Maggie was sitting back with her hands behind her head.

'No luck?' he asked.

On the contrary, my friend, on the contrary. I've found another generation, two possibly, I think. Michael O'Donnell's wife, Bridget Cusack was from County Clare, not Dublin. Her parents were Timothy and Ellen Cusack. They also came from Cappa or at least at some point from a small hamlet that must have been close by, although I can't find it on a map. It's called Moy. Michael O'Donnell was named after his father also a Michael. His parents were Michael O'Donnell – explains why the name keeps appearing throughout the generations – with a wife called Mary Ellen Corcoran. I've found six children. They're: Ellen born in 1834 – mother's mother; Daniel born in 1836 – father's father; Timothy born in 1841 – mother's father; Johanna also born in 1841 – more twins, must run in the family, and named after father's mother and her mother, – Mary born in 1843 – named probably for her mother's eldest sister; and, finally Michael O'Donnell, baptised in November 1846 – named for his father. Classic naming conventions.'

'Are you certain it's the right family? I mean, I know you are, but I always like to check.'

'Of course, we should evaluate this rigorously. There's a lot riding on it.'

'OK. What makes you so certain?'

'For now, places of birth and baptismal sponsors. Of the six children, four have an O'Donnell as one of their sponsors, and two have Joseph and Ellen Corcoran, who were either Mary Ellen Corcoran's parents, or Joseph was her brother. Then, there are the named places. Four places of baptism are Kilrush, the details of the eldest, Ellen and the youngest, Michael, say Moy and give the name of the actual road or street. It was called Clamhunger Row,'

Chapter 6
Liverpool 1849

If Dublin had been a shock to the village girls, Liverpool was how Father Jerome had described a vision of hell in his fiery Sunday sermons. The size, the roughness, the smells, the fighting everywhere. The three clung together as the ship docked, watching the sailors and portside workers arguing and shoving each other around as the carters loaded the cargo of other ships and ran with their carts towards the warehouses further along the quayside. Even the girls who had struck up friendships with the onboard mariners – some going a little too far, in Ellen's opinion – were silent.

'You can stretch your legs on the quayside,' one of the mates said, 'but don't be thinking about moving further away. There's a steamer on its way to take you to Portsmouth, but it won't arrive until tomorrow. You'll eat on board tonight, then onto the steamer first thing in the morning.' His speech was rough, but his eyes kind. 'Good luck to you all.'

Norrie stepped forward. 'When will you be returning to Dublin, sor?'

He spat on the ground. 'Tomorrow, after you lot's gone.'

She put her head down and whispered to Ellen and Peg. 'I have something to tell you. Come with me.'

She led them down the gangplank and they walked amongst the carters and carriers, Norrie pushing her way through until they reached the end of the quay where no ships were tied up and no-one to overhear.

There was an old broken wooden spar from some long since abandoned ship, next to the quay wall. They were close to the Mersey itself now, with no ship to shield them from the biting wind that reddened their cheeks and caused Peg's cough to worsen.

'Here, wrap this around your head and shoulders,' Ellen said to Peg, taking off the tattered shawl that had belonged to her mother; the only thing she had left of any of her family. Peg tried to refuse, but Norrie grabbed the shawl and tied it firmly. She gave Ellen a quick look, shook her head and bit her lip. They both knew the signs. Peg should never have been chosen for this journey. Yet, what would have happened to her if she had stayed in the Workhouse? At least with them, for as long as she lasted, she would live with friends, and die with friends.

'Why are we here, Norrie? I'd rather be on the ship. At least it's a bit warmer.'

'I'm not coming.'

Ellen gave her friend a questioning look. 'What do you mean, Norrie?'

'I mean I'm going no further. I'm not staying in this terrible place, either. I'm back to Dublin, tomorrow.'

'I don't understand. Why? What's for you there? Norrie don't do this. We need you, Peg and me.' She had leaned forward as she spoke and taken Norrie's hands in hers. Norrie pulled away and stood up.

'I don't want a new life. I want my own life, decided on by me, not that swine of a Workhouse master.'

'Norrie,' Peg whispered. 'Such language.'

'And I want to use whatever language I choose. You two will do fine without me. I have plans. I have a little money. Once I'm back in Dublin, I'll find something to do, some work to get more. I'm going back to Cappa and Moy.'

'But why, Norrie? You've no family; our homes are gone. What will you do there?'

Norrie Madigan turned her back, muttering something that the wind snatched away.

Ellen stood, moved around to face her. 'What are you going to do in Kilrush, Norrie? That's where you're really headed, isn't it?'

'Best you don't know, Ellen O'Donnell.'

Ellen put an arm around Norrie's waist. 'What if you're caught?'

'I won't be.'

'I'd beg you not to, to come with us, take our chances together in this Melbourne place. But I know you better.'

Norrie turned around and hugged her friend. 'You do. Now, I'll need your help, both of you, because I need you to tell lies for me.'

Once, Ellen would have been horrified at the prospect. Lies would take you straight to Hell, Father Jerome always said. But hadn't he also said that what was happening in Ireland was all part of God's plan for his people? *Well*, Ellen thought, *God makes bad plans as well as good ones.*

Norrie was speaking again. 'Each of us can read and write. I'll find a way to keep in touch with you, somehow.'

'Norrie, please let me know about Michael. I fear he'll die in the Workhouse.' *If he's not already in heaven*, she thought.

'Write to me, care of Father Jerome, as soon as you get there,' Norrie said. 'Give me where you are, and I'll write back.'

As they reached the ship the sailors were already loading cargo to take back to Dublin. They walked through the usual shrill cacophony of whistles, gestures and unsubtle comments about what the sailors would like to do to them – none of which Ellen understood – held their heads high and went down to their sleeping mattresses.

**

In the early hours of the morning, Norrie watched in delight as three of the girls crept from their mattress, making their way up through the ship onto the quayside. Two didn't get far. The sailor on watch saw them as they reached the end of the quay and yelled out a call. Other men came running and within ten minutes two had returned, weeping. They couldn't catch the third one, who disappeared off into the night.

Good luck to her, Ellen thought. She turned over, and saw that Norrie wasn't on her mattress. It had been stuffed with rags and bits of wool, the best they could do to make the shape look human.

The men who returned the two weeping girls took a quick look around, saw one empty mattress and left.

The call came in the morning at six. It was still dark. The Captain was in no mood for banter and the men were silent.

'Collect your boxes. Your steamer is here. You'll be going on to Portsmouth.'

'But, sir, we haven't had no breakfast yet.'

'You'll get none on here. I want you all off my ship.'

The girls hurried, Ellen and Peg praying that no-one would notice they were two short of their original group. One man had noticed. He sidled up to Ellen as they stood shivering on the quayside.

'Where is she, the fine looking one with the black hair?' It was the mate, who had spoken kindly before.

'She went off in the night, with the others. They'd planned to try their luck in Liverpool, find a bit of work, like,' Ellen stammered, not able to look him in the eye.

He paused, then said, 'I don't believe you.'

''Tis the honest truth, so. I wouldn't lie to you, honest I wouldn't. Liars go straight to hell.'

She looked so earnest that he hesitated.

'Off you go then,' he said.

'Yes, sir, thankyou sir,' she replied. 'You've been kind to us. Not like some of the others.'

He said nothing.

'Have you a family back in Dublin, sir?'

'I have.'

'You'll be pleased to be seeing them again later, then.'

'Indeed I will. What's your name, girl? How old are you?'

'Ellen O'Donnell, sir. I'm fourteen years old.'

'You learn to take care of yourself, Ellen O'Donnell.' He lowered his voice. 'You know that friend of yours, the one that coughs, won't last long.'

Ellen bowed her head as the group walked off.

'Ellen?'

'Yes sir?'

'I don't know why she wants to get back to Dublin. It's as bad there as anywhere else, but I expect she has her reasons. I'll make certain she gets ashore.'

Ellen bit her lips together, then smiled at him. 'Thank you, sir.'

'I hope I won't regret it,' he muttered as the group of girls walked along the quayside to the steamer that lay waiting for them. He turned back to the ship and barked an order at the men to make ready to sail.

**

The steamer was a bigger vessel than the ship in which they had made the initial crossing, yet it took three days to reach Portsmouth. A heavy gale blew up in the Channel and the steamer had to put into the port of Charlestown for twelve hours. Despite the rain, Ellen went up on deck and looked around at the pretty little Cornish village surrounding the harbour. She thought that if she hadn't Peg to take care of, she might herself consider running away here. The more she thought about Australia, the more her trepidation increased.

She knew Peg was dying. She wasn't even sure her friend would reach their destination. Peg's destination was heaven. A woman on the quayside smiled up at her and Ellen smiled back. Could she do it?

'Ellen, what are you doing up here? You'll catch your death of cold.' Peg stood in the doorway to the lower part of the ship. Her face was white, both from the storm and the disease. The previous day she had coughed up a little blood for the first time. The remains of her once shiny blonde hair had dulled. She held out her hand.

Ellen took one last look at the woman on the quayside, then turned back to Peg. 'Just coming. I needed a breath of air. The stink down there was too much for me.'

Peg took Ellen's hand.

Two hours later the storm had blown itself sufficiently quiet for the steamer to continue its journey.

Twenty-four hours later, they arrived in Portsmouth, another huge, noisy, angry port. This time they were greeted kindly by a group of ladies, who said they would be staying overnight in a hostel and given a decent meal, before leaving on the "SS Pemberton" the following day. That was some comfort, at least.

They left Portsmouth the following morning on the rising tide, sailing out into an ocean, on a voyage that would last ninety days.

Ellen, who had become used to the rolling motion of the sea, leaned on the rail on the edge of the ship. She put her hands together and prayed; that Michael was still alive, and that Norrie Madigan had made it back to Dublin, from her hiding place behind the cargo stowed at the bottom of the "Mary Jane".

Norrie hadn't told Ellen her plan. But she knew Norrie was intent on revenge, on the man who had stood and smiled as the inhabitants of Clamhunger Row watched, mute with horror, their homes being destroyed, Norrie's grandfather killed when he refused to leave.

One thing of which she was certain – Norrie Madigan would get that revenge. Ellen's final prayer before she went down below was that the name "Clamhunger Row" would remain on the lips of the British for a long time.

Chapter 7

'You look disappointed,' Nick said with a sideways glance at Maggie.

'Not disappointed, exactly.' she replied, looking up from her screen and the software she was using to complete Mike Walker's family tree. 'I thought I felt something special about this one. Take a look.' She put the tree up onto the white screen that filled the top half of the wall opposite the window. Nick spent a minute taking a look.

'There's a lot more you can do.'

'Not in terms of finding direct origins,' she replied. 'The birth of Daniel O'Donnell around 1780 and his wife Johanna Barrett – those dates of birth are speculative on my part, based on the date of their marriage and the only child I can find, Michael, in 1804 – I think that's pretty good. I can't get beyond that. No records.'

'You've found similar on the other side, with Michael O'Donnell's wife, Johanna Corcoran and her parents. You can show they kept strictly to the naming conventions which carry on well into the next century in the United States.' He paused for a few seconds, staring at the screen. 'There is something up there that intrigues me.'

'Tell me,' Maggie said urgently. 'I've found Mike's one confirmed direct ancestor, the Michael O'Donnell born in 1846.'

'He was the youngest of six children, right?'

'Yes.'

'And he was born as the famine worsened, yet he survived.'

'Again, yes.'

'And all of these births were in the hamlet of Cappa, which is in the Kilrush Union.'

'Yes, for the third time; well, almost. Clamhunger Row was in Moy, about half a mile further on from Cappa. What's your point, Nick?'

'From what I've been reading, the Kilrush Union had one of the worst reputations in Ireland for its Workhouse. And one of the highest death rates from famine related diseases. Some of the highest death rates overall were in Clare. So, what happened to the rest of the family? Don't you want to know? Given the history of the famine in Clare, don't you think Mike might want to know what happened to that family? You've a good history up there, but little context. When you put all of the baptismal and birth information together, you know that the family lived in Clamhunger Row, Cappa, Moy in the Kilrush Union in County Clare. Don't you think there's more to find out about them?'

Maggie sat with her arms folded, staring at the history. 'OK, you have a point. I'll email this chart off to Mike today, with some notes about the Kilrush Union, which I hope you can let me have, pretty please, Nick?' She paused for a moment, then asked, "So what was Kilrush Union particular famous, or notorious for?'

'Apart from the shocking management of the Workhouse, it was the clearances.'

'Go on.'

'One of the most notorious was the agent of a landlord, name of Seamus McMahon. The landlord was…' He paused, frowning as he drummed his fingers on the desk. 'I can't remember the name now but not an absentee, like many of the British aristocracy owning land in Ireland. He was a local landowner. Like many of them, he felt he was suffering because the devastation of the potato crop year after year meant that his tenants, which most of them were, couldn't pay their rent. So, the landowner – Vandeleur, that's it – ordered McMahon to remove them from their homes and destroy those homes. These were mostly one room cabins for the poorest of the poor, some had a second floor, but even so, once the potato crop failed again, they had nothing.

These were the destitute and starving. McMahon gave them no more than one day's notice in many cases. He just turned up with a company of soldiers and a band of his own thugs, specifically employed for this one purpose, and ordered the residents out of their cabins with whatever they could carry, and had the soldiers raze the homes to the ground. Even the sick and dying, children and the elderly were dragged out if they couldn't walk.'

'That's absolutely shocking. What happened to those people?'

'Many had no choice but to go to the Workhouse which was already overcrowded. If they had a contagious disease, where better to spread it than in a crowded environment with little sanitation and poor food?'

'I have to add this information to my email to Mike. I might also suggest a trip to Clare for a couple of days. He may want me to follow up over there.'

'I wouldn't be surprised,' Nick said, turning back to his laptop.

'Nick, once I've sent the email, can I borrow some of those books you've been reading?'

'Thought you'd never ask,' he said. 'They belong to Maze, anyway. I put them in the bookcase.' He nodded in the direction of the latest bookcase that had been squeezed into the office.

'We're going to run out of space in here soon,' he said.

'I've been thinking about that for some time now. We need a discussion about it with Zelah. It may be time to find Maze a new office.'

**

The email sent, with Nick's succinct notes about the probable situation of the O'Donnell family during the famine, Maggie took three books and a coffee out onto the patio and began to read.

At eleven Nick joined her.

'I see what you mean,' she said. 'I knew about the famine, of course, but I've never read any of this in detail.'

'What are you reading?'

'These books vary between personal accounts and stories and essays, and more academic accounts of the levels of disease and suffering around the country. The latter are actually worse, quantifying the difference between actual starvation and the effects of starvation that killed people. A million dead of famine and its effects and a million emigrating, plus more leaving after the potato infestation was over, because they just couldn't recover back to where they had been.'

'Almost ten percent of the population of the US claims Irish descent, that's over thirty million people.'

'No wonder St Patrick's Day is such a big event. I never understood, 'til now.' Maggie replied. 'Another lovely day,' she sighed. Her phone rang and when she saw who was calling her face broke out in a wide grin.

'Zelah!' she said. 'How are you? Where are you? Just a minute, I'll put you on speaker. We're in the garden. That's me and Nick.'

'We're back,' Zelah replied. 'Back in Caerleon, that is. Are you two up for lunch?'

'Of course,' Maggie replied. 'Will you and Rick come over here or shall we meet somewhere?'

'I can't think of a better place than your garden,' Zelah said. 'Rick wants to see it, especially the roses.'

'He'll see them at their best. What time?'

'How about one-ish? I'll bring food.'

'Excellent. We're both looking forward to seeing you and Rick.'

**

'You both look remarkably well and healthy,' Maggie said as she kissed Rick, hugged Zelah, who didn't struggle to get away, and led them through the kitchen to the deck where plates, etc., had been laid out ready.

'We are, thanks. We got back last night. Where shall I put these?' Rick asked, balancing two trays of sandwiches and another of salads.

'In the centre of the table,' Maggie replied. 'Hot or cold drinks?' They all ordered cold.

When they were settled, Maggie asked, 'What are your plans? Are you off to Ireland?'

'Yes, we're going to visit the boys and Mischa for a couple of days, then we're off to the West Coast. We're going to start in Galway, then make our way down through Clare over the course of a week or so, then across to Cork for a few days in the city, then back to Rosscarbery.'

'I want to see a village called Lahinch,' Rick said. 'I believe my wife had an ancestor from thereabouts.'

'My latest case has ended up in Clare,' Maggie said to Zelah, 'but in the south of the County, in a hamlet called Moy, not far from Kilrush and Cappa.'

'It sounded interesting. What progress have you made?'

'In terms of a line of descent, I've gone as far as the records go, back to around 1780 which, as you know, is pretty remarkable for Ireland. Nick has suggested I start to look at the social history of the family. He told me about the famine in that area, which I've been reading about this morning. It was grim.'

'What does the client want?' Zelah asked.

'I've given him the direct history, and also told him about the effect of the famine on the area. His direct ancestor for whom I have dates, a Michael O'Donnell, was married in 1833 and had six children, one of whom I know survived. I'm not sure about the rest of the family. I'm waiting to see how he responds. I've also suggested he does a DNA kit, see what comes up. He probably has a lot of relatives in the US that he knows nothing about.'

'Maybe he'll find he has some in Ireland, too.'

'That's possible. His next direct ancestor in the line of descent, named Michael O'Donnell, after his father, was the youngest of the six children, born in 1846. If any others of them survived, there'll be a few, I suspect, although they may also have travelled to America.'

'Or Australia,' Zelah replied.

'Or Canada,' Nick put in.

'That would be the story of Grosse Isle,' Rick said. 'The Coffin ships. That's one helluva bad story.' He stopped and shook his head. 'My dad's ancestors survived; Theirs wasn't a coffin ship. They came from England and got treated better than the Irish. The first coffin ships headed for Quebec. The journey was three thousand miles, about three months at sea. When they arrived in the Saint Lawrence, they were supposed to be inspected for disease, and sick passengers taken to quarantine on Grosse Isle, downriver from the city.' He paused to take a sandwich but didn't eat.

'My father told me the story. In 1847, too many ships arriving too fast overwhelmed the medical inspection house. They say there was a line of vessels two miles down the St. Lawrence. It took five days for any passenger to see a doctor and the doctors started to get ill from typhus being brought in by the passengers. Soon, there were miles more ships, so a fifteen-day quarantine got imposed for all passengers, the sick and the healthy. Lots of healthy Irish picked up typhus as they waited and died on board. The authorities didn't know what to do with the bodies, so they dumped them overboard into the river. Some of the healthy ones also got thrown off and had to crawl onto shore, if they could, and walk to the city. Can't imagine what it must have been like.'

'I read about that this morning,' Maggie replied. 'I agree with you, Rick. A dreadful stain on Canada's history. Your ancestors were lucky to survive.' She waited a moment as he stared off into space. Zelah put a hand on his back, gently rubbing it.

'Carry on,' he said, in a low, soft voice. 'Don't mind me.'

'When are you off to Ireland?' Maggie asked.

'First thing tomorrow. I'm just here to catch up on work stuff. Anything else you need to tell me?' Zelah asked.

'Not really,' Nick replied. 'We have five other cases, all of which are well in hand, although there is one other matter we should discuss.'

'Which is?'

'We're running out of space, Zelah. We need a bigger office. Maggie and I were talking about it this morning. We think the time has come to find a new place, as much as we all love working here.'

'Or, what about an extension?' Zelah said, 'to the side of the house. It's a blank wall. The house isn't listed is it, Maggie?'

'No. I hadn't thought about that. It would mean a lot of work and expense—'

'Let me worry about that,' Zelah interrupted. 'How about we talk it over? I don't know about you two, but I like it here. It's a good working atmosphere and it comes with a kitchen and a garden. However, it's your home Maggie. You're decision.'

'I'll think on it. Right now, I can't think of any objection, except for how we'd work whilst it's going on, and of course we'd need proper plans, and a builder.'

'You're not against the idea, then?' Zelah said, with a grin.

Maggie smiled back. 'I've always loved the convenience,' she said. 'I'll talk to Bob about it tonight.'

**

'No, I don't have any objections,' Bob replied later that evening. 'But I do have a suggestion. How about you make it a double storey, not for an extra bedroom, we don't need one, but with a connecting staircase, so you can make an upstairs kind of… library? And somewhere for your files, plus an extra desk. Since you put in the new bookcase and had to remove a desk, I've been surprised you and Nick haven't been bashing each other's elbows whenever you're both at your computers.'

'I like the sound of that,' Maggie said. 'I'll give Zelah a call in the morning. They're leaving about eleven. I suspect she already has an architect lined up, and probably a builder. But Bob, it will take about six weeks, or longer, to do. It'll be very disruptive.'

'I have an idea about that, too.'

'I see a gleam in your eye. Tell me.'

'What I'm thinking is, you don't need it immediately, so how about, when it's being done, we take a long holiday, say, September and October, once the boys and Alice are settled.'

'Someone would have to oversee the work.'

'Nick and Zelah,' he said firmly. 'You deserve a good break.'

'Where were you thinking?'

'Australia and New Zealand.'

Maggie sat up in her chair. 'Wow. I'll have to get this case cleared up well before then. Don't tell me – you've got an idea about that, too.'

He grinned. 'I was thinking, Zelah and Rick are going over to the west coast of Ireland. Why don't you join them? You said your case is based in Clare. Why don't you go investigate for yourself. You never know what you might find. The Client knew you might need to go. You can discuss dates for the building work with Zelah.'

'Actually, I did send him an email after Zelah and Rick left. I sort of suggested a few days in Clare.'

'You're blushing.'

As he spoke, Maggie's phone beeped an incoming email. 'It's from Mike. I'll see what he says.' She skimmed through the email. 'He says yes, go to Ireland. He's amazed I've managed to find out so much so quickly. He can barely take it all in. He'd like a Zoom meeting tomorrow at nine, that'll be about two tomorrow afternoon for me.'

'Sounds like a slam dunk to me.'

'I'll think out some plans for what I do when I'm there. There'll be plenty. Cheers.' They clinked glasses in which Bob had made cocktails, as the sun set over the mountain and a shadow slowly crept up the garden.

Chapter 8

A long call with Zelah as she and Rick were driving down to Fishguard elicited two results. Zelah was onboard with the idea of a double height extension and a second room above the old dining room that had served for six years as their office.

'Brilliant idea,' she said. 'I'll organise an architect to come around to look and report asap. If you like, we could even have a separate entrance.'

'No,' Maggie replied. 'I like the business being part of the house. It's past events in the house that led us to form Maze.'

'Fine. It's your house.'

'Also, Zelah, I'll probably be joining you in Clare. Mike Walker is on board. He's blown away by what I've done so far, but for me, it's just names on a page. I've proposed I find out more about what happened to his direct ancestor, Michael O'Donnell, by going to Clare and examining localities and off-line resources.'

'Good,' Zelah said. 'You thought there was more to this story. Go and find it. Let me know where and when we'll meet up. Have to go now, we're just about to check in.'

**

Maggie was ready at two for the call with Mike Walker, Nick sitting beside her. When he came online, he didn't stop talking for almost five minutes, enthusing dramatically about what Maggie had discovered, at times wringing his hands.

For the tenth time he asked, 'How did you do it?'

'It's a question of knowing how and where to look,' Maggie replied, smiling patiently when he finally ran out of breath. 'Irish records aren't easy, but we were lucky with this case, your case. But, as I said in the email, I think there's more to be discovered about Michael. I don't know yet who else from the family survived. He was just a baby, so someone must have taken care of him.' She drew a breath, then said, 'Mike, I'm so pleased you agreed I go over to Ireland for a couple of days, to Clare. My plan would be to start in Ennis, the biggest town in Clare, which has a good library and a family research centre, then head down to Kilrush, Cappa and Moy, to see what I can find there. It would take about three or four days. Are you OK with that?'

'Absolutely,' he replied. 'I feel a strong connection now, to Michael O'Donnell and his family – my family – and I'd like to know more about his early life. Jay and I have started reading about the famine. We're so shocked and horrified, especially now I know my ancestor was right at the heart of it, so to speak. When will you go?'

'Some time in the next week. I'll let you know the dates and how I get on. Did you send off your DNA kit?'

'Sure did. We both did. I probably shouldn't say this, but I have a friend at one of the labs. He's going to expedite our results.'

'It's good to know the right people. Do let me know when you get the result. You'll probably find a huge number of cousins, both in the US and in Ireland. It may be helpful to let me know any Irish ones, if you get the results before I leave.'

'I should have it in a couple of days, my friend says.'

'That is quick. OK, I'll get on with my planning. I'll keep in touch. Thank you, Mike.'

'No, thank you Maggie. You know, this is all pretty emotional.'

'That's not unusual,' she replied. 'We'll never know them, but they are part of us.'

The call ended and Maggie turned to Nick. She had already told him about the building plans, of which he'd enthusiastically approved.

'I won't be able to go for at least a week. Zelah and Rick are spending a few days at Rosscarbery House before they go on to Clare, and she has to arrange for the architect to come here. I want to be here to take him or her around and explain what exactly we want, and need. In the meantime, I'll flesh out Mike's family tree, find as many as I can of the ancestors' dates of marriage, births of children and death dates, plus any extras like the baptismal sponsors for Ireland. That'll keep me busy. And I'll also find out as much as I can about County Clare. Nick, do you know where I might find details of the inmates of Irish Workhouses?'

'What kind of details?'

'Names of inmates?'

'If you're talking about Clare, then I'd suggest you contact the Ennis Library. They have an extensive set of records for the county. I believe many records have gone to Dublin, to the national library, but for Clare, I'd try the Ennis library.'

She looked it up online, saw that there were records, and sent an email asking for which years they had collections.

**

The reply came the following day. The library held a few records for most of 1849 and part of 1848, with a few from 1847. The most extensive information was for deaths in the Workhouse, but for 1850 onwards. She had been hoping for more but wasn't unrealistic. If Mike's family had gone late into the Workhouse, they might still have been there in 1850. Unlikely but not completely hopeless. Maggie emailed back to say that she would like to view the records and would confirm a date.

She also asked if they had old maps of Clare, with details of the village of Cappa and the hamlet of Moy. The answer once again was yes but dating only from 1850. The reply also said that the list of deaths in the Workhouse was already online. She checked immediately but found no O'Donnells. This was hopeful. Perhaps one of them had survived. She'd wait until she visited the library and the family research centre.

'That's enough for me,' Maggie said to Nick. 'As soon as the architect's been here tomorrow, I'll leave on Monday morning.'

Zelah had been quick off the mark.

When the architect arrived, he spent an hour with Maggie, confirming that he saw no reason why the extension couldn't be built. It would require the usual planning consent, building regulations, etc. He took in all of her suggestions and added a spiral staircase in the corner of the new room to reach the upper floor, plus a door through from the current office, which could return to being a dining room or a second lounge. He promised to have the initial plans ready a week or so later and would hold an informal discussion with the Council Building Department to make sure they had no initial objection.

In the meantime, Maggie had completed the wider family tree for Michael Walker, including all of his relatives she had found so far from the time the family arrived in New York, up to the 1930s.

'But I'm having trouble with the Irish family,' she said to Nick on the Friday morning. 'I'm going to check the Workhouse records for the Kilrush Union – the library has some names from '47 to '49. The current map of the Kilrush area doesn't have a Clamhunger Row. I found one map online for 1900 and it isn't on there, either. Hopefully I'll have better luck in the library in Ennis.'

'Maybe it was cleared and never rebuilt, or if it was rebuilt, given a new name,' Nick said. 'Like I told you, Kilrush was notorious for its clearances. Most of the families had to go to the Workhouse.'

'But if Michael O'Donnell was in the Workhouse, someone had to have taken him to Dublin.'

'Maybe he took himself to Dublin, when he was older.'

'Hmmm. I'll be looking to find out. What I have found online at Ennis Library is a book of the Guardians of the Poor for the Kilrush Workhouse in 1849. It was built to accommodate eight hundred, but by 1849 it had fifteen hundred inmates.'

'Many Workhouses were horribly overcrowded,' Nick replied, 'an indication of desperation in the face of starvation. The problem was that in 1849 they didn't understand the transmission of disease, so thousands who entered a Workhouse disease free, ended up dying from the infections and diseases brought in.'

Maggie shook her head. 'I can't begin to understand it,' she said in a quiet voice. 'I still have a lot of questions; I hope I can find some answers in Ireland.'

**

As she was packing on Sunday night, an email arrived from Mike Walker. *I have my DNA results. Some parts puzzling. Do you have time for a quick call or is it too late?*

No, it's fine. I'll set it up now and send you the link. 15 mins.

As soon as they were on the call, Maggie could see that Mike was puzzled.

'Some of it not what you expected, Mike?'

'Exactly. I have very little in Ireland, although my ethnicity says forty percent Irish. The rest is mostly English and Northern European. I guess that'll be from my Grandfather Walker's family.'

'Sounds about right,' Maggie replied, 'given that your family was one hundred percent Irish when your grandmother married your Yorkshire grandad. You dad would have inherited 50% English and European from him and 50% pure Irish from your grandmother.'

'Then why do I have a very small amount from Australia?'

'What do you call a small amount?'

'A tenth of one percent.'

'Mike, I'm not a DNA expert. I'm surprised that Australia comes into it, as all non-native Australians have a mostly European or Asian background. But, it means that somewhere back along your line, someone went to Australia, married a native Australian there and had children. Have you checked your relatives list? Are there any in Australia?'

'Yes, there's one and the amount of DNA is 8 centimorgans.'

'Only just enough to get on the list,' Maggie replied. 'How about you try to contact the individual, see what they have to say?'

'Already done. I'll let you know what they say.'

'If they respond,' Maggie said. 'You'd be surprised how many don't.'

'Really? Then why do the test?'

'No idea Mike, but a lot of people just want to know their ethnicity, not what distant cousins they might have. Anyway, I'm off to Ireland first thing tomorrow. I'll be in Ennis by tomorrow night, then in the library on Tuesday. I'll let you know what I find. In the meantime, I guess you have a lot of "cousins" in the US?'

He laughed. 'Hundreds. I'm looking forward to seeing who will get in touch.'

'If you find anyone with information about Ireland, do let me know. It may complete a part of the puzzle we haven't found out, yet.'

'Will do Maggie. Have a good trip.'

As she finished packing, Maggie hoped he'd find something useful. The Australian connection puzzled her, too. It had to mean native Australian. She'd need to check with someone who knew more about DNA. Nick was bound to have a contact. It was already nearly midnight. She was setting off at eight the following morning. Time to grab some sleep. She told Bob what she'd found out.

'Sorry I can't come with you,' he said.

'Me too. Who knows what I'll find out. You wanted a holiday, I know, a longer one but perhaps we could fit in a short break? Maybe one of the US connections will tell Mike something we might be interested in finding out more about. I've never been to New York.'

Chapter 9
Port Philip and Melbourne 1850

Ellen had to hold Peg up as they disembarked the ship. After ninety-one days at sea, her body had become accustomed to moving to adjust to the tossing of the ship. On dry land, she swayed, as did all the girls.

Some were chattering, faces gleaming with excitement about what they believed awaited them.

'Ellen had talked to some of the girls from Kilrush Workhouse.

'I'm real excited,' one had said. 'They say there's lots of work here, and they need us. I'm a hard worker. I hope to find a man to marry, too. One day.' The girl sighed. 'Can't be worse than Ireland, can it. I have no family there now.'

'I had a brother left,' Ellen said. 'I had to leave him in the Workhouse. I begged for him to come with me, but they said no. I'm not so sure this is a good thing.'

The girl shook her head and walked away. Ellen didn't think about what was coming. She concentrated only on Peg, who was wilting in the intense heat, the likes of which none of the girls had experienced. Her friend was no more than a shadow and, Ellen knew, near death. She was terrified of their being separated, but knew it was inevitable. She herself had survived the journey well enough, and had kept away from the sailors, unlike some of the other, more brazen girls whose bellies were beginning to swell.

Ellen could see a reception committee of five or six people waiting for them on the quayside. One was a Catholic priest, whom Ellen was both pleased and relieved to see. He was the only one smiling.

One woman looked particularly forbidding. Despite the intense heat she was dressed head to foot in black, her pig-like, scowling face poking out of a tight bonnet.

'More Irish Workhouse sweepings,' she said in a voice loud enough for all around, including the girls, to hear. 'Line up in pairs. Now!'

Ellen was outraged. She was no "sweeping". She and Peg both came from good families, but she said nothing. No point provoking this woman before they'd hardly left the ship. Once they were on the quayside they stopped and the party moved closer to inspect them, walking up and down the line.

'What's the matter with you, girl?' The pig-faced woman had stopped in front of Peg.

'She suffered from sickness during the sea voyage, missus,' Ellen replied. 'She'll be fine once she's settled on dry land, she'll improve fast, you'll see.'

'Speak when you're spoken to,' the woman snapped. She was about to say more, when the priest approached. 'These poor mites have been at sea for over three months, Mrs Donaghue. Let's get them to their housing and give them a little time to recover.'

The woman scowled again but moved off. Ellen gave an audible sigh of relief.

'You do know, this girl is not sick from the sea,' the priest said quietly to Ellen, who nodded.

'She was ill before we left Ireland, Father. They just wanted rid of her from the Workhouse.'

The priest shook his head. 'She's not long for this world. Let's see how we can make her more comfortable. Once we reach the accommodation, I'll have her transferred to the hospital.'

Ellen couldn't help the tears that stung her eyes.

'Thank you, Father. I'd like to be with her, at the end.'

'Of course, my dear. What's your name and how old are you?'

'I'm Ellen O'Donnell and I'm fifteen. All my family is gone, except maybe my baby brother. They wouldn't let me bring him. What's your name, Father?'

He laughed. 'I'm Father Gerard McCarthy and I'm fifty years old. Come on, we're moving off.'

The accommodation proved to be a warehouse, with straw pallets. Ellen was uncomfortable, but at least the floor didn't move. Before the girls were allowed to sleep, a man in a frock coat appeared and explained that they would be in the accommodation place for around a week.

'We'll find suitable work for you, but first we must observe your habits. We want girls who aren't afraid of hard work, who are of a good Christian nature, clean and respectable.'

An exhausted Ellen slept on a pallet with Peg. During the night, ten of the girls disappeared. In the morning no-one seemed concerned. Ellen picked up from overheard conversations that this was not unusual. There were always girls who thought they could do better for themselves than be apprenticed out as servants. The members of The Board of Guardians – the reception committee – would neither look for nor miss them.

Father McCarthy was as good as his word. Later in the day he arrived to transport Peg to a local hospital in Melbourne. This involved an argument with members of the Board, but the priest was adamant. The girl was going to die, and she should be allowed to do so with dignity. He also demanded that her friend Ellen be allowed to accompany him. 'Peg Dillon will die in the next few days. Her ailment is what is known in the mother country as phthisis. There is no cure.'

'Is it contagious?' one of the board members asked.

'No,' the priest replied. 'Just fatal.'

**

Peg died four days later, with Ellen holding one hand and Father McCarthy the other. Ellen shed no tears. 'She's better off now,' she said as they stood by the common grave where Peg would be buried. 'She never wanted to come here.'

'Did you?'

'No,' Ellen replied. 'It wasn't a choice. They may tell you it was, but not for us. One day, we were given a box containing a petticoat, bloomers and stockings, a dress and material, and a Bible. We were told to put on the dress, then we were marched out of the Workhouse.'

'It was supposed to be a choice,' the priest said.

Ellen shrugged, as she looked down at Peg's coffin. 'Who was going to stand up for us? We'd been thrown out of our cabins, which the agent's men destroyed. We all three lived close, on Clamhunger Row, next to the sea. At least we were together.'

'Three? There was another girl? What happened to her?'

'When we reached Liverpool, Norrie – that was her name, Honora Madigan – decided she wasn't coming. She was going to find a way to get back to Ireland. I fear what she had in mind.'

'What do you mean, Ellen?'

'Her grandfather was murdered by the agent's thugs when he refused to leave their cabin. Norrie went off to try to find food for her father and herself, her father had become ill, you see. She was away three days. When she came back, her father had gone to look for work. She never saw him again. He wasn't strong, so he probably died on the works.'

'What were the works, Ellen?'

'Oh, it was some kind of scheme set up by the English to build roads. The roads didn't go anywhere, but the men and women were paid a few pennies. They had to dig and carry rocks. Some just fell down dead. Maybe that's what happened to Norrie's father. She wasn't the same after she came back. She had some money, but she never said where she went or how she got it. She wants revenge. She never said so exactly but I believe she was intending to find a way back to Clare, to our village, and kill the man who did it. His name is Seamus McMahon.'

Ellen hadn't looked up from the coffin. 'And I think she'll succeed.'

Chapter 10

Maggie left early the following morning and was in Fishguard in good time for the ferry. Her trepidation of seafaring settled a little when the captain announced that it should be a calm crossing, but even so, she decided to spend the first hour on deck, watching Wales disappear.

At least the drive across Ireland wouldn't be too long. She expected to be in Ennis by early evening and eventually arrived at her hotel at 7pm, after an uneventful drive. The weather was good, too, a cloudless sky and no sign of rain. After calling Bob to let him know she had arrived, she ate and went to bed early.

The following morning, a little before nine she left the hotel and was at the door of the Ennis library ready for when it opened, which she discovered wasn't for another half an hour. Looking around, she saw a café open across the road and decided to go sit there and check her plan, to decide on priorities.

The first of these was to review the information available about the inmates of the Kilrush Workhouse. Then, she was due to speak to the family history specialist resident at the research centre to see if there was any further information that could help trace more about Mike Walker's Irish family. She was expecting that this would take up most of the day. Zelah and Rick were arriving during the evening, and they had agreed to dine together before she set off for Kilrush in the morning.

The library was a small building, with the research centre in dedicated rooms at its side, around a five-minute walk from the centre of the town.

At nine thirty the doors opened. The librarian on duty was the person with whom she had corresponded; a short, round, middle-aged man with a balding head and a welcoming smile.

'Good morning! You must be Maggie from Wales. I've taken a preliminary look for you, based on the information in your email,' he said.

'Thanks, Kevin. Did you find anything helpful?'

'I've a few books for you to look through. I've also called my colleague down in Kilrush. They have material there written by people who lived in the area during the famine. She'll be expecting you tomorrow.'

'That's brilliant. Thank you so much.'

'We do the best we can and you're very welcome. But I would warn you, finding names for the '45 to '50 period isn't easy. Too many died unrecorded.'

'I think that might be the case for the client I'm trying to help. As you know, I have the name of the one fully traceable ancestor, his parents, plus his siblings. In 1846 they ranged in age from eleven to a newborn.'

Kevin paused for a moment. 'Was the eleven-year-old a boy or a girl?'

'A girl, called Ellen.'

'Who would have been around fourteen by 1849, yes?'

Maggie nodded.

'Have you checked the register of the girls sent to Australia under the Earl Grey scheme? Do you know about that?'

'Yes, I do know, but I haven't checked.' She slapped her hand on her forehead and grimaced. 'I should have done. One of my colleagues is looking into a similar case right now. And my client told me two days ago that his DNA has a 'cousin' in Australia, with whom he has 8 centimorgans in common.'

'Come with me.'

He led Maggie through to another room with a row of computers on desks standing against the wall, indicated to her to sit beside him, fired up the computer, and went straight to the site, the same one that Nick had told her about.

'Right then, O'Donnell, wasn't it?'

She nodded. He entered the search criteria.

'Yes! Here's an Ellen O'Donnell age fourteen. From Kilrush, Clare. Sailed on the Pemberton in December 1849. Went to Port Philip then to Melbourne. It describes her as an orphan, parents Michael and Johanna, both dead. So the parents died before 1849. Let's see how many others went from Kilrush Workhouse on that same ship.'

He returned to the search criteria. The site brought up a list of twenty names. He stared at them for a moment, then sat back and whistled. Maggie felt a thrill of excitement. 'What?' she said, leaning forward. 'What have you found?'

He turned slowly to her. 'There were twenty girls from Clare sailed in 1849 on the Pemberton, two of them from Moy, which is down near Kilrush and Cappa. Ellen O'Donnell, Margaret Dillon and…' he paused again and swallowed. 'Honora Madigan.'

'You know that name?' Maggie asked, 'that last name, Honora Madigan.'

'Indeed, I do. She's a heroin, or a villain, according to what you think about the famine.'

'What did she do?'

He sat back in the computer chair and folded his arms. 'She set off from Dublin to Liverpool but went no farther. She was due to go to Melbourne, according to the ship's manifest, but instead, she found her way back to Kilrush and three months later, she killed a man, an agent, name of Seamus McMahon. She did it because he was the person responsible for evicting all the people from a hamlet called Moy, not far from Kilrush, pulled down their cabins and his thugs actually beat one man to death. The name of the street where it happened is well known, it's called—'

'Clamhunger Row,' Maggie said. 'I knew there was more to this story.'

**

Kevin had allowed her to take the books he had given her, outside, as the day was warming up and the research room becoming stifling, even at ten thirty in the morning.

'I'll sit on the bench out there and read,' she said. 'I promise I won't run off with your books.'

He grinned at her. 'You don't look the type, but you never know. Off you go then. I'll bring you a cup of tea.'

'Lovely, thanks.'

'And maybe you'll need something stronger. There's heavy stuff to take in. Those books aren't anything you'll find on Amazon or wherever. They're locally produced.'

'I'll take very good care,' Maggie replied. 'And yes please to the tea.'

Outside in the warm sunshine, she sat on a bench next to a small table and began to read the first of the three small books, more like pamphlets really, that Kevin had given her. She had chosen at random. This first one was around a hundred and thirty pages long and had been written in 1900. It was a young girl's account of her grandmother's experiences in Ennis during the famine and the following years. Most of the family had managed to survive. They hadn't been offered the fare to emigrate to the USA or Canada – a scheme the landowners hit on to get the poorest off their land – and being exceptionally poor had had to survive alone. The grandmother's father had found work on one of the Government schemes, which had just about kept them alive for a short period. But not all of them. Out of nine children, just three had survived, plus their father. They had had the ignominy of having to go to the Workhouse in 1849, and the grandmother, who was just fourteen at the time, had been separated from her father and two brothers. Such was the rule of the Workhouse – the immediate separation of families. Fortunately, after a year, as the potato crop improved, the father had removed himself and his children – all four miraculously having also avoided disease in the horribly overcrowded conditions – and had been able to return to their home and find work. But the years following the famine had been hard in County Clare. One of the brothers, Stephen, had eventually sailed off to America and had kept in touch for a while. He had gone to Philadelphia, found somewhere to live amongst the thousands of Irish emigrants, and had found work. For a while, he sent money home to help his father and told of the many Clare people he had found. He married and had a girlnever heard from him again. She never found out why. At the time of writing her account, the girl's grandmother had died, but not without telling her story to her granddaughter. The book ended there, and Maggie was on fire to find out what had happened to the granddaughter, whose name was Mary O'Connor.

Kevin arrived with the tea. 'Sorry it's taken a while. I had a couple of phone calls to deal with. How are you getting on?' he asked.

'I've read this one. It's left me fired up to find out what happened to Mary O'Connor.'

'Her family still lives in Ennis,' he said, sitting down next to her and wiping sweat from his head. 'It's a fine day we have today.'

'Do you know if they found out what happened to their grandmother's brother, Stephen O'Connor?'

'Yes. He died, in a construction accident. But not before having a couple of kids of his own. They hooked up with the family through DNA and some of the American O'Connors came to Ennis last summer.' He stopped and laughed. 'It was quite a party.'

Maggie smiled too, then her face became solemn again. 'I've read about conditions in the Workhouses. They sound like somewhere to be avoided at all costs.'

'They were,' Kevin replied, closing his eyes. 'They were all horribly overcrowded. Take Kilrush. Built for eight hundred, but at the height of the famine housed fifteen hundred. So many of those were sick when they went in, too, and having to live in such close proximity to others, disease spread like a wildfire, consuming everyone too weak already to withstand them. Same all over Ireland.' He stopped and shook his head, nodding at the remaining two books. 'Enjoy, or probably not,' he said. 'I'd better get back inside. We have a group of children arriving in ten minutes. My favourite.'

Maggie sat until after lunch time, reading the remaining two books, which were also personal experiences handed down by surviving family members.

As she read on and the sun warmed further, she felt the drowsiness that comes with mid-afternoon, accompanied by the buzzing of bees and the occasional bleat of a sheep in the fields nearby.

'I thought you might need another cuppa.' A soft voice and a gentle squeeze of her arm brought Maggie back to life. Kevin had brought out another cup of tea.

She nodded her head and thanked him. 'How's it going with the children?'

'They left an hour ago.'

Glancing at her watch, she saw it was past three in the afternoon. 'Did I fall asleep?'

'You did. I left you for a while. Here's your tea. You've missed lunch.'

'Oops,' she replied,' grinning at him. 'Never mind, I can make up for it at dinner.'

'Where are you staying Maggie?'

'Tonight, at the Royal Hotel, then on down to Kilrush tomorrow.'

He bit his lip, and his hand shook a little as he handed her the tea. 'Do you have plans?'

'Yes,' she replied. 'My colleague is staying here tonight. She and her Canadian friend are making their way down this afternoon, and we're eating together tonight. She's the senior investigator in our company. She has a place over in Cork, but her friend wanted to see the west coast. He's also interested in this particular genealogy story, so they're both coming with me to Kilrush tomorrow and we're going to fit in a visit to the Cliffs of Moher. Can't miss that out.'

She knew she was prattling on, but hoped she was letting him down gently.

'I see. Well,' he said as he stood, 'I have enough work to be going on with. I'm sure you'll all have a lovely time. Clare's a great place. Just pop those books back in to me when you're finished.'

'I will, Kevin and thank you. These books have been a great asset.'

'Don't forget to ask my colleague down in Kilrush about Honora Madigan,' he said over his shoulder as he went back into the building.

Having finished reading and taken sufficient notes, she returned the books, wished Kevin a fond farewell and more thanks for his help, which he brushed away with, 'you're very welcome, Maggie. I hope your research goes well.'

Before returning to the hotel, she checked one final issue with Kevin, if there might be an archive of local newspapers that went back as far as 1849. If they did, there was bound to be something about the story of Honora Madigan.

**

'No, very little,' she reported to Zelah and Rick as they reached the coffee stage after dinner that evening. 'I thought it might be a headline story, but there was just a paragraph or two. It seems there had been another murder of an agent, a man called Major Denis Mahon – no relation – so the death in Kilrush came a poor second. The report said that Seamus McMahon's death was believed to be the work of the Molly Maguires, or the Young Irelanders.'

'Who were they?' Rick asked.

Zelah replied. 'The latter was an organisation called Young Ireland, run out of Dublin. It was a group of young men and women who believed Ireland should be a separate country from the UK. They were the first to openly agitate for a republic, but by persuasion rather than force. They were generally political but there were some hotheads – not amongst the leaders – who would have been up for taking down one of the hated agents of the absentee landlords.

'The Molly Maguires was more of a secret society, nothing political about them. Angry agitators were the Molly Maguires. They were violent and threatening, they attacked and assassinated land agents, the middlemen, when prices were too high, or when the landlords were evicting tenants for non-payment of rent. They had a set of rules, but some went out of the window during the famine.'

Maggie asked, 'When Honora Madigan returned to Dublin, might she have got herself involved with one of these groups?'

'The Young Irelanders had their own newspaper,' Zelah replied. '*The Nation*. They wanted an Irish independent republic. No compromises. They tried for a rebellion in 1848, but it failed, and the leaders were sentenced to death by hanging. Queen Victoria agreed to commute their sentences to transportation. Only one got off. The Young Irelanders was the forerunners of The Fenians.'

'I don't suppose they kept records,' Rick said. 'So how would you find out more about this girl, Honora Madigan? Do you need to, though? I mean, it's not like she's the family you're here to look for.'

'No, Rick, she's not,' Maggie agreed. 'Yet, I have a feeling—'

'And when she has one of those, stand well back,' Zelah interrupted. 'Seriously, Maggie, you'll have to talk to the client.'

'I plan to, but after I've been to Kilrush tomorrow. I'm hoping I'll pick up something more, about the three girls out of the twenty chosen from the Workhouse. Ellen O'Donnell was one of them. Michael O'Donnell had a sister called Ellen. It doesn't feel like a co-incidence.'

'You know what I think about co-incidences. Go for it. If the client doesn't bite, it'll be an interesting story for Maze.'

'Thanks, Zelah. Are you still coming with me to Kilrush tomorrow?'

'No, change of plan. We'll leave here after a leisurely breakfast and drive across to Lahinch. Then Rick wants to see the Cliffs of Moher. We'll probably stop for coffee in Lahinch, so we should be at Moher around lunchtime. You?'

'Early breakfast for me. I want to be in Kilrush for ten o'clock, when the library opens. I have the name of a contact there. Let me know how your journey's going. I can probably meet up with you in time to see the Cliffs. I think it's about an hour's drive back up from Kilrush. I went once with my parents, but it's too many years ago to remember.'

'Sounds like a plan,' Rick grunted. 'Zelah's driving so I'll be giving you the call.'

'Great. How are you liking Ireland, Rick?'

Rick had two facial expressions: grumpy and more grumpy. His face didn't change as she asked the question. 'It's wonderful,' he said. Maggie cocked her head to the side and saw Zelah grin but decided not to respond.

'I'm off to bed. See you both tomorrow,' she said, with a quick wink at Zelah, who threw her back a sarcastic grin.

Chapter 11

It was less than an hour's drive along the direct route from Ennis to Kilrush and Maggie was there well before ten, which gave her time to locate the library, then take a walk around the small market town. The weather had held; even now, just after nine, it was already warm enough for a skirt and t-shirt.

Her pre-trip research had told her that Kilrush had a smaller population now than at the time of the famine. It had been built up at one point in the 19th century by the Vandeleur family. They had been one of the worst landlords in terms of evictions, with over twenty thousand being evicted throughout the Kilrush Union.

It was a pretty town, though. A market town, celebrated nationally as an Irish National Heritage town. It had the usual multi-coloured buildings, so typical of Irish small towns, with a central square that housed a monument, erected in 1903, dedicated to "heroic" Fenians from Kilrush who had played a part in freeing the Fenian leaders from gaol in Manchester in 1867. The inscription said that although the movement leaders had escaped, the Kilrush men did not, and were caught and hanged. The monument called it "judicial murder by a tyrannical government".

Although the town had the usual large supermarkets, there were many small local businesses and today a group of people were setting up tents and stalls for a local farmers' market.

After her walk around the town, she wandered down to the marina. Kilrush was technically a seaside town but was on the mouth of the River Shannon estuary. It reminded her of Conwy in North Wales, which she had visited with Zelah for a previous case.

By ten she was ready to visit the Kilrush Library.

A middle aged, slim woman with brown hair turning grey at the roots, was waiting at the door. 'You must be Maggie Gilbert,' she said, holding out a hand, which Maggie took for a brief, firm shake. 'Kevin told me about your American client. Come on in. I have some papers ready for you. I'm Mary, by the way, Mary Dillon.'

'Are you from Kilrush?' Maggie asked as Mary led her into a room off the main entrance hallway.

'Born and bred,' Mary replied. 'For seven generations. I've been able to trace my family back to the time before the famine, which I think is quite a feat, given what happened here in Kilrush.'

Maggie sensed someone more than willing to talk about history. 'Would you have time for a chat, after I've read the documents you have for me?'

'Delighted to,' Mary beamed. 'I have a group in just now, but I'll be done in an hour. I don't think what you have to read here will take longer than that.'

She took Maggie into a research area.

The information consisted mainly of documents Maggie had already found on the internet. A few referred to general matters of the Workhouse; correspondence from the trustees complaining about the number of people they had to deal with and the lack of financial support, but there was little pre-1850. After that time it was just the recording of deaths; both of inmates and staff. She already knew that Michael O'Donnell didn't appear on that list, nor any member of his family. Was it Ellen O'Donnell who had taken him there and if so, why hadn't she taken him on the journey to Australia? Was it not allowed? Could a three-year-old have been left alone in the Workhouse? From what she had learned, the answer to that last question was probably "yes".

She had more luck with the newspaper of the time, *The Clare Journal.* It had a report on the death of Seamus McMahon in January 1850. His death was attributed to a gang of local thugs. Neither the Young Irelanders nor the

Molly Maguires were mentioned. The paper said he had been going about his lawful business when he was attacked, on his way home, late at night. There was no mention of what his "lawful business" might have been. Maggie thought there was more to be read between the lines than on them.

As she finished, Mary Dillon returned, rubbing her hands together. 'How are you getting on?'

She sat down next to Maggie at the machine on which Maggie was reading the fiche.

'Interesting,' she replied. 'There's nothing specific in the Workhouse about the client's ancestor. His name was Michael O'Donnell and I believe he had a sister called Ellen O'Donnell. She was one of the potato famine girls who were chosen to go to Australia in 1849. I found out about her yesterday, but I don't know if she was related to—'

'Let me stop you there,' Mary said.

Maggie's gut did a somersault. *Information incoming,* she thought.

'Come with me back to my office. It's more comfortable.'

Maggie followed Mary out of the reading room, across the hall and through a small door marked "private", jiggling with excitement as she sat in the armchair Mary indicated.

'Like I said, I can trace my ancestors here in Kilrush back seven generations. The first was a Cornelius Dillon, who had a brother called William. William had a daughter called Margaret, known as Peg. She was born in 1833. Con's family survived. God himself only knows how. William's did not. He lost his wife Margaret and all his children except Peg. She lived in Clamhunger Row, down in a place called Moy, just beyond Cappa. An agent called Seamus McMahon had all of the cabins pulled down and what was left set on fire. Peg had to go to the Workhouse. She was one of the girls chosen for the Earl Grey scheme – set up to send female orphans to Australia..'

Maggie knew all of this but coming from a direct descendant of the family of one of the girls, it felt more powerful.

Mary took a deep breath. 'Peg was weak, chosen because she was sick with an illness that others could easily catch, which we know now but they didn't know back then. She fitted the bill in terms of age and being orphaned. So she left, with Ellen O'Donnell and… there was another girl, called—'

'Honora Madigan, age seventeen,' Maggie said.

'You know already?' Mary replied.

'Very little. I only learned yesterday, from Kevin, about the girls and about Clamhunger Row. I know nothing about what happened to them.' She decided not to mention that she knew Honora Madigan didn't go to Australia but returned to Ireland. She wanted to hear Mary's version of events – if she had one.

'Well, Peg died, just after they arrived,' Mary said. 'I found out. It took a few years, but I found a record of her death, in Melbourne. She was sixteen and had tuberculosis, which she must have had when she left here.'

Mary's face had reddened, and her voice became harsher.

'Still makes you angry, doesn't it,' Maggie said softly, 'even after all this time.'

Mary nodded and swiped at an eye. 'Dust,' she said. 'I'm sorry to say, I don't know for sure whether Norrie made it to Australia, or what might have happened to her.

'I'll find out, somehow,' Maggie replied. 'I'd like to know what happened to Honora Madigan, too. I think they must have been good pals. My client has a DNA contact in Australia, so Ellen O'Donnell must have survived and had children.'

'Good for her,' Mary replied. 'As for Norrie Madigan, well, who knows?'

'What can you tell me about her?' Maggie asked. As she spoke, a cloud passed across the previously blue sky, making the room dark and suddenly cold. Maggie shivered.

'I only know a few small pieces of information. Do you know about the death of Seamus McMahon?'

Maggie nodded. 'That was believed to be Norrie Madigan, but I understand it was never proven. She was from Moy, too.'

'I know. Clamhunger Row. Is there anyone who can tell me more? There's very little in the newspapers, the one here in Clare or in Dublin, of the time.'

Mary paused. 'There is someone, but I don't know if I should tell you. It'd be like sending you into the lion's den.'

'Tell me more, Mary.'

'Down in what's left of Moy, there's an old woman. She's the descendant of a family, one of whom was housekeeper to the priest who served the community of Kilrush and who ministered to those poor souls in the Workhouse. I believe – the library believes – she has letters and maybe other material. We think the letters may have been sent by Ellen O'Donnell from Australia to the priest. The women of the housekeeper's family have guarded them fiercely down through the generations and despite us begging her to let us or Clare Library, or even the national library have them, she's refused. She won't speak to anyone about them or what's in them. Anyone who tries is chased off her property.'

'Sounds like a right old devil,' Maggie said. 'But I'd be willing to have a go. Will you tell me her name and where she lives?'

'Yes but on your own head be it.'

'Is she violent? Should I be worried about her attacking me?'

'I wouldn't think so. She's in her early nineties. She's no living family and we're terrified about what she'll do to the letters when she realises she's dying. Not that there's any sign of that happening soon.'

Maggie sat back in her chair. 'I'm willing to give it a go,' she said. 'If I come away with nothing, so be it. I'm here now though, I might as well try.'

Mary turned to her desk and picked up a post-it note and a pen. She scribbled on it and handed it to Maggie. 'That's the address. It's right down by the sea. Good luck.'

The sun came out from behind the clouds again. Maggie smiled and stood up. 'You've been really helpful, Mary. I'll let you know how I get on. Shall I call here after I've been to see the woman?'

'Yes do, please. Her name is Johanna Regan, known as Joan. I'll be thinking about you.'

'I'll tell her about my client. Perhaps I can offer to find out what happened to Ellen and Honora.'

'Worth a try,' Mary said, as they walked to the door and out into the street. She waved Maggie off.

Maggie's car was just around the corner. The drive down past Cappa took five minutes. Two minutes further on she came to a row of cottages. There was no sign to show this was Moy, but it had to be the right place. She parked the car and began to look for the address. It wasn't difficult. A row of cottages that looked as if they'd been built in the late 19th or early 20th century ran in a straight line up across the road from the seashore. The one she wanted was at the bottom end of the row, closest to the sea, so close the lapping of waves breaking on the sand must be a constant background noise. She could imagine that a storm might even reach the cottage. It looked run down and rather sad. The others had all been painted in pretty pastel shades; this one was a dull grey. The gate had fallen off its bottom hinge and weeds had taken over both the garden and the many cracks in the path up to the front door. She took a deep breath and knocked sharply, three times.

Nothing happened. She tried again. Nothing. Perhaps the woman wasn't in. One more try. Nothing happened at the door, but from around the side of the cottage came the sound of shuffling feet. A hand appeared on the wall, then a head edged around, a very old head on top of a scrawny neck, with a heavily wrinkled face and topped off with thick white hair.

'Who are you and what do you want? Are you from the social, because if you are, you can clear off. I've told you I don't want anything from you. Leave me alone.' The voice was strong and firm.

'No, I'm not from the social,' Maggie replied, standing up straight, smiling but answering in a voice of equal strength. Something told her not to cringe or beg in front of this woman, nor patronise her in any way. 'I've come here from Wales, looking for someone who can tell me something about Ellen O'Donnell, who went to Australia. I research family histories and I have a client descended from a man who might have been her brother, Michael O'Donnell. I've been told you may be able to help me. I don't want anything other than information. But if Mary at the library is wrong and you don't have anything worth telling me, I'll just go away and leave you alone.'

The head dropped to one side, considering. 'If I had information, and I'm not saying I do, what would you be doing with it?'

'I'll be passing it on to my client. He's American, from New York. His name is Michael Walker.'

'And he's descended from Michael O'Donnell? How can you be sure? How do I know you're not just trying to worm your way in?'

'If you tell me what you know, I can show you a chart of Mike's family history. He began by thinking his ancestors were from Scotland, because the name was incorrectly recorded when they arrived in the States, but I found out the correct version. How? Because I'm good at what I do. Why? Because I genuinely want to know. I'm like that with a client. It's their story, but I can't help myself getting involved. What do you think? Will you talk to me?' She kept smiling, but her body was tense. The waves lapped in the background.

The rest of the body appeared around the corner. Maggie could now see just how old Johanna Reagan was. From the round shoulders and curled up body, which was dressed in a woollen skirt, jumper and wool stockings despite the warm day, plus an old, food smattered apron, Maggie could see that she was well into her nineties. Johanna shuffled towards her, only stopping when she was less than a foot away and peered at Maggie.

'That's better, now I can see your face. You've Irish in you.'

Maggie laughed. 'Yes indeed, my mother's family was from Cork.'

'Hmm. Alright, then. Come in.' She turned around and began to shuffle back around the house. She led Maggie to a door at the back, which led into a small kitchen that looked as if it hadn't been updated since the cottage was built, although it did have a few mod cons: a fridge-freezer, a microwave and a conventional oven. She noted a small piece of land at the back of the house, neat, with flowers and vegetables growing. 'Who looks after the garden?'

'That would be me,' Johanna replied without turning around.

They moved from the kitchen across a hallway into a small living room. It held a grey three-piece suite that looked at least fifty years old but was as good as new, a piano, an old cabinet with some china and a few other ornaments, and an old wooden box. It reminded Maggie of her grandmother's "best room", the one into which she was occasionally allowed to go to play, but never for long. Here, this was a room for visitors only. There would be another room for daily use, probably through the third, closed door she had noted as they crossed the hallway. Johanna indicated Maggie to sit on one of the two armchairs, placing herself opposite on the other.

'What do you have to tell me about Michael O'Donnell?'

'I don't know how, but he got away from Kilrush to Dublin. He married when he was twenty, the girl was called Bridget Cusack. They had five children in Dublin. One of their children, Timothy, married a girl called Bridget Mary Reilly in Dublin, and they emigrated together to the United States, in the 1890s. They lived in New York for most of their lives, with one short period in Philadelphia. He and Bridget had five children, all born in New York. The youngest of those children, a girl named Ellen, had a daughter, also called Ellen, who in her eighties, is still alive and remembers her grandparents, Timothy and Bridget.

Timothy's father, Michael O'Donnell from Moy, is my client's two times great grandfather, on his grandmother Ellen's side. Here, I can show you the family chart.' She took her laptop out of her bag, opened up the file and passed the machine across the room to Johanna.

'Can you make it bigger?' Johanna asked, staring at the screen.

'Of course, Mrs Reagan.'

'Call me Joan.'

Maggie stood and crossed the room and knelt next to the armchair. 'How big do you need it? I can make it any size, but if it's too large it can't all be seen at the same time on the screen.' She paused. 'Do you wear glasses, Joan?'

'Broken.'

'Oh. Would you like to try mine? They are reading glasses.'

'Yes.'

Maggie handed hers over. Joan slipped them on, resting them on the tip of her nose, then put her face a few inches from the screen. Maggie went to speak, but Joan hushed her. After staring at the chart for about five minutes, as Maggie tried not to move, she said, 'What's the descendant like?'

'He seems like a good man,' Maggie replied. 'He's keen to know his roots.'

One more minute of silent staring followed. Maggie's knees were starting to feel like she was kneeling on nails, which were probably underneath the thin carpet on the floorboards.

'Right then. What do you want to know about the O'Donnells?'

'Anything you can tell me, Joan. I'd also like to know about Margaret Dillon and Honora Madigan.'

'Then you'd better go back over there and sit down. This is going to be a long story.'

Maggie sat and Joan's gaze drifted off into a faraway place in her head.

'Everything I know came from my own ancestor, who was housekeeper to the priest who cared for the people of Kilrush and around. His name was Father Jerome O'Brien. He was an educated man. He could read and write, and he wrote a diary during the famine. I can show you that, afterwards. It has some names in it.

'Now, about the girls who went off to Australia, three cousins, through their mothers, the Corcoran sisters – Kitty, Johanna and Margaret. Of the three cousins, Norrie Madigan was the eldest, then Peg Dillon, then Ellen O'Donnell. My ancestor, my three times great grandmother, Breda O'Shea, knew that every member of the three girls' families had been lost to the famine. She got that from the list of names in Father Jerome's diary. She didn't know that Michael had survived. Apart from the girls and Michael, that would have been eighteen people in three families, if you include Norrie Madigan's grandfather, who was beaten to death when he refused to leave his cabin.' She paused and shook her head.

'The three girls and little Michael had no choice but to go to the Workhouse. There was a chance of survival, albeit a small one. Not long after they went into the Workhouse, this Earl Grey scheme came up. So grand it must have sounded, the chance of a new life. And what was there to stay here for? No family, no work. Not that they had a choice, Ellen explained that. She was heartbroken to have to leave Michael behind.'

'How do you know all of this?' Maggie asked.

'It's in her letters.'

'There are letters? Ellen could read and write? Can I read them, Joan?' Maggie asked, her voice trembling at the thought of the breakthrough she was about to make.

Joan stared at her for a long minute. She bit her lips, grimaced. 'I've rarely shown anyone these letters. They're like tissue paper now. They'll need handling like they're made of air.'

'I know, paper deteriorates over time and these letters must be up to a hundred and seventy years old. I have special gloves; I always keep a few pairs on me. It's the handling that does much of the damage, because of the acid in our fingertips. The gloves ensure I won't transfer anything onto the paper.'

Joan nodded. 'In the cabinet, you see the box?'

Maggie turned her head and looked through the glass-fronted cabinet at an old wooden box sitting at the centre of the middle shelf. She stood, wincing at the pain in her knees, opened the cabinet and took the box out, then unlocked the lid with a small brass key. Inside, she found papers, each folded into four and neatly stacked.

'Before I take them out Joan, can you tell me why you haven't given these over to the library, or even the national library?'

'Breda promised Father Jerome that she would always take care of them. They were precious to him. He'd lost so many parishioners but here was one that survived. At least…'

Maggie frowned. 'Something went wrong, for Ellen?'

'I'm sorry to say it did,' Joan whispered. 'I'm tired. I'm going for a lie down. My bedroom's just next door. You read. There are four letters, all in order, the first one on the top. Call me when you're done.'

The old woman stood, pushing herself up, groaning with the effort of moving upwards, and shuffled out of the room.

Maggie picked out the first letter, opened it up; there were two small sheets of paper, with writing on both sides. The handwriting was clear and neat. The letter was dated 24th November 1852. She began to read. It became clear as she began that this was a response to a letter received from Ireland.

Chapter 12
Melbourne 1852

Ellen closed the curtains, went to the door to listen again to make certain that Mrs Donoghue wasn't moving around, then took out the wooden board from under her bed, where she had hidden her paper, pens, and ink. Once again she gave thanks to Father Gerard for giving her these wonderful gifts, and for allowing her to use his house as her postal address, so that Mrs Donoghue would never find out that she was writing home.

This was going to be a long letter, for her, given the news that Father Jerome had sent her. His letter had been written three months before and she had re-read it so many times, with both joy and anxiety – joy that Michael was alive and well and away from the Workhouse, but anxiety that Norrie would be caught and hanged for what she had done. It would have been about the same time they had arrived in Australia.

She pulled her shawl tightly around her shoulders. It had taken time to get used to the reversal of the seasons, that they should be heading into summer now, as they would be in Kilrush, but here it was turning colder and would soon be winter. She was not to be allowed a fire in her room. Mrs Donoghue didn't approve of warmth for servants; said the cold was good for their constitution, as she warmed herself in front of a blazing hearth.

A few more seconds' check that the old bitch had gone to bed and was well asleep, then Ellen dipped her nib into the ink bottle and began.

Dear Father Jerome,

It was with so much pleasure that I received your Letter. Such a consolation it was, to Heer a little of good news. I thank God that Michael is well and his safety is in hand. I cannot blame Norrie for what she did. She had the Intention to do it, right from when we came to Liverpool and she told us she would not be coming onward. I never expected that she would think of taking Michael. Whatever she has done, she has saved my Brother. If you Heer more news from Dublin, I beg that you will be good to inform me. I long to heer what has happened to him. It is indeed sorry I am sad to heer there is no good news of our naybors. And to heer of so many passing away in the Workhouse. That terrible Place. I am grateful that I was able to get away with Peg and Norrie for I am sure we too would not have lived so long there. But if I had nown then what I now find, perhaps I wood not have allowed Myself to be taken.

Have you news of my Uncle yet, Edward Corcoran? I pray for news that is good.

I cannot give such a good account of myself. I have worked for Mrs Donoghue for nine months now. She is not a kind woman and I am sure she picked me out to work for her dislike of Irish girls. She has beeten me twice now. For what I cannot say for I did nothing Wrong, that I can tell. She lets me no time off, so I have no frends and am sore sad since I lost Peg. I see none of the girls from the Boat no longer. I believe Some have done well for themself. Some have work, others married.

I find the wether here strange. Summer is just finished and so hot it was that I cood hardly bare it. And the flies! So many there are and when they Bite, you can becom ill. I have been lucky. Bite me they have indeed, but I did not suffer so much.

They say the harvest hear was good this year. There are many from England who have come here to try there Fortune. But it is not as easy as they did expect. Some have brought there familys. I heer them talking when I go to the shops. But also there are the Convicted ones. I am greatly affeered of them, ruff as they are.

Winter will come here soon. I do not know How it will be. I feel the cold a little already. How I long for Kilrush and Cappa and Moy. When I close my eyes I see them all. Melbourne is not a bad place, but I feel such loneliness for home.

Your humble and grateful friend
Ellen O'Donnell

She folded the letter carefully, wrote the address in a steady hand on the envelope, then hid it under her bed. It would be another two weeks before she could go into town and deliver the letter into the hands of Father Gerard, who would ensure its safe passage back to Ireland, to Father Jerome in Kilrush. She would not, she knew, receive a reply for at least six months, but she could wait. Just knowing the connection with home was there, gave her hope.

She jumped into bed, shivering, her shawl still around her shoulders, and with her eyes tearing up, dreamed of happier days in Clamhunger Row, when her whole family was still there and nothing, it seemed, could spoil their happy life.

Chapter 13

Maggie re-read the letter several times, making sure she had a good understanding of what had happened to Ellen once she arrived in Melbourne. She already knew that there was a receiving house for the "potato famine girls" as they had come to be known and that many of them had done well for themselves. But she also knew that they had not all been welcome and that by 1851, after Ellen had arrived, they were positively unwelcome. Ellen's ship was followed by only one more before the scheme was abandoned.

She thought about using her phone camera to record the letter but decided against. Joan had trusted her, and copying it, without Joan's permission would be a betrayal of that trust. She would, however, ask Joan when she returned from her rest, but with the expectation that the answer would be a firm "no".

The most important revelation from this first letter was that Michael O'Donnell had been taken out of the Workhouse by Norrie Madigan. Following on from there it would have been she who had taken Michael to Dublin. What did she do with him? As her story – be she heroine or villain – was well known in Kilrush, then it was also known to the British, making Norrie Madigan a wanted criminal. She had made her way back across to Dublin. Michael, as well as being the only remaining relative of Ellen, to whom Norrie had made a promise about keeping him safe, would also ensure Norrie would be less suspicious walking with a small child. Had she kept him as her own child until he was grown up? But he married under the name of Michael O'Donnell. Perhaps the next letter would give her a clue. She picked it out of the box. The date was 1854 – two years after the previous letter.

Dear Father Jerome,

I beg your forgiveness for such a long time since my last letter. So much has happened to me. Yet before that I must thank you for giving me news of Michael and of Norrie. So happy I am that she write to let you know of his news. The family with whom he now lives seem good people who will take care of him. He will be eight years old by now. I try to imagine him, a fine, tall strong boy. And Glad I am to heer that Norrie manage to escape to America. I bless the kindness of her friends in Dublin for giving her money for her passage and Uncle Edward Corcoran to find when she arrived. I pray for her safety, away from the English who would have hanged her for what she did. I know that killing is wrong. You Yourself did say so. But I cannot condemn her for it.

I am happy to hear that Uncle Edward Corcoran lives, in New York. I am so filled with joy that he and Norrie will find each other there. It would be so happy to have such dear family close by. And the Cullinan family too. I pray for their safety and comfort.

As for me? I no longer work for Mrs Donoghue. You Might think that to be a good thing, but she turned me out. And has had me married to a man who was convicted of stealing, in England. His name is Harold Smith. He is a rough man, twice married before myself.

But I have a blessing. I have a daughter now, named Kathleen for his mother. I am Ellen Smith and she is Kathleen Smith. I have made sure to have her baptised by Father Gerard. My husband is not of our faith. He despises what he calles Popery. But he is now my husband and I must obey him. So I cannot attend Mass regular, only when I go into town without him.

I lived at first on a sheep station, a lonely life, in a place called Ballarat. Then, Gold was found not far from here. My Husband became crazy for it. We moved away from the sheep station and are now living in a tent on the goldfields. He does not have luck with his searching. We barely survive. There are many thousands the same in this place. If I had not my Kathleen, my sorrows would be great indeed.

I will be sending this letter when I am able to meet with Father Gerard in Melbourne. It is becoming a great town now, bigger each time I see it.

This is my news. If you have any more from Norrie, or from the people who have my Michael, I beg you write to me of them. I miss my home,

Your friend and humble servant,

Ellen Smith

When Maggie had finished reading, she folded the letter and put it back into the box with the first one. Taking a deep breath, she left the room, peeped around the bedroom door, saw Joan was sleeping, and left the cottage, to stand in the garden, looking out over the estuary and across to Scattery Island, the site of a pre-medieval tower. In the distance, across the mouth of the estuary, was the County of Kerry. A soft wind blew across her face, and she took a couple of deep breaths. She closed her eyes for a moment, then looked up into the cloudless blue sky. Given what she'd just read, and Joan's warning, she knew that the final two letters were going to provide even worse news about Ellen, but she had to go on.

Back in the cottage she picked up the third letter. The date on this one was early 1858 – four years on.

Dear Father Jerome,

It was with great pleasure that your letter of 17 July came safe to hand. How Glad I was on the reseeving of it. How long it is since I last had news of home! And how happy I was to hear that Norrie is doing so well in America. She was always a strong girl. Married to a policeman indeed! In charge of a shop, And with a baby of her own. I send my love and hope to her and her family, and to Uncle Edward Corcoran. I culd not tell from your letter that Norrie and him found each other. I wood be grateful to heer more news of him.

Here in Ballarat we are not so good. My Husband's dream of finding riches through Gold has come to nothing. I think we shall soon return to the sheep station. He is to see the Manager next month.

My Kathleen is growing into a beautiful girl, of five years old. But my two little boys did not live beyond a few days. God bless and keep them in his Mercy. I was allowed the naming of them. The first I called

Michael, the second Jerome, after your good self. They are together in a little grave in Ballarat. If we return to the sheep station, I must leave them. I visit them often. Harold does not know of my visits.

This letter must be short. It may be some months before I can reach Father Gerard in Melbourne and have this sent to you.

I pray to God to keep you safe in our lovely Kilrush. When I close my eyes I can see the Island and the far coast of Kerry.

May God bless you always,

Your grateful friend,

Ellen Smith

Maggie folded up the letter and put it back with the others. She felt sick with a premonition of what was to come and had to force herself to read the final one. The date was 1863. A further five years had passed.

Dear Father Jerome,

This will be my last letter to you. I write to you from the gaol in Melbourne. Father Gerard visits me often and will continue to do until my death which will be soon. I pray you will forgive me and God will grant me Mercy and Understanding for what I have done.

I killed Harold Smith. I found him trying to force himself onto my Kathleen. She is just ten years old. He was steeped in drink. I pushed him away from her. I took up his shotgun and fired it at him. They said it was murder and I am to die.

I am not sorry and I must believe God will forgive me. I had to save Kathleen. I have been visited by a daughter of one of his first marriages. I thought her to abuse me. But she did not. She told me a story so dreadful that I still shudder to think of it. She believes he murdered his second wife, the woman that was her mother. She also had a sister, upon whom he visited his vile lusts, after he killed his wife for her lack of being able to perform her wife's duty. The girl, who was fourteen years in age, became with child. The child was dead when it was delivered. The girl jumped into the river and drowned herself. Is it so terrible That such an evil man no longer walks this Earth? My Kathleen is with good people. She had a friend called Billy when we returned to the sheep station in '60. No one of the white familys would take her in after my sentence was pronounced, not even the Irish familys, even from Clare itself. So she is with Billy's family. They are the aboriginal people. Billy's mother has visited me, and ashured me that Kathleen will be safe with them. She is a kind and good woman. I expect that Kathleen will be cast out from the local community, but I do not care. As long as I know she is loved and cared for, it is enough.

Soon I will be with God, to whom I pray constantly with all my might, to forgive my terrible transgression in committing my sin, against His Comandment not to kill. I live in hope of seeing my family again, my mammy and daddy, the little ones. They did no harm to anyone and must surely be in heaven.

Father Gerard will be with me when it happens. He is with me as I write this last letter to you and will send it once I am gone.

Please forgive me. Your letters have been a wonderful source of consolation to me over the past ten years.

Your faithful friend
Ellen Smith

Maggie folded the letter carefully, and slowly placed it in the box with the others, before returning the box to its place in the cabinet.

She sat quietly, her mind far away, until a noise brought her back into the room. Joan had returned. She shuffled over to Maggie and took her hand.

Maggie teared up and gave her eyes a quick wipe with her free hand. 'Dust,' she said, smiling at Joan.

'Upsetting, aren't they,' Joan said, letting go of Maggie's hand and going to sit in her armchair.

'Dreadful,' Maggie replied. 'Do you know if there's any more information in Australia?'

'No idea,' Joan said. 'Is it important?'

'I think so. My client, Mike Walker, did a DNA test and has found he has a distant relative in Australia, not an immigrant. A person with possibly aboriginal DNA.'

Joan's eyes lit up.

'Maybe the friendship between Kathleen and Billy became more than friendship,' Maggie said. 'My client Mike plans to contact the person, who I hope will reply to him, although if whoever it is had a relative who was hanged for murder, then perhaps they won't want to know about it.'

Joan made a snorting noise. 'Ellen did what she had to do and anyway, it sounds like it was more of an accident.'

'The ancestor may not know that. If they don't, then we have the true story for them.'

'Good luck with that,' Joan said.

'Was there any more news of Norrie Madigan?' Maggie asked. 'She must have written to Father Jerome, too.'

'There's nothing more, only those four,' Joan said. 'I often wondered myself what became of her. Sounds like she did all right for herself, doesn't it.'

'Yes.' She paused for a moment. 'Joan, did Father Jerome have any part in the murder of Seamus McMahon?'

'Maybe, maybe not,' the old woman replied, smiling so widely it looked like her false teeth might fall out.

'Come on, Joan. You know something.'

'I'm not going to besmirch the memory and reputation of a great man of this town.'

'That would be a "yes", then?'

Joan's smile turned to an angry frown, and she banged her hand on the arm of her chair. 'Don't you go suggesting anything. He was a great man, so they say.'

'I won't, I promise. What happened?

'He hid her. It's in his diary.'

'Good for him,' Maggie replied. 'But, thinking about it, if he kept Ellen's letters, why not Norrie's?'

Joan tapped the side of her head with her forefinger. 'Think about it. Ellen died. Norrie didn't.'

'Ah. He destroyed her letters, to make sure no-one could ever find them and know where she was.'

'He told Breda the whole story, of where Norrie was in America, but said she should never write anything down.'

'Can you remember the story, Joan?'

The old woman shook her head. 'I remember a few parts, but most of it's gone now.'

'Can you tell me what you remember?'

'I remember she put Michael with people, a married couple from the Young Irelanders. They were the ones who helped her when she returned to Dublin from Liverpool. They looked after him. Father Jerome died in 1870, so there was no more news after that, except that one reference to Norrie in the third letter.'

'Do you know where she stayed when she first reached America, or the name of her contact?'

'That I do know. It was Manhattan. The contact was supposed to have been her Uncle Edward. After that, I don't know how long the correspondence went on before Father Jerome died.'

Maggie stood and walked across the room, and gave Joan a brief hug, which she shrugged off. 'Joan, is there anything further in the diary, about the O'Donnells, the Dillons or the Madigans.'

'Just the names and dates of their deaths. Like I said, they all died, except for Ellen, Michael, Peg and Norrie, between '45 and '49.'

'From hunger or disease? Did he say?'

'From both. You can't separate them, not really. Now away with you and take your glasses. You've left them on the arm of that chair.'

'Deliberately,' Maggie said. 'They're for you. I have other pairs. I always have more. I keep putting them down and can't remember where I put them. I can spare a pair. Now, Joan, why aren't you getting more help, and don't you shout at me, or tell me you don't need it.'

Joan had opened her mouth but closed it again. 'I don't want anyone putting me in a home,' she whispered. 'I manage well enough.'

'No-one's going to put you in a home, especially if you can see properly. I think you might have cataracts, which could be removed. You'd have to see a specialist, but if they could be removed, you'll be able to see so much better. Unless you're scared, of course.'

Joan pushed herself up and stood in front of Maggie, who didn't flinch. She went to speak, then gave another wide grin. 'You're a sly one. I might give it a thought.'

'Good for you. I'm going back to the library. I'll tell Mary Dillon to come see you, and before you start up again – I can see that look – she's a lovely woman. I'll make sure she doesn't push you to give her the letters, or even look at them.'

Joan nodded. 'I suppose she's alright. I used to take out books there.'

'I'll go now,' Maggie said. 'But just one more thing. What's your intention for the letters when you've passed on? I dread the idea that anyone who didn't know their value would just burn them as useless old paper.'

'I'm not going to die any time soon, so don't worry yourself on that score.'

'We all die some time, Joan, sooner or later. Please, think about it. Here, take my card.' She pushed a card into the old woman's cardigan pocket. 'If you want to talk about it, let me know.'

They went together to the back door of the cottage. Maggie turned to Joan and hugged her again. This time she wasn't pushed off.

'Goodbye Maggie Gilbert. Good luck to your client too. I'll remember his name. Michael Walker.'

Maggie started to walk away, but turned around as she had another thought. 'Joan, what happened to Clamhunger Row, after it was knocked down? Was any of it ever re-built?'

This time, Joan gave a huge throaty laugh. 'Now where is it do you think you're standing?'

With a lump in her throat, Maggie walked to her car and drove back to Kilrush.

Chapter 14

She had just parked her car outside the library when her phone rang. It was Rick. She'd forgotten he was going to call.

'Where are you? Are you still planning to join us at Moher?'

She glanced at her watch. It was almost eleven thirty.

'Hi Rick, this has taken longer than I thought. I've had an interesting morning, beyond interesting, actually. I'm just at the library in Kilrush for a quick chat with the librarian, then I can head up to you. I'll be there about…' she stopped for a quick calculation, 'one o'clock. Is that going to be too late? How's it going with you?'

'No, that works just fine. I was calling to say we're running late. We're just in Lahinch now and it would be good to spend another hour here, so it works out just fine. They tell us it's gonna be real busy up at the Cliffs. Zelah says it's changed a lot, so it's a long walk from the carpark. Are you OK with that?'

'No problem for me. Perhaps we can do our walking then find somewhere to have a late lunch. Tell Zelah I have a lot to tell her.'

'She hears you. Apparently there's a shopping area where tour buses park. We'll meet you there.'

'Great. Right, I'm just walking into the library. See you there.'

As she walked in, she practically fell over Mary Dillon, who had seen Maggie's car pull up and was waiting in the hallway.

'You've been over an hour, so I'm guessing she didn't throw you out.'

'Indeed not,' Maggie replied. 'Can we go and sit in your office?'

Once they were seated Maggie took Mary through the visit. As Maggie recited the detail of each letter, Mary's mouth dropped open, then shut, then dropped again.

When Maggie had finished, she added, 'She needs help, Mary. She can barely see. Do you think you could—'

'Stop there. I'll get down to her after work. I finish at three today. Do you think she'll let me see the letters?'

Maggie shook her head. 'I would suggest you don't push it. If you can get her on side, in time you'll get to the letters. It's going to be like walking on eggshells, but your best approach would be to help with the eyesight issue first. You can tell her that I've told you I've read the letters and what a sad story it is, but I would suggest you leave it at that, for now.'

Mary nodded. 'If she needs her eyes sorting out I know one of the opticians here in town. I'll ask her if she'll do a home visit. I can stay with her whilst she does, provided Joan agrees.'

'I think she will,' Maggie smiled. 'She'll be trying to prove she's not frightened and, secretly, she knows she needs help. She's terrified she'll be taken out of the cottage and put in a home.'

'That won't happen,' Mary replied. 'Once she can see better, perhaps we can get her a bit of help, to make sure she can stay at home.'

'I think you'll do really well with her, Mary. I have to go now. I'm meeting my colleague and her friend up at the Cliffs of Moher. I last went there over forty years ago, with my parents. It had just a small, rough car park, back then.'

Mary laughed. 'You're in for a shock, then. It's a major attraction on the tourist route now. A proper carpark, farther away, shops, a café, and a long walk up the hill. The Cliffs are spectacular and well worth the walk. They haven't changed; not at all.'

'Good, then I'll be on my way. I'm so grateful for your help, Mary. I hope we meet again.'

'I'd love to hear about your client's progress,' Mary replied. 'Perhaps he has some relations here in Kilrush.'

'I'll make sure you know. And you can tell me how the "dance macabre" goes with Joan.'

**

The drive up the Wild Atlantic Way from Kilrush to Moher was so spectacular that Maggie didn't have time to think any more about Ellen O'Donnell, being too taken up with the scenery along the way. Although it was a major road, she had to drive carefully; long straight stretches of countryside would come to a sudden ninety-degree bend, as the road touched the edge of the ocean, where Atlantic waves would be suddenly crashing onto a beach beside the car.

Thanks to there being only light traffic, she arrived in Moher a few minutes before one. Her first reaction was shock. She was expecting something like an upgrade on what she had seen at her previous visit, but nothing prepared her for the sight of an area with a dozen huge tour buses, a row of shops and a visitor centre gouged out of the hillside. Nor the crowds. The road to the top of the Cliffs split into two parts and the walk was much farther than it had been on the previous occasion. She couldn't blame Ireland for taking advantage of one of its most breathtaking sights, despite this upgrade.

As she walked from the carpark to the area where she would be meeting Zelah and Rick, the accents around her were multiple; American and Canadian, French, German, Japanese and other languages she didn't recognise. She saw Zelah and waved.

Zelah was frowning. 'Hello. Changed, hasn't it?'

'Yep.'

'I came here with Martin, about forty years ago. It was us, a few other windswept people and sheep. Lots of sheep, in the carpark. And just a short walk to see the Cliffs.'

'Global commercialism,' Maggie said. 'That's the world we live in now. Come on, let's get going. The Cliffs won't have changed.' She turned to Rick. 'You won't be disappointed.'

He didn't look too sure, but set off after Zelah, who had begun a route march towards the top of the cliff.

She was right. When they reached the best viewing point on the summit of the hill, they joined the crowd of people staring in awe at the seven-hundred-foot-high Cliffs of Moher, that stretched out to a far point. It was windy at the summit, and huge Atlantic waves crashed down below on the rocks, over and over, as if trying to beat their way inside. Even this high up, you could hear the boom as wave met rock.

Zelah said something to Rick, but he didn't reply. He was just standing, staring. Maggie thought he couldn't hear Zelah, then realised that he was just lost in the sight, his eyes drawing it into his memory. It was mesmerising.

After fifteen minutes they walked slowly back down, then up the other side, where they had a more distant but fuller view of the entire range of cliffs. It was even more windy on this side and Maggie soon suggested they return in one of the little shuttle vehicles back down to the entrance area and hit the café.

When they all had food and drinks, Zelah asked about Maggie's morning, and she told the story again. She had begun by saying it was going to be depressing. Despite the many sad stories they had come across in the years they had worked together, for Maggie this one was at the top of the list.

Zelah and Rick listened in silence for the next fifteen minutes, Rick shaking his head from time to time. Zelah took an occasional sip of her coffee.

'What's your next move?' Zelah asked when Maggie finished.

'Honestly, I'm not sure. When we get back to the hotel I'm going to email Mike to tell him I have a story, going right back to Daniel O'Donnell, who married Johanna Barrett in 1796, and their son, Michael, who married Johanna Corcoran, and then the direct ancestor for whom I have all of the dates, Michael himself, born in 1846, who survived the famine. I can offer to flesh out the rest of the family tree for him, although I now know how many of them died during the famine.'

'The three sisters,' Rick said.

Maggie and Zelah turned to him.

'The three sisters,' he said again. 'If I were him, that would be the hook that kept me on the line: Johanna, Margaret and Kitty Corcoran. All from around Kilrush, all living in the same row in that Moy place. They married three local men. One of each of their daughters was chosen for this Earl Grey scheme. Two went to Australia. Of those two, one died from Phthisis, the other hanged for murdering her abusive husband. The third one, well, seems like she also committed a murder, then disappeared. Two killers in his family, neither of whom would be condemned by anyone for what they did. If you take out the emotion, it's a great story, for him and for you.'

Zelah, her cup to her lips but not drinking, thought for a moment, then said, 'That's a brilliant idea.'

Maggie wasn't so sure, but she knew that Zelah's commercial instincts were usually spot on. 'I can put it to Mike tonight, see what he thinks. What are you two doing next, after here?'

'Back to the hotel,' Zelah said. 'Rick wants to know more about Lahinch and his wife's ancestors who came from the town.'

'What's it like? I didn't get to drive along the front. The road takes you around the back of the town.'

'Spectacular,' Rick replied. 'Great place for surfing.'

'Probably in the winter too,' Zelah added. 'The Atlantic can be a real beast along this coast. I have a feeling,' she glanced at Rick, 'we'll be coming back here later in the year.'

'Yeah,' Rick said. 'Not for surfing, mind you. I don't like sand.'

Maggie laughed and stood up. 'I'll leave you to it. Rick, thanks for the idea. I'll let you know at dinner tonight what the client thinks.'

**

Back in Ennis she sent Mike Walker an email with a precis of the story, telling him they should speak as soon as possible for the full version. He replied at once but suggested the following day. This was fine with Maggie. On the drive back from Moher to Ennis she thought over what Rick had said and had the beginnings of a plan; one that would involve a change of timetable.

The day was still sunny, so she went out for a walk along the River Fergus. She stopped to look at the ruined Abbey, walked along the bustling high street, with its local cafés and pubs advertising Irish music, stopped in one for a cup of tea and to write a few ideas in her notebook, then walked back to the hotel, to the restaurant which sat on the banks of the slow flowing river, to wait for Zelah and Rick.

'A change of plan,' she said, as they joined her on the balcony over the river. 'I'm going across to Dublin tomorrow, to the national library. I want to know if they have any information there about the murder of Seamus McMahon and if they have anything about the famine in Clare.'

'Won't most of the information be here, in the Ennis Museum and library?' Zelah asked.

'I'll visit the museum tomorrow morning first thing before I drive over to Dublin. I've booked a hotel for tomorrow night, and a passage over to Holyhead on the ferry the following morning first thing. I'll drive back home from there. It should only take about four hours to get back once I land.'

'What did your client say?' Rick asked.

'I've told him the plan. I gave him a quick update by email and we're going to speak on a video call tomorrow. He's very excited.'

'You haven't told him about the murders,' Zelah said.

'No,' Maggie replied. 'I thought I'd keep that for when we speak face to face. It won't be an easy thing to take in. What about you two? Back to Rosscarbery?'

'Tomorrow morning, for a couple of days. Rick wants to take another day in Cork. As the weather's so good, we might as well make the most of the warmth and sunshine. You know Ireland, it could change any minute.'

'Then I'll see you back home in a few days.'

'I've had an update from the architect,' Zelah said. 'He'll have more ideas ready for us early next week.'

'Brilliant,' Maggie replied. 'Right, let's get on ordering some food. I'm starving.'

**

The following morning, she was away from the hotel at nine. There was no sign of Zelah and Rick. She guessed they were having a late breakfast before setting off.

Her visit to the museum was interesting but didn't supply any further information.

She was on the road to Dublin by eleven. She stopped for a break in Athenry, where a river ran through the middle of the town on its way to Galway Bay. A pretty little town, she thought, with its medieval abbey and castle. Maggie knew the name best from the song that her mother and grandmother used to hum to her when she was a child, the haunting ballad called "The Fields of Athenry", about a young man caught stealing corn during the famine to feed his family and transported to Australia. It seemed a fitting place to stop, given her reason for being in Ireland.

It was another uneventful journey across Ireland, mostly quiet until she reached the outskirts of Dublin and the usual traffic madness of a big city. Here she forgot everything except how to navigate her way into a city full of crazy drivers who all seemed to know where they were going apart from her and keep herself alive. Despite the SatNav's clear instructions, she took a wrong turn, too early or too late, and cursed out loud. At last, with much relief, she crossed the river and, avoiding the trams, which she loved riding on but hated driving amongst, found the hotel, where she had reserved a parking space.

After booking in Maggie decided to take a walk, for some deep breathing and to stretch her legs after the long drive. Previously, she had been north of the river, but today she was south. The streets teemed with tourists around the Trinity College area. As the weather was holding, the street cafés were full, the atmosphere buzzing. She found a café with a walled garden through at the back, where it was relatively quiet, ordered a fruit tea and sat down to think about what to do next.

She was going to spend a day in the national library, having requested papers from the Vandeleur estate in Kilrush, deposited by some long dead member of the family. She had asked for anything relating to events of 1850 but wasn't sure they could be that precise. Whatever, she'd find out tomorrow. In the afternoon, she planned to go into the family history room where she had also booked an hour with the experts there, to see if she could find out more about what Norrie Madigan might have done in between arriving in Dublin after killing Seamus McMahon and going to America. She also wanted to find out more, if she could, about Michael O'Donnell. She already knew about his marriage and the births of his children, but she wanted to see what the available census records held for 1901 and 1911, in particular the names of his children still at home, if any. Timothy, she knew, had emigrated to America in the early 1890s. That left the twins, Michael Cornelius and Ellen, plus Mary and Bridget. They would be aged between thirty-one for the twins and twenty-one for Bridget, the youngest. There might be a possibility that an elderly parent also lived with them.

After she had checked in with Bob, her dreams were punctuated with people on ships, crying to get off – possibly the result of her forthcoming boat trip over to Holyhead – and being on an endless journey.

The following morning, she was at the library when it opened at ten, and the Vandeleur Estate papers were ready for her.

To her disappointment, it wasn't a huge bundle. In the main it consisted of accounts and letters about tenants and some instructions for repairs. If there had been any instructions to remove tenants from their homes, such instructions had not been in writing. Perhaps Seamus McMahon couldn't read, so the orders were made verbally.

After an hour of reading the old papers, she was yawning and not expecting to find anything further. She had reached the end of 1849 and was tempted to give up, but she had made this additional journey to find any available information, so she wouldn't be doing her job properly if she ignored the last few pieces.

Only five pieces remained. The first was a note to a tenant farmer, dated April 1849, thanking him for his letter and saying that his agent, Mr McMahon would call to discuss the terms of his payment. Here was the proof that Seamus McMahon was working for the Vandaleur estate.

The next seemed innocuous at first, just a list of names, until she saw that it was a list of tenants in Cappa and Moy, and – listed separately, the tenants of Clamhunger Row. There were the names she was looking for: Michael O'Donnell, David Dillon, and James Madigan with his father Denis Madigan. There were eleven others on the list. She turned the paper over. It was addressed to Major J Henderson, of the Militia. There was no further information. Why would such a list be sent? Had there been a letter accompanying it? If so, it no longer existed. The date of the list was July 1849.

Then came a letter of instruction to a new agent, dated January 1850, to inform him of plans to be forthcoming for "reformation of the land recently obtained in Moy".

Next, another letter, written in December 1849 to the same Army Major, thanking him for his service in relation to the events in Moy, and his ongoing efforts to find the murderers of Seamus McMahon, known to be two men and a woman, still in the area, and urging him to continue to be vigilant, to spare no household in the town of Kilrush, where the writer was sure the perpetrators were being hidden. Maggie guessed the soldiers must have searched the home of the priest, Father Jerome O'Brien. This was his part in the story: he had successfully hidden Norrie Madigan.

The fifth and final piece was a letter, written to Major Henderson, in February 1850, expressing sorrow that the killers of Seamus McMahon had not been found, and thanking him for his service, now he was to return to Dublin.

Maggie had taken photographs of each of the papers, which she would send to Mike Walker when she got home. Thanking the librarian, she returned the bundle and went out into the sunshine and back to the café courtyard, to put her thoughts in order until the library re-opened after lunch, and she could speak to the family history experts.

As she was eating, a text arrived. It was from Kevin in Ennis. He had found a reference to the murder of Seamus McMahon in a local paper, and could she contact him, so he could share it with her. She replied immediately that she was about to spend an hour or two in the national library. Could he do a video call later? He replied that he could. She set up the call and sent him the details, then went back to the library, buoyant with anticipation.

Chapter 15
Melbourne 1863

Ellen had taken her focus away from the courtroom. When she had been led in, there had been whistles and jeers, but the judge had soon silenced the crowd on the benches below the bar, threatening to have them removed.

The chains had been removed once she was in the dock with her back to the crowd. She glanced up at the jury, a group of solemn men seated to her left in a gallery above the court. The judge was dressed in the British fashion, with his wig and red gown. She noticed that his nose was red and bulbous and that he winced as he stepped up to his high chair. *Gout*, she thought.

The Prosecutor began his speech, his tale of what a dreadful murdering woman she was, having killed a man who had, it must be said, come to Melbourne as a prisoner himself, but had stayed when he could have returned to England, had made a good life, produced children who were now citizens of this land, and had been cut down in his prime by a woman who refused to say why she had killed him.

Flies buzzed around the stifling hot room. She flicked them away from her face, before realising that she was being addressed.

'Have you nothing to say for yourself, Mrs Smith?' the Judge demanded.

Ellen stood up. 'Yes, Sir. I have something to say. There was nothing honourable about Harold Smith. I am – was – his third wife. The first one killed herself. How the second one died is a mystery. They say it was an accident.' She shrugged. 'He had three daughters besides my Kathleen. One is dead. Neither of the others would go near him and got away as soon as they could. I have saved my Kathleen. I came to this country against my will. Us Irish girls were promised hope and a good life. I was employed by a woman who beat me, then sold me off to that evil man for marriage. My family all died in the great hunger in Ireland, except for my baby brother, who I was not allowed to bring with me, but made to stay in the Workhouse. I am twenty-eight years old. I have met with nothing but contempt here and been treated bad. Harold Smith was an evil man. I did what I had to do. I had no thought of killing, only to stop what he was trying to do. My only friends have been Father Gerard McCarthy and Mrs Barambah, who is the mother of my Kathleen's friend Billy. That is all I have to say.'

She clung onto the rail at the front of the prisoners' dock, squeezing until her knuckles turned white. She knew what was coming. Father Gerard had spoken passionately in her favour, telling of the terrible state of Ireland, the starvation, the disease, the deaths, the lack of proper action by the British Government. He described her as a decent, hard-working girl, of good character, and hadn't held back on his comments about Mrs Donoghue, who was not present in the court. He talked about Ellen's daughter, and her two dead babies. He talked about how Harold Smith had beaten her, broken bones on more than one occasion.

However, he had not been able to persuade either of Harold Smith's two remaining daughters to speak about the other unspeakable things he had done to them, nor of the unmarried sister who had had a child and then killed herself. Ellen had refused to speak of what he had tried to do to Kathleen. She knew it would do the young women no good. It was all to no avail. There were likely men amongst the jury who had done the same, in a country with such a great surplus of men, most of them convicts.

The judge summed up. The jury retired. Ellen sat. The jury was back in ten minutes. She wasn't surprised. She had taken a shotgun and fired two shots into the back of the man she had been forced to call her husband and steadfastly refused to tell why she had done it. Only Father Gerard and Mrs Barambah knew the whole truth.

'The Prisoner will stand.'

The crowd, who had been chattering away behind her back, settled to silence.

'Foreman of the jury, have you reached a verdict.'

'We have, your Honour.'

'How do you find the prisoner: guilty or not guilty?'

'Guilty, your Honour.'

The judge turned to her. 'Ellen Smith, you have been found guilty of the murder of your husband Harold Smith.' He paused and put what looked to Ellen like a black square of cloth over his head. She thought it looked ridiculous on top of his wig.

'The sentence for murder is death by hanging. You will be taken from this place to a place of execution, where you will be hanged by the neck until you are dead. May God have mercy on your soul.'

In a steady voice she said, 'He will have mercy on mine, Sir, of that I am sure.' She looked up at the jury. 'But he will not have mercy on yours. There are those amongst you who knew what Harold Smith was and what he did but had not the courage to say so.'

Two guards pulled her hands away from the rail, put the chains back on and led her out of the courthouse, back to the gaol.

There were whispers amongst the crowd, some having taken in the implications of her speech. They filed out of the courtroom with less enthusiasm than when they had entered. They waited outside by the wagon that would take Ellen back to the prison. Amongst them was Mrs Donoghue. For the first time, Ellen felt a surge of emotion.

'You knew what he was. I hope you spent your blood money to your liking.' She spat on the ground at Mrs Donoghue's feet. The woman turned and walked away without speaking, the crowds parting silently to let her through.

Hands reached out to her as she walked. She looked up and tears came to her eyes as she saw girls she recognised from the ship that had brought them here, girls from Clare with whom she had walked across Ireland.

'We wanted to speak for you at your trial, Ellen. You remember me, Mary Forde, I was from Ennis. We were on the boat together. You were a good girl, I know that.'

Ellen couldn't speak, but nodded as she was pushed into the carriage.

**

She was to hang the following morning at eight. Father Gerard spent the night with her, in prayer.

'A small group of women from Clare and other parts of Ireland is gathered outside, Ellen, keeping vigil for you. A plea for clemency has been made to the governor. He's been informed of your circumstances. There's hope, Ellen.'

She knew there wasn't. The State Governor was known for his insistence on carrying out the punishment of crimes as ordered by law, in particular for "foreigners" as he termed them, although he himself was English. The reply came at midnight, delivered by the governor of the gaol.

'I'm sorry, Ellen. He says an example must be made. No-one can take the law into their own hands and expect mercy.'

She nodded silently, and went back to praying to the God she was finding it hard to believe in.

At seven thirty, guards arrived to change her into a simple shift and tie back her hair. They chained her hands and walked slowly with her to the hanging room. As she approached the door, she began to shudder. Father Gerard took her elbow.

'Close your eyes, Ellen. Think of your family, who you'll be with soon in heaven. See them, waiting for you.'

It was as if something had touched her skin with a caress, light as a feather, filling her with joy. She opened her eyes. In front of her was the Governor, the hangman and two more guards. But she didn't see them. She spoke in a low voice to the priest. 'I see them, Father Gerard, I see them. Mammy and Daddy, and the little ones, Daniel and Timothy, Johanna and Mary. It's like... it's like they're surrounded by light. Mammy is singing, our favourite song and Peg is there with them. She's holding out her hands to me. And Father, there's no Michael and no Norrie. They must still be alive.' Her face was filled with joy and tears.

'Have you anything to say before sentence is carried out?'

Ellen didn't reply.

The Governor read out the sentence. A hood was placed over Ellen's head. Father Gerard began to recite prayers.

The hangman stepped in and placed the rope around Ellen's neck.

'I'm coming,' she whispered.

It was over in minutes.

Bodies of executed persons were usually put into a rough box and buried within the prison grounds, but Father Gerard had insisted Ellen's body be released into his custody. He took her to the small church and performed a mass, for which he knew he would be in great trouble with the Bishop. He didn't care. He had seen what he had never seen before – the face of God on a human being. He was joined at the service by the women of Clare and their friends, by Harold Smith's two older daughters, and Billy's mother, Mrs Barambah.

After the mass, Ellen was buried under a false name, so that her final resting place could never be desecrated, as was known to happen to hanged criminals' graves if they were identified. He wrote to Father Jerome in Kilrush, to tell him about the name under which Ellen was buried, so that, should any family members want to find her, they would know where to look.

After thanking the small gathering, he spent a few minutes discussing with Mrs Barambah what Kathleen should be told about her mother's death, which they decided was that it had been an "accident".

He walked back into the church, filled with sorrow and disgust. He would make a visit to Mrs Donaghue the following day, to ensure she would never attend his church again. If she did, he would make her part in Ellen's history known to all, to her everlasting shame. Not that he believed the woman had any shame, but at least he would never have to see her sitting piously in front of him again.

Chapter 16

Having found no further references in the Vandeleur papers – she had briefly checked them again – about Seamus McMahon, after lunch Maggie made her way back to the family history research room and began with the 1901 census at the suggestion of one of the genealogy experts.

'By that time Dublin was a city of four hundred thousand people, only a third of its current population but sizeable enough. Provided Michael O'Donnell's name wasn't changed, you should find him without too much difficulty. Remind me what age he was by then?'

'He would have been around fifty-four. He had a wife, Bridget, and children. I have their names but it's doubtful they'll still be at home. Still I can give it a go.'

'Try 1911 too. I'll take a quick look at other databases for you.'

'Thanks, John.'

Maggie made her way to one of the dozen or so desks in the old, high-ceilinged room. There was just one other researcher at a computer and the room was peaceful and quiet. No traffic noise penetrated from the busy streets of Dublin. She sat at the first available machine and began her search.

With a deep breath, she opened up the file that would give her access to the Irish 1901 census. It took only a few minutes to locate the Michael O'Donnells in Dublin. There were dozens, but just three in the right age range, with a wife called Bridget, and only one with just one older child, single and living with her parents. This was the youngest child, the daughter, Bridget, now twenty-one years old. She checked the other two, just to be certain, but knew she had the right one. Everything fitted.

Michael had given his age as fifty-four and Bridget's as fifty-one. Their daughter Bridget was twenty-one. Michael's profession was listed as "dock labourer". Bridget had none. Young Bridget was a shop worker. They were all Catholic. But, for Maggie, the best information was that both Michael and Bridget had been born in County Clare. They didn't give anything other than the county, but this was enough.

She moved on to the 1911 census. This time, they were easy to locate as young Bridget had left home and it was just the older couple. Michael's given age was now sixty-three and Bridget's sixty-one. Michael was still working as a dock labourer. Bridget again had no recorded work. This was the census where years of marriage and number of children, both dead and alive, were recorded. They had been married for forty-three years, had five children, four living. One of Timothy's siblings had died. Which one? Maggie steeled herself. This was not part of her remit. It might even be something Mike Walker would want to find out for himself. She would put it to him when she spoke to him later.

That all changed when John came to sit beside her. 'Doing OK?' he asked.

'Great,' Maggie replied. 'I've found him on both census records. Everything matches. The only puzzle is that one of their children died. But I'm going to leave it to the client, see if he wants to…' She paused. 'I know that expression. You're about to tell me something I won't like.'

'That depends,' John said. 'I believe the child who died was the male twin, Michael Cornelius O'Donnell.'

'I presume he died as an adult?'

'Yes. He was believed to be a member of the Irish Republican Brotherhood. Do you know about that part of history?'

Maggie nodded. 'Not to any great extent, but if you can recommend some books, I'll get reading. What about Michael Cornelius?'

'It sounds like he was quite a hothead. From an early age he had prosecutions for minor crimes. Then, in 1910 he shot a policeman and was hanged for it.'

'1910? He would have been around forty?'

'The report says thirty-nine. I've a copy for you.' He handed her a print-out of a newspaper article. She read it then looked up. 'Son of a formerly imprisoned Fenian? Wasn't that a pejorative term?'

'Yes, depending on where and when it was used. Sounds like your Michael O'Donnell himself was strong for home rule.'

'Will the prison record be available? Maggie asked.

'Should be,' John replied. 'I can't tell you the reason for his imprisonment, if it was an act committed, or just political. Would you like me to go on looking?'

'Thanks, but no, John. I'll do it myself, but if I don't get anywhere, perhaps I can come back to you. This is the client's direct ancestor, so I'm sure he'll want to know. Can you tell me when he was imprisoned?'

'It was 1880.'

'All of the children would still have been at home and young Bridget would have been a baby. I wonder if that's why Timothy decided to go off to America? It could also explain why he never amended his incorrect name, particularly after his brother was hanged. That makes three murderers in the family. Sorry, just musing.'

John smiled. 'There's a lot to muse about in this family history. Good luck.'

'Thanks, and I'd better go. I have a video call at four thirty with Kevin in Ennis, who's found some actual information about the death of Seamus McMahon.'

'Is this what you expected when you took on this client?'

'Although I rarely have expectations, John, I did have a feeling about this one. So far, I've been right, and I feel like there's more to come.' She stood up and began to pack her briefcase. 'I'm not so sure about the client, though. This is going to come as quite a shock to him.'

**

Maggie began the call with Kevin at four thirty and found him already waiting.

'How's it going?' he asked.

'Interesting. I've found Michael O'Donnell on both the 1901 and 1911 census records. I've also found he was jailed around 1880 but I'm not sure why, yet. I'm going to see if I can find out this evening, before I head back to Wales in the morning. And, the final surprise, his eldest son, Michael Cornelius O'Donnell was hanged in 1910. He was a member of the IRB, and he shot a policeman in Dublin.'

There was a few seconds' silence. 'Wow,' Kevin said. 'That'll be a heavy load for your client. And I've more to add.'

'Do, please,' Maggie said. 'What have you found?'

'It's a newspaper article about the death of Seamus McMahon. Quite detailed, but on an interior page of the paper at the time, which was *The Clare Examiner*. Mind you, the front page was usually taken up with advertisements, so it wasn't a headline; they kept those for news of Royalty and War. Anyway, the gist of the article is that McMahon was with one other man walking home at night, when they were surprised by a gang of three, one of whom was a woman. They were overpowered. At first, it was thought a robbery, but soon became clear when the accompanying man – his name isn't given – was held back by the two men and the woman pinned McMahon to the ground, then slit his throat. The report says she gave out a wild, screaming laugh, but that may just have been embellishment by the unnamed friend. Then, the two men knocked the friend to the ground and the three ran off.'

'Does it say if they said anything throughout any of this hold-up?'

'It says that the woman whispered something to McMahon, and when she stood up, presumably after finishing her wild laugh, she shouted, "*You'll not kill more poor folk, nor remove them from their homes*"; sounds too much like a speech to me. It was probably just a few words but again, this is presented from the point of view of the witness. The important issue, for you, is that it says the woman was believed to be a young woman from Kilrush, recently removed from her family home for non-payment of rent.'

'Anything else?'

'There was a search. This happened just outside Kilrush. There was an army barracks not too far away and the soldiers searched the entire town and surrounding area, but despite a good description from the witness, none of the three was found. That's about it.'

'Was there any further information about the woman?

'Yes, the paper was offering a reward of ten pounds – a fortune back then – probably put up by the Vandeleurs. She was young, around twenty years, tallish, thin, with black hair and green eyes.'

'If it was dark, how could the witness have known the colour of her eyes?'

'Good point. It may be she got close to his face, or he just made it up. That's about it, Maggie. I've checked as many other sources as I can find, but that's all I could find.'

'Seamus McMahon was a hated man, so I'm guessing the reward was never collected. The Vandeleur papers don't even refer to the murder, apart from a letter thanking the army Major Henderson for his – failed – efforts in finding the killers.'

'Do you think this was your woman, Norrie Madigan?'

'I do, Kevin. We know that she was determined on revenge, so much so that she returned to Dublin. The timeline fits. The girls reached Liverpool in December 1849. I'm guessing Norrie returned immediately, as she never reached the ship in Portsmouth. There's a month or so gap between her return to Dublin and the murder of Seamus McMahon in January 1850. Father Jerome's letter to Ellen O'Donnell confirms when McMahon died. This gave her time to cross Ireland again, with accomplices. Perhaps they were members of the Young Irelanders, or the Molly

McGuires. Whatever, she found someone to help her in those three months. But then, she disappears.'

'What do you think could have happened to her?'

Maggie pondered for a few moments. 'Two possibilities. One: she remained in Dublin under an alias and looked after Michael. Two: she left Ireland. We have little chance of finding her on a shipping record. And what did she do with Michael if she did leave Ireland? I'm going with the second option. Based on information I discovered in Kilrush, she went to America, but most likely under an assumed name. If she did that, what did she do with Michael?'

'She must have left him with someone she trusted,' Kevin said.

'If so, all he would likely remember of his life would be in Dublin, not in Clare. Yet, the information in the census records, and in the names of his children, tells me he did find out about his roots. It could be that, if she trusted whomever she left him with, they eventually told him the truth. I wonder if he ever went back to Clare? If they told him everything, then he'd have known his family died in the famine, except for Ellen. Might he have gone looking for her?

'I have a thought.' Kevin said. 'Find out why he was in prison in 1880. If it was political, or just theft or vandalism, it might tell you something. Let's face it, there's nothing else between 1850 and 1901.'

'Good point, Kevin.' She glanced at her watch. 'I have to go now. I've promised the client an update on progress. I'd better tell him to be prepared. Kevin, I can't thank you enough, for—'

'Stop there. I'm glad to have been of help. The history of Irish independence is well documented, but in the end it's about people, and these small discoveries increase our knowledge. It's me should be thanking you.'

Enough,' Maggie said with a grin. 'I'll keep you in the loop about any progress I make.'

She ended the call and sat for half an hour making notes before she started the next call – with Mike Walker.

Chapter 17

Mike's response was stunned silence. A little unnerved, Maggie decided not to try to intervene in whatever thought processes he was going through. After all, it was a lot to take in. In just over a week, he had gone from thinking his ancestors came from Scotland to knowing that, not only were they from Ireland, but that almost the whole family died during the famine, and that one was imprisoned, and one hanged for their commitment to nationalism. And that was only the immediate line.

It was Mike who filled the silence gap. 'I'm stunned,' was his response. 'I don't know what to think about first.'

'Mike, shall I sum up all of this in writing for you and send it on to you now, before we go any further? I can do this tonight, so you'll have it before the end of your day. I'm here tonight, then taking the first boat back in the morning. I then have a five-hour drive to get home. We could do this again tomorrow afternoon. That'll give you twenty-four hours to read through everything and we can talk about each of the people in more detail. Would that work for you?'

He nodded slowly. 'I need some time with this, thank you Maggie. Let's say three for me, tomorrow afternoon. That's 8pm for you. Would that be too late?'

'No Mike, that's perfectly OK. I'm hoping to be home around three. The ferry is at six in the morning, docking around nine thirty. With five hours to drive, I should be home by three at the latest in South Wales, which will give me five hours to rest up and be ready for you. I'll send you details for joining the meeting.'

'Thank you. Jay and I can spend the evening and tomorrow morning working out questions. Be prepared. There are going to be a lot.'

'No problem, Mike. Pile them on. I'll speak to you tomorrow.'

They ended the call and Maggie got to work on her synopsis. It took almost three hours, as she included a family tree with names and dates as far back as she knew, although she also knew there would be more to add once she accessed US records – if she was going to do that. She wasn't sure from Mike's reaction if he would want Maze to continue. Well, whatever. She had decided on what she wanted to do next, and already had the beginning of a plan.

She was done by ten, satisfied that her report was as accurate as it could be, sent it off, then phoned Zelah.

'Doesn't sound to me like he wants to go much further,' Zelah said when she heard Maggie's description of the video call.

'Fifty-fifty, I'd say,' Maggie replied. 'There's so much more I could do, but I'll wait to hear what he has to say tomorrow. Zelah, there's something else on this, but—'

'Yes. I agree,' Zelah said.

'You don't know what I was going to say,' Maggie protested.

'Of course I know what you were going to say. You want to follow up on the three sisters. Rick was right, it's a great story. You want to follow the trail of Norrie Madigan in the US. You want to go to New York.'

Maggie laughed. 'What can I say? That's it exactly.'

'If he doesn't want you to do any more, then just go. I could do more than one of my usual books out of this. I might even write an actual book.'

'Become an author?' Maggie stopped and thought, then said, 'Why not? Depending on what the outcome is for Norrie Madigan, it would make a brilliant genealogy book. You'd have to add some tension, throw in a death, or something threatening in America. But yes, a great story.'

'Sounds to me like you should write it,' Zelah replied.

'No, I like what I do. I have no delusions about my ability to write fiction. I'll leave that to you. Let's see where we are after tomorrow. What are your plans?'

'We're heading off tomorrow to Rosscarbery. Mischa has passed her third year with flying colours. She'll be getting in front of real patients next. We're going to have a celebratory meal out somewhere. Then, Stephen and I have to discuss the revised plans for the extension. After that, it's another couple of days in Cork city, for Rick. He really loves that place. Then, after a few more days in Rosscarbery, we'll be back. Make sure you keep me up to date on your discussions with Mike Walker.'

'Will do. I'm going to grab a bite to eat, then it's sleeping for me. I've an early start.'

'Drive safely. Enjoy the boat trip.'

'Sarcastic to the end, Zelah. The weather forecast is perfect. It'll be a smooth crossing and I've booked myself into the first-class lounge.'

'Good for you.' Zelah ended the call.

Maggie went down to the restaurant, ate a light meal then back to her room and bed. It was a while before she slept. She didn't think about what Mike Walker's response would be. It didn't really matter. What would be, would be. He was related to Norrie Madigan through the three sisters, but it was so long ago he might not be interested. In a way, this was better. Without an obligation to a client, she could work the case entirely for Maze.

Her head was full of Norrie Madigan; of finding out what had happened to her in New York, and planning when and for how long she could go.

**

The sea was calm, the boat on time and the drive long. Maggie reached home at three thirty. She'd needed a stop on the way for some fresh air and to stop herself falling asleep, despite the music, the podcasts and the audio book.

She had called Bob to let him know she was on her way. He said he wouldn't be late, the South Wales crime scene being still sleepy. She arrived to an empty house. No sign of Nick. She called him to check if there was anything to catch up on. There wasn't. He had taken a day off and he and Stella were at the seaside with Flora, who was now seven months old, crawling around, loving the sea and the sand.

'Are you loving it too, Nick?'

'Absolutely. Mind you, the water's still freezing.'

'British kids don't notice. I remember. I think we're born with an "immune to seaside cold water" gene.'

'Definitely. We'll catch up tomorrow. I have to go. Flora's heading for another kid's sandcastle which she intends to knock down.'

Shaking her head, Maggie ended the call. Whoever would have thought the quiet, dour fifty-five-year-old Nick would end up gleefully chasing his tiny daughter around a beach. Her Alice had always hated sand and sea. She recalled their summer in Cornwall, when they stayed at the wonderful house on the clifftop at Sennen Cove and Zelah had told them the true story of her own youth. Happy times.

After quickly unpacking, she took a cold drink into the garden, where Bob joined her at five.

'That's a lot of notes,' he said, glancing at the pad on the table in front of Maggie. What are you planning next?'

She spent the next twenty minutes going through the story of Mike Walker's relatives, and of the discoveries she had made in Ireland. She was surprised that he nodded enthusiastically when she reached the end, then mentioned the prospect of a trip to New York.

'How about I come with you, if it's on. It'll be more fun if you're not on your own.'

She reached out and hugged him. 'That would be wonderful,' she replied. 'You're a good man, Chief Inspector Pugh.'

'I know,' he replied, grinning smugly. 'Mind you the crims will have to behave themselves if I'm going to take five days off.'

'Five days? Who said anything about five days?'

'Has to be,' he replied. 'You know, jet lag, your research, lots to see.'

'I'll know better after this call at eight.' She yawned. 'This is a long day.'

**

Maggie was ready at eight, with her notes, as was Mike Walker. He began to talk at once.

'Maggie, you've done an amazing job, a wonderful job. Jay and I are still stunned at what you've found out. And I've discovered I have thousands of cousins, through the DNA test, both here in the States and in Ireland, as well as the one in Australia.'

'For some of them, when you get down to the "5th-8th" range, it may be difficult to find the connection. At that distance it will go back many generations.'

'I know. The Irish ones are mostly in that category, but now I have the history and the names,' he stopped and coughed. Maggie knew what was coming. 'We – uh – we want to take it ourselves from here. I'm sorry.'

'Mike, that's absolutely fine with me; please don't apologise. I'm always delighted when a client becomes more deeply involved in their own story. It tells me I've done my job.'

'Your job has been superbly done,' he replied.

'What plans do you have?'

Maggie could see the blush on the screen. 'We've thought about it overnight, and we're going to take a trip to Ireland. We'll start in Dublin, then go across to Clare. I've found two cousins from Clare. I've written to them. So far, one has replied, so we're going to meet up with her. I want to see Kilrush and Cappa and Moy—'

'Mike, Moy isn't really there. It was destroyed. It was only really a line of cabins, that was called Clamhunger Row, and they're gone.'

'Oh, OK. But it'll still be good to just go stand there.'

'I think you'll love Clare. It's wild but beautiful.'

'We're setting off in two weeks. We'll be away for two weeks, then we're thinking about coming over to England, to visit Devon, and see the places Jay's ancestors came from.'

'Sounds like a great trip,' Maggie said. 'Perhaps we can arrange to meet up.'

'I'm expecting it,' he replied with a beaming smile.

'What about you? Onto the next case?'

'Not exactly. Mike, there's something I want to tell you. It's research that I want to do for Maze. It wouldn't be fair if I didn't tell you I was planning to do it.'

His smile turned to a puzzled frown.

Maggie decided to push on. 'I told you about the three sisters. I'm interested in the third one, Catherine Corcoran, known as "Kitty". She was Norrie Madigan's mother.'

'The Norrie who killed the agent?'

'That's right. From—'

She had to be careful here. She had told him she had information obtained in Cappa about the cousins, including Norrie Madigan, but she hadn't told him about Joan or the letters. She had promised Joan and she wasn't going to break that promise. On the other hand she could ask Joan about meeting Mike, and only if Mike wanted to, but not yet. 'From the information I found in Kilrush it looks like Norrie went to America, as you know. I'd like to see if I could find out more about what happened to her. Of course this will be at Maze's expense entirely. So, I'm planning to go to New York, quite soon.'

To her relief, he laughed. 'When you said you were a fanatical genealogist, I wasn't too sure what you meant. Now I get it. It would be ironic if you were here, when we're going to be there.'

'I'll just be going on a short trip, about five days should be enough. I'm sure I'll be back by the time you reach Devon. Let's exchange dates and set something up.'

'Good plan,' he replied.

They said their goodbyes and the call ended. Maggie sighed again with relief. She was free now to follow her own plan.

**

Two days later, on Monday morning, the architect called to tell Maggie that he had initial drawings for her and asked if they could meet. They agreed on two days' time, which would give Maggie enough time to do the research she needed for her and, hopefully, Bob's trip.

Bob called at midday to say he had no problem booking in the five days, but preferably including a weekend. They agreed to begin planning flights and hotels that evening. Maggie felt the excitement mounting.

That evening she spoke to Jack and Alice, both of whom were delighted at the prospect of having the house to themselves for five days. Maggie suggested Max move in also, and Alice asked if Matthew could join them, which was fine with Maggie.

'And if you have any plans for bigger get-togethers, or, God forbid, parties, forget it. You can do those when you have your own homes. And, of course, Nick will be here every day.' She made a note to tell Nick. 'If you need anything, he'll be able to help. And Stella too.'

They all agreed it was fine, although Jack's fixed smile told her he had formed an immediate plan, on which she had just thrown a full bucket of cold water. If they wanted a party, Max had a flat. They could go there.

Chapter 18

Bob was going to take care of the arrangements for travel and accommodation, and other matters concerning their trip to New York. Excited about the trip as she was, Maggie wanted to arrive in New York armed with as much information on Norrie Madigan as she could find. Not that it would be much, with just two names to go on: Edward Corcoran and the Cullinan family. Ellen's letter naming her uncle and mentioning the Cullinan family had been written in 1854, and she mentioned him again in the 1858 letter. She had also talked about Norrie being married to a policeman.

The following morning, she began researching.

When she had seen the list of the tenants of Clamhunger Row she thought there might have been a family named Cullinan or something similar. She checked her phone for the list. Yes! The name on the list was Cullinane. Edward Corcoran was not there. That meant that some at least of the Cullinanes had survived and reached America, or Australia. The letter hadn't been specific. Edward Corcoran, however, would either have been living elsewhere or would have departed before Clamhunger Row was destroyed. He had gone to America and the suggestion was that he was in New York. Did Norrie find him?

Her first idea was to check census results for the United States, knowing that they had probably the longest set of surviving records in the world. She had no idea when Norrie had gone there, or under what name. It would have been after 1849 and before 1854. She couldn't, for now, pin it down any closer. And if, as she suspected, Norrie had not used her own name, there was no point even beginning a search for "Honora Madigan".

Thinking logically, she knew that it would be helpful to have a rough idea of Edward Corcoran's age. He was brother to the three Corcoran sisters, but elder or younger, or somewhere in the middle? There was only one possible source – the Clare church records. It was unlikely she would find his birth record. She had found the names of the three sisters from the baptisms of their children. Knowing how important sponsors were, she looked again at the records of the baptisms of Ellen O'Donnell and her siblings. Edward Corcoran was not there, but there was a Joseph Corcoran, as a sponsor to Michael, and an Eliza Corcoran for Johanna, one of Ellen's sisters. She would have to try the siblings of both Margaret "Peg" Dillon and Norrie Madigan. This was going to be a long morning. However, not as long as expected. She had begun with Norrie and had found two siblings; one had a Timothy Corcoran another a Jeremiah Corcoran as a sponsor. After a quick tea break, she looked at Peg Dillon, and there he was. Peg's baptismal sponsors were a Margaret Reilly and Edward Corcoran. The year was 1833. Guessing that Edward would have been at least sixteen when he stood as sponsor to Peg, she began with a birth year of 1815 – unlikely – and went back as far as 1800. There were no records of any Corcoran children born in Kilrush in that period. However, she did have a family tree now. No parents' names, but at least eight children. If any of them apart from Edward had survived the famine, their ancestors might be in Clare, or indeed in America. Having drawn up the tree she sent it to Mike Walker, in case a Corcoran came up in his "cousins" list. You never knew.

'How's it going?

Maggie was so deep in thought about her next move, that she hadn't heard Nick arrive and enter the office.

'Maggie? Hello, anyone home? Earth to Maggie Gilbert.'

She spun around. 'Sorry, deep thinking. How are you?'

'Sunburnt, but it was a good day. What's happening?'

As Maggie filled him in, Nick asked no questions. He gazed frowningly at her, with the occasional 'hmm'. His eyebrows shot up when he heard that Maggie and Bob were going to New York for five days.

'Sorry, Nick. You'll be holding the fort.'

'Not a problem. When are you going?'

'We wanted to speak to you about dates before we actually book anything. It has to include a weekend, so could be as early as next Thursday or Friday, unless that interferes with anything you have planned. Zelah should be back by then, too. She and Rick are in Rosscarbery now and on their way back, I think, in about a week. She'll be in and out. She has an idea about this story.'

'Which is?'

'She wants to write a book about the three sisters,'

Nick grinned. 'From what you've just told me, there were at least five sisters and three brothers.'

'When would a small detail like that stop Zelah, once she's got her teeth into an idea?'

He shook his head. 'Where are you going next with this research?'

'I'm not sure, Nick. Do you have some ideas about databases I could search? I've not dealt with the famine years in Ireland before this and I know there aren't any reliable passenger lists until at least the 1880s.'

'I do,' he replied, starting up his laptop. 'And that's an incorrect assumption. There are two I'd suggest to begin with. The first is the New York Passenger Lists 1820 – 1891. It lists everyone entering the USA through New York. The records from the very early dates are fragmentary, but later on they become more comprehensive. There was no immigration entry point as such, before Castle Garden in 1855, but each ship's captain had to provide a manifest to the New York authorities. The details are vague. Ireland was just part of the UK then. The list gives a name, age in years and months – and people in the early years only had a vague idea of the year in which they were born, never mind the month – sex, occupation, country of departure and country in which they intended to become inhabitants, and whether or not they died on the voyage. There were always corpses during the famine years when the ship docked. Then, if you can pin down the age of Edward Corcoran, there's the United States Irish Famine Immigrants List, which goes from 1846 to 1851. It gives birth year, arrival year, name of the ship and destination. Then, when you get onto an actual record, you'll find much more information, such as occupation and, if you're very lucky, county of birth, as well as just "Ireland". Birth year comes with an "estimated" tag. After that, you can go on to census records.'

Maggie shook her head. 'You're amazing, Nick.'

'Not really,' he replied, turning back to his laptop.

'Coffee?'

'Yes please,' he said, still not turning around, but Maggie thought she caught a side glimpse of a smile.

She began the search with the New York Passenger Lists, which proved disappointing. Even with age and arrival ranges as wide as was feasible, she had only two results, one of which was too early, in 1842 and the other too late, in 1854.

She moved on to the United States Irish Famine Immigrants list. It was a useful resource, even though it only went from 1846 to 1851. She began with "Honora Madigan", just in case, but nothing came up. Searching on "Honora", then "Norah" then "Norrie" brought up hundreds of results in the age bracket she had allowed for – a birth year between 1830 and 1835 – even the latter date had fifty-seven potential surnames, and she didn't know if Norrie would have even used her own first name, never mind her family name.

Next, she tried Edward Corcoran. This was better. There were eight Edward Corcorans, born between 1800 and 1820, arriving in New York between 1846 and 1849. She had made 1849 the top end of the scale, as the girls had left Kilrush in 1849 and from Ellen's letter it appeared she already knew that her uncle had gone to America at the time of their own departure.

Eight names, ranging in age from twenty-one to thirty-one. Widening out the possible year of birth brought no more Edward Corcorans onto the list. So, if he were one of the eight, he could have been born anywhere between 1817 and 1827.

'Was he married?'

Nick's voice made her jump.

'I don't know. I'll check the database. I know that Ellen's parents were married in 1833. Records start in 1830, but some are hard to read. I'll give it a go.'

Ten minutes later, she gave a whoop.

'You found it.'

'Yes, I've found his marriage. He married in Kilrush in 1840. No age given, so I still don't know when he was born. But it's definitely him. His wife was called Ann Sullivan and the witnesses were Johanna Corcoran and Michael O'Donnell – Ellen's parents. Johanna was already an O'Donnell, but it wasn't unusual to give the mother's maiden name as a witness, same as you find sometimes for baptismal sponsors. I'm going to look to see if they had any children.'

Another fifteen minutes and she whooped again.

'Enough with the whooping,' Nick said.

'Ok. But I'm excited. I've found two children: Timothy born in 1841 and Ellen in 1843. That means he must have emigrated shortly after the birth of Ellen.'

'Or maybe he lost them in the famine. Ellen's letter only asked about her uncle; no mention of his family.'

Maggie's shoulders sagged. 'Yes, a definite possibility. It also means I'll have to research both a single man and a family on immigration and census records.'

'That's the job,' Nick replied. He turned around to face Maggie, who had sat back with her arms folded and was frowning. 'I'll help, if you'd like me to.'

The frown turned to a beam. 'Please, Nick. If you aren't too busy yourself.'

'Nothing that can't wait a couple of hours. Right, how about we start with the databases of immigration and see if we can find Ann, Timothy and Ellen. That'll tell us if he went alone or with his wife and children. You take the New York Passengers list, I'll take the Famine Immigrants list. Shouldn't take too long between us, given we know the ages of the children.'

'Right. Nick, what about Castle Garden, wouldn't there be some info there?'

'Didn't start until 1855. Before that the ships just unloaded them all at a New York pier and left them to it. They had to make their own way.'

'That may well come into the story of Edward Corcoran and Norrie, but for now, let's keep to the plan,' Maggie said. 'You know what I'm like about disappearing down rabbit holes. If I start to get interested in what the immigrant experience was like, we'll still be here this time next week.'

'Definitely. Let's give it an hour and compare notes.'

An hour later, at twelve thirty, they stopped for another break, each with a solemn face.

'Let's head outside,' Maggie said. 'compare stories, although I think we've reached the same conclusion.'

Once settled under the pergola at the bottom of the garden, next to the fence which separated the end of the garden from the canal, Maggie sighed and opened her notebook. 'I have two good prospects. Two out of the four family members in each case. They both landed in New York in 1848. What about you?'

Nick nodded. 'I have two – both called Edward and Timothy, arriving in 1848, one in May and one in December.'

'Same.'

They were both quiet for a moment, gazing over the fence at the black, still water of the canal.

'Both of my Edwards and Timothys were aged thirty and seven respectively,' Maggie began, 'but it's impossible to tell which might be the correct one. Place of birth just says Ireland for both.'

'I have more details on both Edwards. One – the May one – was a tailor. The December one was a carpenter.'

'But no sign of Ann or Ellen on anything I've looked at. I've seen a few more Edwards, with women I think were their wives, but no wife called Ann nor child called Ellen. It must be one of the two we've identified,' Maggie replied. 'It seems fair at the moment to say that Ann and Ellen died, and Edward headed off to America with Timothy.'

'If there's nothing further in these records, then we can move on to the 1850 census, assuming they stayed in New York.'

Maggie nodded. Ellen's letter asked after her uncle in New York. They could have had news back, somehow, that he was there.'

Nick leaned forward and picked up a sandwich. 'Let's think it through.' He lapsed into silence and Maggie knew there was no point in trying to push him for initial thoughts and ideas. They would come when he was ready. Sandwich finished, Nick stood and walked to the fence, staring intently into the water, as if he might find an answer come popping up from the blackness. The only thing that popped up was a frog, that landed on the bank, then jumped back in. He turned back to Maggie.

'Even if we can trace the right Edward through the census records, it doesn't help with Norrie. Ellen's 1858 letter indicates Norrie was married, with a child. The next census wasn't until 1860, so she'd probably have a different name and address by that time. They just about got the census in before the start of the Civil War.'

'We know that she married a policeman,' Maggie said. 'It's not much, but it's a start.'

Nick picked up his tablet and tapped away for a few minutes. There was a police force in New York in the early 1850s. Says here they didn't have proper uniforms until 1853.'

'Can you find something that says how many men served in the New York police in the 1850s?' Maggie asked.

'I'll go back inside and start researching,' Nick replied. He left, leaving Maggie in the garden. 'Talk about finding needles in a haystack,' she muttered. 'Still, we have to try.'

Chapter 19
Dublin 1850

Norrie Madigan squeezed herself into a door entry and held her breath as the soldiers rushed past. She had missed curfew, being determined to reach the office of *The Nation* newspaper before it closed for the night. It was dark enough to keep her safe on the streets, she thought, but it had been her bad luck to run into, not just a small troupe of soldiers policing the curfew, but a group led by Major Wilfred Henderson. She had run, praying he had not recognised her, that she was just a woman out alone on the streets after curfew.

He would have recognised her, she was sure, or at least been curious enough to wonder why a woman matching the description of Norrie Madigan, killer of Seamus McMahon, whom he had hunted relentlessly in Kilrush, was now running on the streets of Dublin late at night.

At the office of *The Nation*, David would be worrying. She was only supposed to have been visiting Michael at the family who had taken him in, just a quick visit, she had promised, one of the few times she would see him before she, David and Norah set off for America as brother and sister, David and Ellen Margaret Dillon, and David's wife Norah.

When she had arrived back in Dublin she had gone straight to the office of *The Nation*, asking for help to get back to Clare.

'And why would you be wanting to go back into the death-house?' David Dillon had asked.

'I have business there.'

'In the Kilrush death-house?' David had asked. He always referred to any Workhouse as a "death-house". As far as he was concerned, that's what they were.

Despite much questioning Norrie had refused to give her reason for going back. She didn't want to allow anyone to know part of her plan, despite her sometimes overwhelming need to talk about her family and what had been done to them by Seamus McMahon, and her pain when those memories rose up into her throat – just in case she was caught, and names of accomplices were demanded. The less anyone knew, the better. But he had seen the look in her eyes, the fanatical hatred. When she asked for a name of someone who might assist her in carrying out a particular task she had to fulfil, he had understood.

The name provided, Joseph Power, was a giant of a man, over six feet tall, and muscular, with the darkest eyes and thickest neck Norrie had ever seen, all of it muscle. He barely spoke but listened with fierce intensity. When the time came, he turned up with another man, shorter but equally powerfully built. They had walked together across Ireland without any trouble. When the deed was done, the two men had disappeared into the night, silently. Norrie had never seen either of them again.

She waited another ten minutes, until her breathing steadied and she felt it was safe to re-emerge and make a run for the office. It was only a few streets away.

There was just one scare before she reached the back door of the office – a family of a mother and two children, barely clothed, wandering the streets, walking skeletons. She wanted to offer them shelter but knew that could be dangerous, so gave them a couple of pennies. The mother wept her thanks, wringing Norrie's hand, not letting go until Norrie yanked her hand away, smiled and ran off.

David was ready behind the door.

'Where have you been, Norrie? I was beginning to worry.'

She told him about the soldiers and Major Henderson. He shook his head. 'Do you think he recognised you?'

She thought for a minute. 'No. He spent a long time looking for me in Kilrush. He didn't even try beyond the townland. He thinks I'm no more than an ignorant peasant, being hidden by my own kind. He hasn't the imagination to believe I could have crossed to Dublin.'

'What about Michael? Might Henderson know you took him?'

'Major Henderson would not have entered the Workhouse,' she said with a ferocious grin. 'Much too scared. He'd have sent in one of those young lads he commands. Only a couple of people saw me, and I swore them to silence.'

'Would they comply, Norrie?'

'Totally.'

'Well, it worries me, nonetheless. We may have to advance our plans. Norah is ready. Tomorrow I'll be checking out the next sailings. We can't risk another two months. We'll see if we can get away next week.'

Norrie threw herself into a chair and put her hands over her face. Tears began. 'I'm so sorry, David.'

'Norrie Madigan, stop that crying, would you. You're one of the strongest girls I know, and we have a few in the organisation. We're off to America. No-one will know us; we'll have a new life, a better, safer life. And we can be sure of arriving before our child is born.' He smiled gently. 'My child will be an American, but I'll be sure he never forgets Ireland.'

'Might be a girl.'

'Then she'll never forget. Nor will his – or her – children, and their children. Right, I'm for home.' David and Norah shared a room with her parents and her two sisters, in the building next door.

'I met a woman in the street,' Norrie said, now looking up. 'She was in rags, with two starving children who could barely walk. I gave her my last few pennies. I loved my family and my friends, my cousins, in Australia. But when I remember Ireland, I'll remember that woman, the despair, the hopelessness. I'll never forget her.'

David paused at the door. 'Who was she? What was her name?'

'I don't know. I didn't ask her name.'

'She was Ireland,' David said.

Norrie went to her straw pallet at the back of the office and lay for a long time, unable to sleep, thinking about the woman and her children. She would be able to buy bread in the morning. But what after that? She'd probably die, if she couldn't find a place in the Workhouse, or something to eat at a soup kitchen, as would her children. If this was Ireland now, she wanted no more of it.

**

They departed Dublin two days later, for Queenstown, from which David had found berths in steerage for the three of them on a sail ship, *The Wanderer.* The trip to New York would take around ten weeks, provided, David said, there were no storms.

As she watched Ireland disappear, Ellen Margaret Dillon, aka Norrie Madigan knew she'd never see home again. But, she was determined to make a success of America, for her family and her friends. She would be the one who got away, the one who survived.

Her final meeting with Michael had been heartbreaking, for her. He hadn't understood that this was his final time with her. He was three and a half years old. He would forget her. The new family – also called O'Donnell so that Michael would never have to change his name – promised to tell him his real story as soon as they felt he was old enough. James and Sarah O'Donnell were no relation to Michael, but they already loved him as much as their other two babies. They had lost two young children to the famine, both of typhus. They were not going to lose Michael. James now had work at the Port of Dublin. They would survive. She hugged him to her.

'Ouch, Auntie Norrie. You hurted me.' He struggled to get himself out of her grasp.

'Sorry, Michael. Didn't mean to hurt. Goodbye now. Don't forget Ellen, will you, like we talked about? Now, off you run. Sarah has bread and a bit of jam for you.'

The little boy ran away to Sarah, who gave Norrie a pitying smile, and took him to their shared kitchen.

Norrie walked to the prow of the ship, towards America. Ireland was gone. A new life was about to begin, for Michael O'Donnell, and for herself.

Part Two

America: 1851 – present day

Chapter 20

New York scared her, at first. Maggie decided within five minutes she'd never experienced anything like it: the heat, the humidity, the crowds, the noise. She had visited many cities, but this was a unique experience.

From the time she and Bob stepped out of the airport building at JFK International and into the cab that Bob had pre-booked, she was awestruck; not just the way the cab driver made his way into and through the city, which felt like he would have been happy to eliminate any and everyone who got in his way, but the level of aggressiveness, in both other vehicles and the fast striding, angry looking pedestrians she glimpsed as the taxi whizzed past.

They had landed at five fifteen in the evening. It took over an hour to reach the centre of Manhattan. Bob had chosen a hotel with a pool. When they reached their room on the 30th floor – a luxurious double with a wide balcony fronted by a high glass panel, onto which she was definitely not stepping, Maggie scoured through her suitcase, found her swimsuit and took off to find the pool. It turned out to be on the roof, enclosed only by a high glass panel surrounding it. There were just two other swimmers. Half an hour of swogging relaxed her sufficiently to return to the room, where Bob was on the balcony with a cold beer, gazing out at the view of the sun setting over the city, with the corner of Central Park in view on the left-hand side. He had adjusted the air conditioning to a reasonable level; comfortably cool.

'Beer?' he said without looking round. 'If you can handle it, you should come and see this.'

'I'm going to take a shower, then I think I'll just stand behind the window. See you in a few minutes. By the way, what are we going to do about dinner? I'm starving, but I don't feel I have the strength to go down to the restaurant.'

'Room service,' he replied. 'I've ordered some hot sandwiches and fries. OK with you?'

'Fine,' she replied. She was used to Bob making these kinds of decisions without consulting her and anyway, after five years together he knew what she liked to eat.

She was back out in five minutes and ventured to the edge of the open balcony access.

'It's OK,' Bob said. 'Just don't look straight down.'

Maggie edged her way around the glass door and dropped into the chair next to Bob, who had moved his chair back. She picked up the beer from the table, as a knock came at the door. Room service had arrived. Back on the balcony, Bob put the tray of food on the table between the two chairs.

'Shall we make a plan for tomorrow?' he asked.

'I'd like to start with the Tenement Museum. We'll need a cab. There's also the Merchant's House Museum. The middle- and upper-class merchants had Irish servants, so definitely worth a look. Then, perhaps we can go on down to Battery Park and take a boat across to the Statue of Liberty.'

Whoa!' Bob said. 'We have four and a half days. Let's pace ourselves.'

'Ok. What do you suggest?'

'I'm happy to go to the Tenement Museum in the morning, but I thought you wanted to find out more about the New York police force in the 1850s, see if you could identify a marriage for Norrie Madigan, or whatever she was calling herself. What's your plan for that?'

Maggie slumped back in her chair, ate a fry and closed her eyes. 'I don't have one. Nick is looking through any information he can find online. There used to be an NYPD Museum here, but it closed some years ago. I need a name.'

'Which shouldn't be too difficult. You already know she married a policeman before 1858 and she was in Ireland in early 1850, so probably mid 1850 when she arrived in New

York. By 1858 she was married with a child. Think about a timeline, for her to settle here, meet a young man, get married and have a child. Ellen's 1858 letter said "baby" and was in response to one written to her, which would have taken three months to reach her, probably more, as she says she only travelled into Melbourne to see Father Gerard infrequently. Therefore, the letter to her must have been written in 1857 or even 1856. It narrows down the timeline. The child would have been born in 1854 or 1855, so the marriage would have been around 1853 to 1854, allowing for a courting period of around six to twelve months. And she had her own shop. Now that really would have taken some doing for a destitute girl, from 1850 to 1856. It adds to the narrower the timelines, at least.'

'Yes, that's good. But still, without a name…'

Maggie yawned.

'You're very tired,' Bob said. 'How about we do the visits Monday, instead of tomorrow. With a bit of luck we can find someone at the Tenement Museum to speak to. If we have any time left after that we can do some sightseeing. For tomorrow, I think we should have an easier day, maybe just stroll around, take in Manhattan. You'll be more refreshed.'

Maggie yawned again. 'I need to sleep. It may be ten at night here, but for us it's three am. Let's go to bed. We can think some more in the morning. My head's about to drop off.'

'That would be an interesting sight.'

'Good night, Robert.'

Chapter 21
New York 1850

New York scared her, at first. Norrie Madigan, who had never had a fear of anything before in her life, took one look at the raucous, arguing, crowds on the quayside, some terrified, others aggressive and fighting already, and wanted to turn around and go straight back to Ireland, to take her chances there.

But that would mean the possibility of facing another storm. Despite having lived by the ocean and witnessed spectacular winter storms, none of those had prepared her for what they had experienced for three days during their sea voyage. She had been up on deck when she sensed that the ship was buffering harder against the waves and the wind, stronger than it had been since they left Ireland. She had had to get out of the steerage accommodation, where she shared a family bunk with David and Norah. The smells and the fetid air had become too much. She was used to living in their cabin with the pigs, but the smell being given off by the vomit of sea-sick humans, together with the other smells produced by the buckets that weren't emptied nearly often enough in her opinion, was nauseating. A few families were out cooking their daily meal but were having trouble keeping everything steady. Ahead the sky was black and roiling, coming down lower. The rain began as a drizzle but as an hour passed, it became hard and slashing. The family, who had managed to cook their meal and eat something, packed up and went back down below. Another twenty minutes, and Norrie knew that something was wrong.

The Captain, whom she had only seen once since The Wanderer left Queenstown, now appeared on the bridge, shouting. 'Baton down, baton down, everyone. Get them all below. This is going to be bad.'

Sailors rushed around, shouting at the passengers to get below. She was shoved down into the hold, and the hatch slammed shut above her head. She went to their shared bunk, where David was tending Norah, who was nauseous yet again.

'Something's not right David,' she whispered. 'They've locked us in. The sky is black, and the ship is hitting huge waves, bigger than I've ever seen. The sailors look worried.'

'Nothing we can do,' he replied. 'We'll be fine down here. It'll only be for a few hours.'

The storm continued for three days. Norrie's only thought was that she was going to die. Goods that hadn't been roped down rolled and smashed, and people who couldn't hold on rolled around too. Children screamed as the ship pitched and the sound of waves crashing with a thunderous roar above and beside them convinced them they were going to sink.

Women wailed as they watched their possessions disappear amongst the mess. The worst horror: a mother lost her grip on her baby, which washed down to the bottom of the hold, amongst the filth. It was drowned by the time the mother waded in and found it. The sickness intensified to a degree where the smell became unbearable as did the amount of human excrement that couldn't be contained in the buckets. Norrie clung onto her edge of the bunk, with David on the other side and Norah wedged in between them, and prayed, certain this was retribution for what she had done.

When the storm finally abated, on the afternoon of the third day, and it had become almost impossible to breathe, the hatches were opened, and the stronger passengers kicked the weaker ones out of the way in their desperation to ascend the ladder out of the stinking steerage hold.

No, she couldn't face that again. She had arrived in America and, taking a deep breath and squaring her shoulders, here she would stay.

Baggage was being unloaded for the wealthier passengers who had baggage to unload. Norrie had nothing to her name; just a parcel with one spare dress and bloomers, plus her material from her Workhouse box. She was exhausted, ravenous and anxious – their food had been severely rationed in the last week to last through the delay caused by the storm. Despite the gnawing in her stomach, Norrie gripped her fists together. She had been distraught, frightened for her life in Dublin, so now needed to banish the doubts that were setting in.

She watched from the crowded deck as bodies were removed in their shrouds. Four men, two women and six children, including the baby. The adults and some children had been sick before they got on the boat.

She was torn out of her reverie by the health official who had supervised the removal of the dead and the morbidly sick.

'You, girl, next.' He grabbed her mouth, opened and examined it, then pushed it shut. Then, he examined her arms and hands. 'You got signs of sickness, girl?'

'None at all, sir,' Norrie replied. 'I'm healthy.'

He gave her a leering look, then deemed her fit to enter the city, pushing her aside and moving on to the next shaking, panicked person.

She watched the diseased being taken away next, shrieking families trying to go with them, but being pushed out of the way by the health official and his cohorts.

'Where are they taking them?' She asked a man standing next to her.

'To a place of quarantine, on Staten Island, over there,' he pointed to a building on a small island just off the shore.'

'Is it like the Workhouse, do you think?'

The man laughed. 'Probably.' He walked away to join the line of single men queueing to leave the ship. Norrie suspected many of the poor devils would never be seen again. Families were separated. Husbands and wives begged the health official to allow them to accompany their sick family members, but were refused, as were the parents of sick children.

A tug on her arm pulled her around and away from the sight of the bodies. She knew she must forget what she'd just seen and heard. This America was a hard, unforgiving place.

'Nor… Ellen, David's waiting for us. Are you coming, or what?' Norah Dillon wasn't happy about Norrie accompanying them. A timid creature, Norrie thought. Small, blonde and pretty was Norah, but she had been constantly sick throughout the voyage and David worried about the baby. There were still several months to go, but Norah was sick every day.

David Dillon gave Norrie some confidence. He had that look about him; self-assured, a leader, tall with ginger hair and a wide smile. How could anyone believe they were brother and sister? Still, that's how they had set out and would remain until they were settled, and it was time for them to go their separate ways, which, for Norah Dillon, couldn't come soon enough.

People from steerage were still crowding onto the quayside, huddling together in family groups, unsure of what to do or where to go. Some of the women were crying. What did they expect, Norrie wondered, as she followed Norah down the gangplank? A welcoming committee? A number of the men were fighting youngish lads who were trying to take their luggage, telling them they could find them accommodation at good prices.

'And if you believe that, you'll believe anything,' Norrie said to David as they reached the quayside.

'Many of these people have nowhere to go,' David said. 'I've heard about this. The boys are called "runners". They spot the weak ones, then fleece them. At least there are some people trying to help, look, over there.'

At the far end of the quayside Norrie could see a group of adults trying to gather people around them.

'Friendly societies,' David said. 'Not just Irish; Germans, Russians and Jews too. They were once refugees themselves. They have hostels and take in those who made no provision for what might happen after they arrived here. Most of those people have no money. Their landlords paid for their transport but gave them nothing to survive on when they arrived here.'

'What about us, David? Where are we going?' Norrie asked. Norah was clinging onto David's arm, looking faint.

'I have an address,' he said. 'Somewhere for us to stay for a few weeks, until we have ourselves settled and,' he raised his eyes to the bright blue sky, 'if the job on the newspaper is still available to me. Come on, let's get away from this.'

They walked for over an hour through teeming streets of a Lower Manhattan district called the Five Points, to another, called the Lower East Side. Norrie breathed a sigh of relief as they walked beyond the area, leaving behind its gangs of men hanging around on territorial street corners, its brothels, pubs and filthy people of all types and denominations.

The buildings looked no better than the slums of Dublin. Yet, there was a sense of optimism in the air here, more than there had been in Dublin. People chattered, argued and laughed. In Dublin, indeed everywhere in Ireland, people had become too exhausted by hunger and hopelessness to speak to each other in the street. They had looked, then averted their gaze when they saw no help in the eyes that met theirs.

'We're here.' David had halted as they turned a corner onto Suffolk Street, then walked along until he stopped suddenly in front of a brown building, its front door hanging off one hinge and many of the windows broken and boarded up with whatever the inhabitant of the room could find. Norah looked at it with dismay. David felt her grip tighten on his arm and said, 'It's not for long, darlin', just a few weeks until my job is secure, and we can find a place of our own. It's to be a shared room, but not for long.'

Norah returned an unconvinced weak smile.

'We need to find Patrick and Bridget Allen. My informant said Bridget would be at home with the children, in the basement.'

Norrie looked down through the railings that fronted the house and saw steps leading to the basement level. 'Down here,' she said, striding forward.

David and Norah followed her as she banged on the door. A woman pulled it open and stood gawping at them for a few seconds, before she broke out into a great wide smile and pushed Norrie out of the way to hug David.

'You've arrived early!' she boomed. 'Come, come in. We weren't expecting you for another two weeks. Mr Borowitz is still in the corner, but we'll shift him out soon enough. Someone else can find room for him. You'll have a cup of tea, now.'

She pulled out a chair from a table in the centre of the room, and Norah sank down into it. Pointing at Norrie she said, 'So, this is your sister. I never knew you had a sister, David.' She gave him a sly, questioning look.

David took another chair. 'This is Ellen, my little sister. She's just seventeen.'

'Ah, Mary had another one. Well, she's welcome too.' She walked over to the corner and pulled back the curtain to reveal three rough beds. 'Mr Borowitz took up just one of them. This'll be you, now.'

Norah paled. Four children had entered the room and gathered around the buxom Bridget.

'We have six. Three born here, three in Ireland. Two are old enough to work at the dock with their father. They'll be home later.'

'Where do you all sleep?' Norrie asked.

'The two smallest under the table here. The rest next door with me and Paddy.' She turned to the stove. 'There's the kettle boiling. Let's have a cup of tea.'

Norrie still stood and looked around. After their initial quiet observation, the children had begun to play and chatter. They didn't look emaciated, like the children she'd been used to in Dublin, and the starving, barely clothed children of Kilrush. It was poor, yes, but she'd be able to cope here.

'When does Mr Borowitz find out he's being replaced?' Norrie asked.

'He knows already. He's trying to make an arrangement, but he thought he had a couple of weeks yet. Never mind, I'll go visiting while you get settled. Someone will have a bed for him.'

'How long have you been in New York, Bridget?'

'Must be five years now. Paddy had heard there was work here, and there is. We'd hoped to go inland but hadn't the money. Problem now is, there's hundreds and thousands arrived in the past three years. There's not enough work and the older Americans are turning against us. There's not just Irish, you know,' she said as she put the tea into rough cups and brought them to the table and plonked herself into a chair, shouting at the children to go and play outside. 'There's a lot of Jews from Russia and Poland. Loads of Germans, and Dutch. We all rub along well enough together.' She stopped and looked at Norah. 'You're very pale. Can I give you a piece of bread and butter?'

Norah nodded and Bridget bounced up again.

Bread with butter, Norrie thought, her mouth drooling. She hadn't seen butter for years. The slice, when it arrived, was an inch thick, slathered in the rich yellow spread. Norah looked repulsed but David encouraged her to eat. When she couldn't finish it, Norrie took the rest from her and devoured it in two bites.

'You all look hungry. Have you your cooking things?'

'Yes,' David replied. 'But we've no food left. I have some money, though. I can buy a little food.' He described what had happened during the storm.

'That was a bad one,' Bridget said, shaking her head. 'I've heard of people dying during those monster storms. But good you have your cooking pots,' she added. 'There's a store up the road. Sorry I can't help out there. Feeding eight is all I can manage.'

'As soon as we're settled, I'll go to buy food. We need a decent meal. And the rent—'

'Paddy takes care of that. He has an arrangement with the landlord.'

'Very well, Bridget.' He turned to Norah. 'I have to go out,' he said. 'I'll buy a little food, then I have to find Ben Barry, to talk about the work.' Norah took hold of his sleeve, in a low voice asking him to stay with her.

'I'm here,' Norrie said. 'It's important David makes sure of that work. Come on Norah, let's get ourselves settled whilst he's out. You can rest while I unpack. It won't take long,' she laughed.

She led Norah to the bed closest to the wall, pulled the curtain and began to empty David and Norah's bags and her own meagre bundle. She pushed the second bed up against Norah's, and pulled hers as far away as the curtain would allow, then packed up Mr Borowitz's scanty belongings into a bundle. He has no more than I, she thought, feeling momentary sorry for an old man who was about to be turned out of his accommodation.

When Norrie emerged from behind the curtain there was no sign of Bridget. She sat at the table. She wanted to wash herself but wasn't sure where to go to find water. As she sat she gazed around and began to plan. She had been shocked as she had walked through the wealthier parts of Manhattan. Some of the houses were advertising for servants, but added to the sign was: "No Irish Need Apply". Hundreds of thousands, Bridget had said. Norrie's stomach turned. Perhaps there wasn't work here. If not, she'd have to try another city, where she might be more welcome. In the meantime she considered what she could do. Her first action would be to find Uncle Edward Corcoran. She was still thinking when Bridget came back.

'I've been upstairs. There's a space for Mr Borowitz on the third floor. He should be able to make it up there.'

Norrie asked about the water for washing and the arrangements for ablutions.

'There's a tub out back. Water comes round twice a week. We fill the tub. It's not too bad at the moment. You can wash yourself out there.' She glanced at Norrie's dress, which still bore signs of the vomit and urine from the ship. 'Have you another dress?'

Norrie nodded.

'There's a washing tub with a dolly out there, too. I'll give you a bit of soap and hot water.'

Twenty minutes later Norrie was clean, her hair washed and wearing her spare dress. The former vomit-stained one hung on a line in the sunshine and fresh breeze.

'It's warm today,' she said to Bridget, as she came back in.

'Just look at you now,' Bridget exclaimed. 'Fresh as a pin and a good looker, too. Warm? This is nothing. In a couple of months, the heat'll be so unbearable, you'll not want to go outside if you can help it. It's not like Ireland.' Her face had darkened.

'You miss it,' Norrie said.

'Yes and no. I never thought I'd say I miss the rain, and mind you it could be cold, but it's nothing compared to winters here. I thought our little Pat was going to die from the coughing last winter. He didn't, but it was close. But I suppose we'd probably all have died had we stayed. It was a hard decision back in '44, but Paddy was insistent. It's no joyride here, either. Still, we're not starving, like some of the poor creatures we see walking the streets, begging for food. They're finding the streets are not paved with gold, like they thought when they left, especially the ones without family to take them in. So, miss, where are you from, really? And don't tell me Dublin. You're no more David Dillon's sister than I am. Don't worry, I won't tell a soul, not even Paddy.'

Norrie thought for a moment. Bridget was probably a good woman to have on-side. She'd been here long enough to know the what and who of New York. She'd have to trust the discreet part.

'County Clare,' she replied. 'My family's all gone. I went to Dublin. I was supposed to go to Australia but changed my mind when I got to Liverpool and snuck back to Dublin. I met David and the Young Irelanders. David was already set for America. I wanted – I needed – to come. He agreed to bring me with him and Norah.' Norrie wasn't going to tell Bridget the full story, as she sensed the woman had an inkling already that she had done wrong.

'The English won't find you here,' Bridget replied in a low voice. 'You're Ellen Dillon now. Make the most of what you can now you're here, because I'm guessing you can't go back.'

Norrie nodded.

The sound of steps, heavy slow steps, making their way down to the basement distracted what might have been more probing from Bridget, and Norrie was relieved. An old man entered the room. He gave a questioning frown in Norrie's direction, then his shoulders sank.

'You have arrived early,' he said in a low, depressed voice, his accent thick.

'Now don't you be worrying Mr Borowitz. I've found you a bed upstairs with the Maloney family. They have a spare bed, and they don't want paying. It's only for a couple of weeks, until our nephew and his wife and sister find themselves their own room. Now what'll be the matter with you, Mr Borowitz? You're home early.'

'I tore my shirt,' he said, trembling. 'One of the big Germans did it.' As he turned around Norrie could see the shirt had a ragged rip, where someone had seen a snag and pulled on it.

'Do you have another?' Norrie asked.

The old man shook his head. 'Just my best for church.'

'Then put that on and let me fix this one for you,' she replied. 'I'm not good for much, but I'm a fair needlewoman. I'll have it done in a jiffy, and it'll be my way of saying thank you for the temporary move.' She turned to Bridget. 'Do you have needle and thread Bridget?'

The woman shook her head. 'Sorry no. I need to get more. The kids are always tearing something.'

'I have some,' Mr Borowitz said. 'It belonged to my late wife. I will fetch for you.' He shuffled off to his former corner, found the sewing items amongst his belongings, and now wearing his best shirt, handed the torn one to Norrie. 'You packed my things nicely. Thankyou miss.'

'Ellen,' she said, taking the torn shirt.

He had a few pins, which helped. As she sewed and mended, Norrie thought about what she could do. The basement was quite cool, and she could smell the damp. If it really was going to be as hot as Bridget said, it would be suffocating in the coming summer months. She'd have to find some work, and a better place to live. Yes, the Allens were still in poverty after five years, but they could eat, and keep themselves. The older children worked, and the younger ones were in school, a Catholic school, Bridget had said. The Catholics had come together to set up their own school to make sure their children were brought up in the faith, and they had built their own church.

'We have a proper parish now, organised by Father Klein. It's called St Bridget's. It's only a short walk for us here on the Lower East Side, so we can go to mass on a Sunday.'

Norrie wasn't interested in church or God. As far as she was concerned, He had abandoned Kilrush, so she had abandoned Him. But she wouldn't spoil Bridget's pride and enthusiasm, so she smiled and nodded.

She would need to find out as much as she could about New York, and Manhattan itself, as quickly as possible, if she were to find Uncle Edward. The most important matter was where she went next. Norrie Madigan had no intention of sleeping on a rough pallet shared with a family in a tenement for the next five years.

'Here you go, Mr Borowitz,' she said, handing him back the shirt.

He took it from her with shaking hands and said a quiet thank you. Then, he examined the tear, frowned and looked up quickly at her.

'Is it not alright Mr Borowitz? I'm sorry, I—'

'I cannot see where it was torn,' he said.

'Oh, I matched the pattern of lines. I thought to keep it regular, but if you want me to try again...'

'No!' he exclaimed. 'This is exceptional. My late wife was a seamstress, but even she couldn't sew this good. Thank you my dear. I must pay you something.'

Norrie beamed. 'Indeed you must not, Mr Borowitz. It's me should be paying you for the bed, but I've only a few pennies.'

'Please, call me Jacob. What shall I call you?'

Norrie took a deep breath. My name is Ellen. Ellen Dillon.'

Chapter 22

As it was a Sunday, and they were both still tired, Bob decided they should take a walk in Central Park, the entrance being about five minutes from the hotel.

'Just a stroll,' he said to Maggie. 'Nothing strenuous. We can find somewhere for breakfast first if you like.'

She had been wanting to get on with the research as soon as possible, but she saw the sense in his suggestion. She felt exhausted. It had been many years since she had had jet lag and was finding it hard, having woken at 3am and been unable to get back to sleep.

'Ok with me. But that'll only take up the morning. What about the afternoon?'

'Let's leave that until we've been around the park.' Bob had spotted a deli serving food on the corner of their block. They crossed the road and entered. It was cool and welcoming.

They chose bagels with cream cheese, and coffee, and sat on high stools, watching the traffic streaming up and down 6th Avenue.

When they had finished, somewhat reluctantly Maggie went out into the sunshine and stopped dead in the street, hit by both the heat and the humidity.

'I can't walk around in this, Bob.'

'I've taken care of that. Come on, we'll be late.'

He set off and she followed him, sweat beginning to pour down her face. As they crossed the road one block down to the park, Maggie could see bicycles pulling covered seats and wondered if they could take one of those instead, but Bob walked past and, taking her by the arm, headed into the park. After a few minutes he stopped. Maggie, panting with the heat and the tiredness, was about to say something cutting when she realised that Bob was anxiously looking up and down the roadway, where bicycles and their passengers hurried past, with cyclists and runners in their wake. Then, came the sound of clip clopping. Bob smiled, as a horse and carriage, both white, the horse with a tall plume on its headgear and the carriage covered with flowers, came around the corner and pulled up next to them.

'Your carriage, ma'am,' Bob said, bowing her towards the seat. She climbed up without a word, to find that the inside of the carriage had a small air conditioner. He climbed up beside her.

'This is going to take around forty-five minutes, so sit back and relax.'

'You had this planned all along.'

'Yes. Now, sit back and enjoy.'

The first five minutes was spent in silence, as Maggie settled down into the seat and the horse sedately trotted along. The driver, dressed in a nineteenth century costume, made the occasional comment about the park, but Bob shook his head and the man turned back to his horse.

'You are a wonderful person, Robert Pugh.'

'You didn't always think so.'

'True. I remember when we first spoke, when I told you about Eira Probert and you thought I was a lunatic.'

'Yes. Do you remember when that was?'

'No. Should I?' There was something playing out here.

'Probably not, knowing you. It was exactly five years ago. To the day. This is the anniversary of when we first met.'

Maggie sat up. 'OMG. I'd forgotten. Is it really five years?'

He nodded. 'Not a great start, but it's slowly got better. Hasn't it?'

'Of course it has. It's the best. Honestly, I never thought, after David died, that I could ever be content with another man. I was wrong.' She leaned across and kissed him.

'What are your ideas about marriage now?'

She went to reply, then, hit by a sudden thought about why he had gone to this much trouble, stopped. 'Bob, is this a proposal?'

'No. It's a question. I know you too well to ask a direct question out of the blue. I'm leading up to it.'

'Wow. You're right. It's something I need to think over. I'm not against the idea. I love you, very much, but our previous experiences have been so different. You loved your wife, and she died. I didn't love my husband, which I didn't realise at the time, and he died, in very different circumstances.'

'Have as much time as you need, and if you say "no", I won't be offended. I know we're fine as we are.'

'Have you booked anything else?'

He grinned. 'I may have booked a dinner tonight at a local restaurant. It's Italian, with a good rep.'

'Sounds lovely, but let's enjoy the ride. This park is gorgeous.'

**

When they returned to the hotel, strolling hand-in-hand in the sunshine, Maggie went to swim whilst Bob spent an hour on the balcony.

He was snoring gently in the chair, a discarded newspaper fallen to one side, when she returned. For a few minutes she watched him. He was not the kind of man she had ever thought about spending her life with. Fit and healthy, with a balding, closely shaved head, a leader who was used to giving orders, often to her irritation; on the outside, a commander. But, she knew another side; kind, loving, irritatingly instructive, protective. He had become a father figure to her children, which she knew with Alice hadn't been easy, but he had gently persevered until he won the girl round. Would they both be happy at her marrying Bob? Yes, they would. Her friends would be ecstatic. Her only condition would be a small ceremony, family and close friends, in a place of her choosing. She would tell him at dinner. She showered then went to sit beside him.

The heat was intense, and Maggie felt tiredness creeping up. Preparing to sleep for an hour before they began to get ready for dinner, she closed her eyes, just as her phone pinged an incoming text.

It was from Nick. Found something interesting in the Irish Immigration Passenger Lists. A family of three, on the Wanderer sail ship in March 1850, Dublin to New York. David Dillon, his wife Norah Dillon. His sister: Ellen Margaret Dillon. Checked available church and other records. David Dillon a reporter in Dublin, born in Dublin. Well known member of the Young Irelanders. And – as far as I can tell from church baptisms, David Dillon never had a sister.

Chapter 23
May 1850

Summer arrived early in New York and the residents of Suffolk Street, suffering with the heat, began to sit out on the steps that led to the front doors of the tenement buildings. Inside the basement of number seventeen, the atmosphere was cooler, indeed, had become frosty, between Bridget and Norah.

David's job had not yet materialised, but Ben Barry of the New York Commentator had assured him that he would be taken on at the start of June, in three weeks' time. David had paid the rent but had had a quiet word with Norrie that he could not continue to pay for her. She would have to find work and pay for herself and her own food. As yet her search for her Uncle Edward Corcoran had been unsuccessful. Last week, she had heard about a newspaper that held ads for people looking for relatives. She had taken out an ad, but so far, there had been no responses.

From the day after they arrived, Norrie had walked the streets of the Lower East Side, up into the East Village and across to Broadway, looking for work of any kind. She had not been received well. In addition to the many notices stating 'No Irish Need Apply', she was often spat on, jeered, and mocked. This was not what she had expected from New York. She had chosen to go nowhere near the Five Points, although many of the men in the other areas shouted out to her that she'd find no shortage of customers for a "fine looking Irish girl", as it was "all she was good for". Norrie held her head high, gritted her teeth and walked on.

Now, it being Sunday, David and Norah had gone for a walk and Bridget Allen had taken her brood to church. Norrie walked up to sit on the stoop, where she found Mr

Borowitz smoking a cigarette. His shoulders were hunched, his face pale. She sat down next to him.

'How are you doing, Miss Dillon?'

'Not so good, Mr Borowitz. Nor are you, from the look of you.'

He smiled. 'I'm an old man. What's your problem?'

'I'm Irish. That's my problem.'

'Your people are not well liked here. Some New Yorkers are afraid of you. So many of you arriving every day and I think, more to come.'

'Only the ones that aren't starving or dead, and those left behind soon will be, the way things are in Ireland. What's to fear, Mr Borowitz?'

'Popery. The Protestants, who think of themselves as the original Americans, fear too many Catholics will take over from them, especially at Tammany Hall.'

'At what?'

'Tammany Hall, Miss Dillon. They run Lower Manhattan.'

'Are they good people?'

'No, they are not. Corrupt politicians,' he said and spat on the ground.

Norrie didn't reply.

'Miss Dillon, may I ask you something?'

'Whatever you like, Mr Borowitz.'

'Who are you, really?'

Norrie gave him an appraising look. 'I'm Ellen Dillon.'

'I think not,' he replied in a low voice. 'If you don't want to tell me, then do not. It makes no difference to me.'

'My story is not a good one, Mr Borowitz.'

'Mine neither. Tell me about your home.'

Norrie drew in a deep breath. Instinctively she knew she could trust this old man.

'We lived on Clamhunger Row, on the west coast of Ireland. We hadn't much, but we had our small piece of land with our cabin. It was just the one room, but we had a roof space where daddy and mammy slept. The roof was made of rushes and reeds. Sometimes it let the water in. In winter there were great storms, waves higher than our cabin. Clamhunger Row had ten cabins. We all knew each other. My mother was one of three sisters and I had two cousins, who were like sisters to me, Ellen and Margaret, we called her Peg. We had a pig, and we planted our potatoes. We hadn't much in the way of possessions. There was a bed and blankets, and a settle to sit on near the fire in the winter. We had cups and saucers and plates, and a special dish that came from my mother's mother. When the hunger came, we had no potatoes, they all went rotten, every single one. Not just for us, for everyone. They rotted and stank. At first daddy said it was just the one year, we'd be fine. We paid our rent. But it came again, and we had to sell our pig. Then everything else. Then, it came a third time, and we had nothing left to sell. If someone had something they shared, but after three years, we all had nothing. Everything was gone, everything sold. And still it came. There was nothing to pay the rent. What about you, Jacob?' This was as far as she was prepared to go, to wait to see how he reciprocated.

Jacob Borowitz didn't hesitate. 'I came here because I could not stay in Germany. I wanted democracy and liberalism. We failed. There were riots and I killed a man. My wife and I decided to start again in America. We came here two years ago. But my wife was already sick. She died soon after we arrived. We had a son. He also died. Now, I am alone.'

Norrie thought hard, swallowed and decided to go on. 'I killed a man, too, Mr Borowitz. I slit his throat. He had evicted my family from our home and killed my grandfather because he would not be moved. Then, he and his band of local thugs demolished our cabin and set the ruins on fire.'

'And you killed him?'

'Not right there and then. We'd already lost three of the little ones, of starvation fever. Mammy had hardly eaten. She had the baby. Joseph his name was, a poor wasted creature. It was a miracle he survived being born. But he lived.

Mammy tried to feed him, but she had no milk. One morning we woke up and he was dead. Mammy died the following day, of starvation fever. We managed to bury them proper, at least. Our priest helped, a good man, Father Jerome.'

She stopped and took a deep breath. Now that she had started, it was like a dam being released. So many pent-up feelings, suppressed memories, unspoken horrors, all came to the surface, and she couldn't stop them coming out.

'Daddy had tried to get work on the Government Works, and for a few weeks he brought home a few pennies. But then, the bloody British stopped them. They were supposed to be replaced with soup kitchens, but nothing happened. The little ones were starving. We tried to cook anything we could find: grass, nettles. Nothing helped. Next to go was my brother Thomas. He was four. He just stopped moving one day, stopped speaking. Then, he died. That left my two sisters, Anne and Mary. They died too. They were ten and eight. Daddy couldn't pay our rent, nor could any of the other families in Clamhunger Row pay theirs. My cousins, Ellen and Peg were the same. In one week I lost my mother and all of my brothers and sisters. It was just me, Daddy and Granddaddy. The day after we buried Anne and Mary, a man called Seamus McMahon turned up. He was the landlord's agent, working for the Vandaleurs, the land owners. He put up a notice of eviction. We didn't know what to expect. The following day he came back with a gang of thugs. They began pulling people out of their cabins. My Daddy refused to go. He stood in the doorway and waved a stick at them, saying he was not for moving. There were soldiers with McMahon. My Granddaddy was shouting in Irish, from inside the cabin. He was still in there because he was so weak he couldn't move. One of McMahon's thugs dragged him out and beat him to death with a rifle butt. All granddaddy was saying was "go away and leave us alone" but the thug thought he was being threatened. After that, people began to grab whatever they could, which was very little.

Daddy took a stool and a cooking pot – that was all we had left, we'd sold everything else, and pushed us out. The men moved in and began to tear down our cabins until they were rubble around our feet. Then they set fire to the rubble.'

She had begun to cry. Mr Borowitz put an arm around her shoulder. It was the first time anyone had touched her since she had left Ellen and Peg, but she didn't object.

'I have another secret, Mr Borowitz, a terrible secret, which I haven't told to a soul. Will you listen to my secret, and not judge me.'

'I will. I am no judge; I have no right to be.'

'Daddy was just sitting, with Grandaddy's body slumped across his knees. I knew I had to do something. I told him I was going to go to look for work, that I'd find something and come back within a couple of days. But that wasn't what I was going to do. The soldiers came from a barracks north of Kilrush. There I went, and at night, I sold myself to those godless bastards. For three nights. Then, I couldn't stand it no more. But I had three shillings. I had to wait a day until I could walk again. When I got back, Daddy had gone to the Workhouse. So there I went. What I found…' she stopped, closed her eyes and for many seconds her body shook. 'What I found Mr Borowitz, was that Daddy was gone. He had left to try to find work. I think he was crazy with grief. I never saw him again. I went to the Workhouse to join Ellen and Peg. I had sold myself – for nothing.'

Then she wept. Mr Borowitz tightened his grip on her shoulder until her tears dried up, and she wiped them away with her sleeve.

'I found my cousins, Ellen and Peg. Peg had also gone to try to find some food but had only managed a bit of bread. When she returned, all of her family was dead. Peg was already sick. She had the phthisis. After a couple of weeks the Master came around and said there was a scheme for girls, to take us away from the famine to a place called Australia. Lots of girls were going. He was going to pick out twenty girls to go. We would be given a new dress to replace our rags, some bloomers, for modesty, stockings, a Bible and a bit of material to make a new dress. Then we would go to Dublin and from there to Liverpool, then on to Australia, where there would be husbands and jobs and a good life. A lot of the girls welcomed the chance and asked to be chosen. Not me. But, chosen I was. Ellen still had a baby brother, but she wasn't allowed to take him. Peg didn't care. If we were going, she would go. I reached Liverpool, before the blackness in me decided I couldn't let McMahon live for what he'd done. I hid on the boat back to Dublin. David helped me, there. He found two men who would ask no questions but would travel back across Ireland with me. They were of a group that called themselves Molly McGuires. We didn't speak; not once. One was called Joseph Power, the other never spoke and they didn't know my name.

When we got to Kilrush, we found McMahon. They held him down whilst I slit his throat. Then they disappeared and I never saw them again. I hid out with the priest, for a week, whilst the soldiers searched for McMahon's killer. No-one gave me up. Before I went back to Dublin I went to the Workhouse. My cousin Ellen's brother Michael was still alive. I took him at night, back to Dublin. David was soon to leave for America. He offered to pay my passage. And here I am. That's my story, Mr Borowitz.'

The old man didn't speak.

'So, Mr Borowitz, you may do as you please with my story.'

'Why didn't you bring the boy with you?'

Norrie shrugged. 'Too dangerous. If I'd been caught, I'd have been hanged. He had a better chance without me.' She paused, then added, 'And I without him. He's with a good family now.'

He took his arm from her shoulder. 'I have a proposition for you, Ellen Dillon.'

She shuddered.

'Nothing like that. I have a friend, a tailor. His wife was a wonderful seamstress, who made dresses for ladies of the better classes. My friend is called Edward Mansard. He has come here from England, twenty years before. His wife died two months ago. He has employed two girls, but they could not sew like Louisa Mansard. You, I think, can. I have told him about you. He knows you are Irish but has seen your mending of my shirt. He would like to meet you. He needs a girl who can sew well – well enough to follow Louisa's patterns. Would you like to try?'

'I would love to try, Mr Borowitz. When can we go?'

'Please, I told you, call me Jacob. We can go tomorrow.'

'I am indebted to you, Jacob.'

'And what should I call you?'

'Please always refer to me as Ellen, but my real name is Honora. My family called me Norrie. I am Norrie Madigan.'

Chapter 24

Maggie went straight to her laptop and looked up the sailing of The Wanderer to America. She knew that the 1850 census was taken on 1st June in that year, so if The Wanderer had arrived in New York in time for the Dillon "family" to settle down, there was a good possibility that Norrie, going by the name of Ellen Margaret Dillon – if it wasn't just co-incidence – would be on record.

Her whoop of delight woke Bob, who wandered into the bedroom from the balcony, rubbing sleepy eyes and swaying.

'I think we've found her,' she said.

Bob blinked a few times. 'Found her?'

'Norrie Madigan, sleepyhead. She gave her name as Ellen Margaret Dillon. She was on the manifest of a ship called The Wanderer, that arrived in New York in April 1850, and supposedly the sister of a man called David Dillon. But according to Nick, David Dillon never had a sister.'

'How could he know it's the same David Dillon?' Bob asked, sitting down on the bed and yawning.

'Because David Dillon was a Young Irelander. He was arrested at the time of the failed uprising in 1848 but was let go. He was a journalist working for a newspaper called The Nation, in Dublin. When he arrived in America, he went to work for the New York Commentator and ended up its Editor in Chief. He supported the cause of Irish immigrants. I've found him on the 1850 census, with his wife, Norah. His profession is "journalist" and his place of birth Ireland.'

'So what about Norrie?'

'Ellen M Dillon is no longer with them. She's a seamstress, living on East 5th Street. There are only two other people in the residence: a Mr Edward Mansard, who's sixty-four. He's an English Tailor and Proprietor, and there's a servant, Annie McGrath, an Irish servant, a widow aged fifty-nine.'

'Sounds like a great start,' Bob said. 'I'm going to take a shower, then I'll get dressed for dinner.'

'Is it far?' Maggie asked. 'I'm still getting over the jet lag. I'm not sure my legs will carry me much longer if we have to walk.'

'Just two blocks across, onto Broadway, then down two blocks. Ten minutes. Can you manage that?'

'I'm sure I can.'

The evening was calm and warm as they made their way through the crowds to the restaurant.

'Does anyone ever walk slowly here, or even stop at all?' Maggie asked Bob.

'No, they don't seem to, do they, only to not cross the street if there's traffic coming and sometimes not even then. That's New York.'

'Those bicycle maniacs must get themselves killed on a regular basis,' she added. 'They don't appear to think the traffic, pedestrians and red lights are anything to do with them.'

'Surprisingly, very few accidents take place with the bikes. The traffic, pedestrians, and red lights have all learned to live with each other.'

'Weird,' Maggie replied, as another electric scooter shot past them and around a corner.

'Here's the restaurant,' Bob said.

It was a pretty place, despite being on Broadway and dwarfed by towering skyscrapers. The pavement was wide enough to accommodate room for walkers, and a covered eating area that stretched out almost into the traffic, which was decorated with flowers and candles.

'We're eating inside,' Bob said, amused by Maggie's sceptical look.

Although the restaurant was busy and noisy, it had a cheerful ambience. Waiters with trays dashed around. They were greeted and seated immediately, with drinks served within five minutes and their order placed five minutes later.

'American customer service,' Maggie said, sipping a gin and elderflower tonic.

'They expect a good tip,' Bob replied. 'Leave it all to me.'

'I had no intention of doing otherwise,' Maggie replied.

The food was excellent, reasonably priced and served, not quickly, but efficiently. Afterwards they sat with coffee and Maggie began to talk about the rest of their trip.

'We'll visit The Tenement Museum tomorrow and The Merchant's House, which might also be interesting. And we have the walking tour of the Lower East Side.'

Bob smiled at her.

'Yes.'

His head cocked to one side. 'Yes, what? Am I expected to comment on your timetable?'

'You asked me a question earlier. My answer is "Yes".'

It took him a moment to realise what she meant. Then he stood up and clapped his hands three times, attracting the attention of people on tables close by.

'Ladies and Gentlemen, this beautiful woman has just agreed to marry me.' He bowed and sat down again. Maggie's face had turned scarlet, as the people who had heard started to clap and cheer. The word spread quickly and soon the whole restaurant was cheering.

'Idiot!' she hissed, as the applause died down.

'Yep. Oh, look.'

A waiter appeared with a bottle of champagne and two glasses. 'Congratulations! Compliments of the house.'

Maggie took the gift graciously and drank the champagne, which turned out to be an excellent vintage. People shook their hands and congratulated them as they walked past and out at the end of their meal.

Once they were on the pavement, she said, 'When did you become Mr Loud and Spontaneous?'

'That was it. A once off, never to be repeated.'

‘Good. Thank you. I love you, but that was a little embarrassing.’

‘We’ll never see any of them again, but they’ll remember us.’

‘I hope so,’ she replied. ‘a moment of fun for them. But Bob, no more discussions of marriage whilst we’re here, please. We can talk about it when we get home.’

‘Works for me. And, no more silly romantic stuff either. Back to the day job tomorrow.’

She laughed and they strolled hand-in-hand back to the hotel.

**

The following morning Maggie was awake at four. ‘Jet Lag,’ she muttered to a sleeping Bob. ‘Might as well get on with something.’

Next on the list was Norrie’s marriage, or rather, Ellen Margaret Dillon’s marriage, which she knew had been to a policeman, somewhere between 1851 and 1855.

She began with a general search on Ancestry for all records pertaining to Ellen Margaret Dillon. It was a fairly common Irish name and the list that came back contained fifty-one names, all living in New York, and all born in Ireland around 1830 to 1832. With a clue already from the 1850 census entry, she was quickly able to eliminate the majority of them, being either married women or single servants. After an hour and a half, she was left with one name. It was a marriage in 1853, of Ellen M. Dillon to William R. Kelly. She gave her address as 1 East Fifth Street. William was at 75 Orchard Avenue. His profession: Policeman. Her profession: Dress Shop Owner. This had to be the right couple. Ellen had given her parents’ names as James and Kitty Dillon, birthplace Ireland. William’s parents were William and Maria Kelly, and he was still residing with them, as he had been, Maggie found, in 1850. Ellen gave her age as twenty-two, William twenty-five.

Ellen O’Donnell’s letter had mentioned in 1858 that Norrie had a child. Maggie searched again and found the birth of a James Michael Kelly, in 1854. He was followed by two more boys, William in 1858 and Michael in 1861. Then, there were no more children.

Bob was beginning to wake, and Maggie was surprised to see that it was already nearing eight thirty.

'What time did you wake up?' he slurred.

'About four, I think. I couldn't get back off, so I started on some research. And,' she drum rolled her fingers on the table, 'I've found Norrie's marriage. As Ellen Dillon she married a policemen called William Kelly, in 1853. They had three boys, James, William, and Michael. She used her own parents' names on the marriage certificate, James and Kitty. She probably thought she was safe enough.'

'Well done you. Let's go have breakfast. Back to the same place?'

She nodded. This was the place from the previous day, the small diner on the corner of 6th Avenue and 57th Street. The breakfast was good and large and would keep them going all day.

'We'll have plenty of time to get to the museum,' she said.

'We're taking a cab,' Bob said firmly as he disappeared into the bathroom. 'We might walk back, but it's much too far first thing.'

After breakfast they hailed a cab and set off for their pre-booked tour of the Lower East Side. Maggie had assumed the traffic would, by now, have settled down after the early morning rush. She was wrong.

'This is Manhattan,' the driver replied. 'If this was 2am we'd be moving faster.'

Despite the traffic they reached their destination on time, a narrow tree-lined street on the Lower East Side, not far from the Bowery and Little Italy.

The walking tour, which began at the museum, took an hour and a half, around a local group of streets of about four blocks, which had once been entirely tenanted but was now more cosmopolitan, and with a more mixed community than it had been in the time of Norrie Madigan. As it turned out, it had been a more German than Irish immigrant area, but the two communities had lived side by side. The tour of the Tenement Museum itself which followed the walking tour gave her a good idea of what Norrie's experience must have been on first arriving in New York.

'At least she had had some experience of Dublin slums, so this wouldn't have been the kind of shock it must have been to the rural Irish,' she whispered to Bob as they moved from room to room. 'Knowing what Clamhunger Row was like, this must have felt like another planet.'

At the end of the tour, as Bob explored the shop and began to buy souvenirs, Maggie went to speak to the woman, Magda, who had conducted the tour. She began to explain about Norrie and why she, Maggie, was there, but as she did so, the woman, who had begun to listen with a beaming smile, dropped the smile.

'Sorry, I can't help you. Talk to Ray, over there. He might know something,' and walked away at a firm pace, not even offering to make the introduction.

Puzzled, Maggie walked over to Ray, who greeted her with the same smile, which plunged into a frown at the same rate as Magda's had done, as she began to tell the story. Bob had wandered over, sensing some tension in the conversation.

The man was biting his lip. 'Come over here, into the corner. We can't talk about this too publicly.'

Maggie and Bob gave each other a quick glance, and followed him, to an area where there were no other tourists.

'I don't know much,' he began.

'I think you do, and it's bothering you,' Maggie interrupted. 'Why?'

The man put his head down, unable to look her in the eye. 'Ellen Kelly,' he said, 'is one of the best-known stories of Irish success in New York.'

'If that's the case, I don't understand why you're so reluctant to tell me about her,' Maggie replied.

'Because there's obviously more to the story,' Bob said, tapping the side of his nose. Maggie knew that this meant "copper's nose", Bob's name for his intuition, gleaned from his experience of years of criminal cases where someone was not the person they pretended to be. Maggie caught on at once but couldn't leave it there.

'Look,' she said to the reluctant man, 'where can we find the information we need about this woman? She's dead. She can't do anyone any harm and we're just looking for family history information for a client.'

'We get a good grant from the City,' the man muttered. 'Talking to you about Ellen Kelly could jeopardise that.' He paused. 'Go up to St Bridget's. Talk to Father Jimmy. He may be willing to talk to you, but please, don't mention my name.'

They nodded and left the shop.

'We seem to have stumbled over something interesting,' Maggie said to Bob as they stopped to consult a street map.

Bob sighed. 'It was ever thus,' he said. 'It must be in your DNA, getting yourself into trouble.'

Maggie had been rapidly thumbing her mobile phone. 'Guess what,' she said, grinning at him. 'Father Jimmy is actually the pastor of St Bridget's Church, and his full name is Father James Kelly.'

'Then we'd better go talk to him,' Bob replied, 'and find out what mess you've gotten us into this time.'

They decided to walk, even though the church was seven blocks away. Approaching, they could see it was older than many churches in Manhattan, built in a plainer style, small and compact amongst its giant companions. It was also quite plain inside. There were a few worshippers, but no sign of a priest. Maggie asked if Father Jimmy was available and was silently indicated towards a door at the side of the altar.

As they walked towards the door, a man stepped out. He was tall, over six feet and built like a boxer, with the marks of a man who might once have been a fighter – squashed nose, puffed lips. He was around six feet tall with wide shoulders, a thick neck and a head of thick black hair. His eyes were a deep dark green, so dark they were almost black. He had divested himself of his priest's regalia and was now dressed in jeans and t-shirt. He stopped when he saw Maggie and Bob walking towards him. He held out a hand.

'Jimmy Kelly,' he said in a strong New York accent. 'And who might you be?' There was friendliness in the greeting, but his body language was guarded.

'I'm Maggie Gilbert and this is my partner, Bob Pugh. I'm a genealogy investigator, from Wales. I'm here on behalf of a client, whose DNA has shown a relationship to a woman called Ellen Kelly. I've been told you may be able to help me.'

The priest stared at her for several seconds. Maggie's return gaze didn't falter. 'The day has come at last,' he said in a quiet voice. 'I always knew it would. Come with me to the rectory and tell me what it is you want to know.'

Chapter 25

Bob nudged Maggie and whispered to her as they walked past the altar and through the side door. 'I didn't know Mike had any DNA relationship to Norrie Madigan.'

'He hasn't,' she whispered back, 'but he could have, possibly. I haven't spoken to him about who exactly he has on his list. I'll do it later.'

The priest led them out through another door onto a small lawned area, across the lawn and into another door which led straight into a living room. It was sparsely decorated with mismatched furniture, a carpet that had seen better days and was showing threadbare patches, a display case of trophies, a bookcase overflowing with books, and a fireplace with an electric stove over which hung a flat screen TV that took up most of the wall.

'My nephew,' the priest said, seeing Maggie looking at the size of the TV. 'He lives with me. It's our extravagance.' He said no more, and she didn't ask. If it were important – and she had a gut feeling it was – an explanation would be forthcoming at the appropriate time.

'Please take a seat,' he said, sweeping away papers from the settee. 'Can I get you something to drink; coffee, a cold drink?'

Maggie was about to refuse, but Bob got in ahead of her. 'A cold drink would be excellent, Father, thank you.'

'No problem. Give me a few minutes and please, call me Jimmy.'

'Something is off,' Maggie said in a low voice to Bob. 'I don't know what, but there's a chill in this room. You can feel it, can't you?'

'Yes, but not in the sense that he's going to be a lunatic who comes back in with a gun and mows us down. He has something to tell us. Let him do it his own way. Have you noticed something about the layout of this room?'

'Not especially.'

'The space between each piece of furniture; the door to the kitchen is wide, as is the front door. It's been adapted for a wheelchair.'

Maggie looked around again and nodded. Bob stood and walked over to the bookcase. He had expected religious texts. Most of the books were old and tattered, but the themes were nothing to do with religion. All were police procedurals, by well-known authors.

The priest returned with a tray, humming a tune that Maggie recognised.

'That's a sea shanty,' she said.

'I used to be a sailor and before that I was a semi-pro boxer,' he replied, pointing to his nose, as he set down the tray. 'Before I joined the priesthood. The book collection not what you were expecting, Bob?'

Bob turned back, smiling. 'These are some of the better ones, by the authors who did their research. Police work can be pretty boring, but it does have the occasional thrill.'

'You're police?' the Priest said, his lips pursing.

'I'm a Detective Chief Inspector with South Wales Police, but here I'm helping out, taking notes and sightseeing when I get the chance.'

'Interesting. I like a good mystery and a chase, always provided it ends up with the bad guy being caught. Now, I have cordials and water. Please help yourselves.'

'You must have come across a good number of bad guys yourself,' Bob said in a casual voice, as he poured a dark red cordial and added water.

'Probably not as many as you, Chief Inspector,' Jimmy Kelly replied. 'Now, Ellen Kelly, or the Blessed Ellen, as she's known within my family, and to many others.'

'Why is she called that?' Maggie asked.

'Because my sister, Marilyn Kelly, has her on a pedestal, as the woman who encompasses all of the virtues of the Irish immigrant; an orphan, originally called Ellen Dillon, a girl who left her home and family to seek her fortune in America; a hard worker, a fair, decent woman, who was widowed when she had three small children, getting no help from anyone, with the strength of character to keep working, bring up those children and turn herself into a great success, despite the opposition against the Irish at the time, and the obstacles thrown in her way. She overcame them all, to establish the Kelly dynasty. A true heroine. A woman to be not only admired but revered.'

'Marilyn Kelly?' Bob said. 'The Marilyn Kelly?'

'The very same,' Jimmy replied. 'The toast of New York, the girl from an immigrant family who's become a multi billionaire.'

Maggie looked puzzled.

'Kelly's Emporium,' Bob said.

'Not just the stores,' Jimmy replied. 'The real estate, the diners; Marilyn's reach is colossal, like a giant octopus. Now, she's looking to politics, here in New York and beyond. You know what I'm saying?'

'I think so,' Maggie replied. 'What's the problem?'

'Marilyn holds up Ellen Kelly as an example of how an honest woman, with a high standard of morality and principles, can not only succeed, but reach high office. She has a picture of Ellen, taken around 1880. Would you like to see it? The original hangs in her office.'

He stood and went to a desk in the corner, returning with an A4 sized copy of a portrait. The woman looked stern, but that wasn't unusual. It was the look in her dark green, almost black eyes that was mesmerising. Not a woman to be trifled with.

'Says to me you crossed Ellen Kelly at your peril.'

'Damn right.'

'Jimmy, you're speaking nothing but good about this woman, but your tone doesn't match your words,' Bob said.

'Nobody is that perfect, not the way Marilyn makes out. Everyone has flaws. But Marilyn can't make a speech without talking about Ellen Kelly. She'd have her canonised, if she could.'

'This woman certainly wasn't perfect,' Maggie replied, handing the portrait back to him.

'You know something, Mrs Gilbert?'

'It's Maggie, and yes, I do. But I don't know you, and for me to tell you what I know I'd have to have total trust in you. You're Marilyn Kelly's brother. Why should I trust you?'

He stood up, walked to the desk and came back with a Bible. He laid it on the table and put his right hand on the top. 'This Bible belonged to Ellen's husband, Billy Kelly. It was returned to her after his death.' He stopped and took a deep breath. 'Billy Kelly was a good man. I swear on this Bible that nothing you say to me will be repeated by me.' He had spoken slowly and with a deep conviction, staring unblinking at Maggie as he spoke.

She took a few moments, looking at Bob. 'Nose?

'Nose says go ahead.'

The priest looked puzzled, then his face lit up. 'Copper's nose. An English expression. I've read about it. So you trust me?'

'I'm going to,' Maggie replied, 'although I do believe I'm about to open a can of worms that will wriggle their way out and fill Manhattan.'

'Wow. That's a lot of worms, Maggie.'

'Let's start with the first one, the head worm, the leader of the pack.' She took a deep breath. 'That woman was not Ellen Dillon Kelly.'

Chapter 26
New York 1850

Norrie's meeting with Edward Mansard had gone well; unexpectedly well. What Jacob Borowitz hadn't told Norrie was that Edward Mansard had decided to close down his business and had no need of a new seamstress. However, Jacob being an old friend, he agreed to meet with the girl and might be prepared to give her a good reference if her work was really as good as Jacob had told him.

Norrie had been practising on Bridget's children's clothes. The scamps, as Bridget called the little ones, tore their clothes often and Bridget was no needlewoman. 'You look like little beggars,' she would yell at them, despairing as yet another ragged tear appeared in the only garment they possessed for summer. Norrie would take the clothes, mend the torn material, wash and iron the dresses, shirts and trousers, and have them ready by morning, having dried them above the steam vent at the back of the tenement. Bridget was amazed, grateful, and thankful.

It was a walk of around thirty minutes from the Lower East Side to the shop on the corner of East 4th Street. Norrie had put on her best dress, the one she had made from the material given to the girls who were supposed to go off to Australia, and which she kept for Sundays and feast days, then wrapped her shawl around her shoulders and set off with Mr Borowitz.

'Good luck,' David said to her, and hopefully good riddance, he thought. He had been working on the newspaper for two weeks now, his trial period, and yesterday had heard that he was to be kept on as a reporter. News had arrived that a woman called Honora Madigan, a notorious murderer, had been sighted in Dublin and was actively being sought out. A warning had been put out to all of the ports in Ireland and Liverpool. There was a description of her, but apart from the dark hair and dark eyes, they were looking for an Amazonian, from the description given by Seamus McMahon's companion, who couldn't admit that McMahon had been killed by a small, thin starving girl. David knew that no-one would recognise Norrie from this description, except possibly her uncle, Edward Corcoran, which might explain why he hadn't tried to contact Norrie since their arrival. He knew she had been asking around all over Manhattan, but no-one had come forward.

They arrived at the Mansard premises shortly after ten. A conversation ensued between Mr Mansard and Norrie, during which it became clear to her that he was not enthusiastic about hiring her. She sighed and was about to leave, when the doorbell rang and a woman entered, followed by a girl of around nineteen.

'Mr Mansard, I am not happy with the standard of work on this dress.' Behind them was a Black woman, holding a cardboard box.

Mansard rushed forward. 'Mrs Poole, I am so sorry. Please tell me, what is the problem, which I am sure can be fixed.'

The woman turned and nodded abruptly to the servant, who put the box down on the counter, opened it and took out a dress in cream satin, covered with red lace and pearls. Norrie winced.

'The neckline is too low, the patterns on the sleeves are not balanced. Sir, I will not pay for this dress in this state. It's a disgrace.'

'Mrs Poole, I—'

Norrie stepped in. 'Madam, you are absolutely correct. And it's also not in fashion in the way in which English ladies are wearing their evening dresses right now. May I make a few suggestions?'

The woman looked suspiciously at her but nodded.

'The colour is exquisite and suits your lovely skin tone well. A good choice, but the red lace is too strong for the dress. I would suggest a delicate shade of pink transparent satin, not lace, with less flounce. The neckline suits your beautiful neck but could be improved with the addition of pearl buttons and a scattering of tiny roses in red and gold. Also, the sleeves should finish just above the elbow.'

'That sounds more like it, but how can you have it ready for my dinner tomorrow evening?'

'Madam, if it takes me all night, I will have it ready for you, and I will deliver it to you myself, so I can make any last-minute alterations.'

She hadn't looked at Mr Mansard throughout this exchange.

'That will be acceptable,' the Poole woman replied. 'Have it with me by five tomorrow evening.'

She turned and left the shop.

As soon as the bell clanged, Edward Mansard turned on Norrie, his face purple. 'How, how… how dare you? It cannot be done. You have ruined me.' He slumped onto a chair and put his head in his hands.

'Of course it can be done,' Norrie said. 'You have the satin, I saw it there on the shelf. She sat next to him. 'Mr Mansard, that dress was going to ruin you anyway. Please, let me show you what I can do. Do you have small rosebuds and gold trimmings, and some pearl buttons?'

He glanced up, nodding.

'Right, then let's not waste time. Let me get to work. There's a lot to do. By the way, whoever made this monstrosity, dismiss her. Where's the sewing room?

He pointed to the back of the shop. Norrie picked up the dress and began to examine it as she stepped through the curtain, tutting.

Edward Mansard looked up at Jacob Berkowitz, who had squeezed himself into a corner. 'My friend, what have you brought me? Just because she can sew a shirt doesn't mean she can bring about this miracle.'

Jacob smiled. 'I have witnessed her in the past two days sew a complete communion dress for one of the little Allens. The child will stand out amongst her peers. Watch what this girl will achieve. I bet you she'll stay up sewing all night. Trust me. I have to go to work now.'

He turned and left the shop, leaving a bewildered Edward Mansard still sitting in his chair; a man who didn't even know the name of the woman now sitting next door, examining the dress and beginning to detach the offending red lace. With a pounding sense of fear in his gut and a headache, he decided he couldn't bear to watch. He closed the shop and went upstairs to his bedroom.

**

The following morning, he crept down the stairs at seven. Norrie, whose eyes were red-rimmed, sat at the table, sewing on pearl buttons in a pattern around the neck. He could see that the delicate transparent pale pink satin was sewn at the waist at the back, and layered in folds over the skirt, which now had a small bustle reaching to the floor. The satin had tiny rosebuds and gold flakes sewn into it.

'It'll be ready in an hour or two, Mr Mansard. Let me be for a while yet, please,' Norrie said without looking up.

'I don't know your name,' he whispered.

'I'm Ellen Dillon. Nice to meet you.'

'Can I bring you a cup of tea, Miss Dillon.'

'Later, Mr Mansard. I don't want to risk anything falling or splashing onto this dress.'

He went away, went out to eat breakfast, then returned at nine.

'Norrie was standing behind the counter. Her face was white, her eyes red, but she looked excited.

'It's finished, Mr Mansard. Please, come and look.'

He took in a deep breath and walked through the curtain, where he stopped abruptly. 'You did this? Overnight?'

'Uh, yes. It was hard work. Are you satisfied? Is my work good enough?'

Edward Mansard walked around the dress, which Norrie had set on a tailor's dummy, three times, stopping occasionally to examine a seam, the sewing on of a button and a rose, the set of the sleeves. Finally, he stopped. 'It's exquisite,' he said. 'I can't hardly believe it's the same dress.'

'I've let out the waist. I've a feeling part of Mrs Poole's frustration was that she couldn't make it fit around her waist without wearing a girdle that was going to stop her breathing.'

He blushed, not used to talking about such intimate matters.

Norrie rolled her eyes. 'Mr Mansard, I'm wicked tired. I was wondering, if there's a spare mattress or pallet somewhere that I can rest for a few hours before the dress is to be delivered, would you allow me to use it?'

Edward Mansard was conflicted. It was not right for an unknown woman to be sleeping under his roof. But, then again, the dress was exquisite and if he could hire this woman, all his worries would be over. Avarice won out.

'Up on the third floor, Miss Dillon. There's an unused room with a small mattress. You may use it.'

'Thank you. Please call me at four, so I can be ready.'

As she hauled herself up the rickety staircase, Norrie heard the clanging of the shop door bell, followed by a great deal of shouting. She didn't care. There'd be time to find out later what had occurred. She was asleep as she laid down.

**

At four in the afternoon, loud knocking on the door roused her and for a moment she was panicked, not knowing where she was.

A timid voice said, 'Miss Dillon, Mr Mansard said to call you.'

Of course, the dress. She sat up quickly. 'Come in. Who are you?'

A young, scared looking, red-haired girl appeared around the door. 'I'm Eugenia, Miss. I'm the new maid.'

'Bring me some hot water, please.'

The girl curtseyed. 'Yes, ma'am.'

Norrie was non-plussed for a moment. Ma'am indeed. Who did the girl think she was? Had something happened whilst she slept? When the water arrived Norrie quickly washed her face and tidied herself up. Her best dress was crumpled and her hair a mess. She did the best she could and went downstairs.

'What was all that commotion and shouting earlier, Mr Mansard?'

'That was my former dressmaker. She was none too happy about losing her job.'

Norrie's heart leapt. 'Shall I be coming to work for you then, Mr Mansard?'

'Let's see how Mrs Poole likes her dress, Miss Dillon. Then we can talk terms.' He pointed to a pile of material on the workshop table. 'It's one of my wife's old dresses, and a cape. It's a little more suitable,' he paused with a blush, 'than what you are wearing, for going to Mrs Poole's house. There's also a cloak.'

Norrie had thought her dress good enough, with some ironing out, but she picked up the dress and saw the sense of it. Without speaking, she took it back to the upstairs room and put it on. It was plain, but well made, in fact, beautifully made; Mrs Mansard had been a fine seamstress. She also used the hairbrush that had been wordlessly included. By the time she returned downstairs, she looked more mature and confident.

'Thank you, Mr Mansard. Perhaps you would give me directions to Mrs Poole's house.'

'There's a carriage waiting outside, Miss Dillon. I took the liberty of ordering one. The package is heavy.'

Norrie nodded her thanks, silently amazed, having never before ridden in a carriage. She picked up the box, which had been tied with pretty pink ribbon, and took it to the carriage. 'I shall tell you Mrs Poole's reaction on my return.'

On arriving at Mrs Poole's house ten minutes later, Norrie had to steel herself to approach the front door. She stood anxiously, as the loud doorbell clanged and was answered by a Black man in a dark uniform.

'I have a dress for Mrs Poole,' she said in a loud confident voice.

'I shall take it,' he replied.

'You will not,' Norrie answered, as she stepped over into the hallway before he could stop her. 'I shall need to be present when Mrs Poole sees the dress, to ensure that no last-minute alterations are needed.' Her legs shook, but Norrie held her ground. The man frowned, turned, and walked away.

A few minutes later he returned, with an older woman, stern looking, dressed in another drab uniform. 'I am the housekeeper. You may come with me.' She glanced at Norrie. 'Don't touch anything.'

They ascended a circular staircase and Norrie was shown into a bedroom, the likes of which she had never imagined. Sumptuously decorated, with a canopy over the bed and floor length rich silk curtains, this was like something out of a dream. The butler put the dress box down on a chaise longue. Mrs Poole entered.

'Well, Miss Dillon. This had better be good.'

'With shaking hands, Norrie untied the pink ribbon. Inside, she saw that the dress had been wrapped in fine paper. Mr Mansard knew what he was doing. She carefully, very carefully, lifted the dress out of the box and held it up, giving it a shake. From behind her came a gasp. Relief flooded through her, as she turned around.

Mrs Poole was staring at the dress, as if she could hardly believe her eyes.

'Please try it on Mrs Poole, to be certain the fit is good. I can make some quick alterations, if needed.'

The woman nodded and, accompanied by a maid, left for another room. The Butler retired. The housekeeper remained. She and Norrie sat in silence for ten minutes. Norrie's foot began to shake, and she had to fight to stop it tapping on the thickly carpeted floor.

Mrs Poole entered again, and Norrie breathed a sigh of relief. The dress fitted perfectly. And suited Mrs Mansard well. In a business-like way, Norrie stood and walked over to Mrs Poole, who was admiring herself in a mirror. 'The bustle is smaller, Madam. That's how the English ladies are wearing their evening dresses now. And their day dresses,' she added, noting the look of interest in Mrs Poole's eyes.

'It will do well enough, Miss Dillon,' Mrs Poole said without looking around. 'Please thank Mr Mansard and tell him I will be calling again in a few days. Perhaps I will consider a new calling dress or two.'

Norrie bowed her head. 'Thank you, Madam. I hope your dinner is a great success.'

The woman ignored her, too taken up with looking at the dress in the long mirror, turning from side to side as the servant and housekeeper made admiring comments.

Norrie was shown out by the Butler, through the back entrance. On the way, she was able to glance into the parlour.

'One day, this will all be mine,' she thought, as she returned to the carriage. 'All mine.'

Chapter 27

'I don't understand. What do you mean, that's not Ellen Kelly?' The priest sat forward in his seat, stared at the photo of the old portrait, then put it on a table beside him. His words were clipped and seemed agitated, but there was a light in his eyes.

'I've been trying to find out about the husband. Was Billy Kelly a policeman?' Maggie asked.

'Yes, he was. Is that important?'

Maggie nodded. 'Do you know when they were married?'

'Yes, it was in March 1853.'

'And before they married, she was Ellen Dillon?'

'Again, yes.'

'Do you know who the witnesses at the ceremony were?'

'I do. They were a Bridget Allen and a man called Jacob Berkowitz.'

'Not David Dillon?'

'Her brother, you mean? No, he had not long lost his wife in childbirth and wasn't able to attend the ceremony. Are you going to explain what this is all about?'

'Yes,' Maggie replied. 'But remember your promise. You do not discuss this with anyone.'

Jimmy Kelly hesitated. 'There is one person I must tell, but he won't be talking about it. I'll explain why once you've told me your true story.'

Maggie frowned, but before she could say more there was a sound of something being dragged along an upstairs corridor and then the sound of an electrical device being implemented.

'Excuse me for a moment,' Jimmy Kelly said, and left the room.

'That sounds to me like a disability lift,' Bob whispered. 'The nephew?'

Maggie shrugged. The noise stopped and a few seconds later Jimmy Kelly pushed in a wheelchair.

Maggie worked hard to keep her face neutral. The young man in the chair was aged around twenty but hunched, with the look of a man at least twice his age. His face had been subjected to a severe beating. One eye was glassed over, and where his jaw had been broken and re-set, the lower part of the face was slightly out of line with the top half. He had a scar running from the side of the blind eye down to his chin. His head was held in a device to keep it upright and still.

Jimmy pulled the wheelchair up to the side of his own seat. 'This is my nephew, William Kelly. As you can see, he was attacked and badly beaten. He's paralysed from the waist down and can't speak. But his brain is all there. He can hear you. And he can use his hands.'

Maggie stood and went over to William. She held out a hand. The boy took it in his own shaking hand, held it for a moment, then let it go and turned his eyes to his uncle with a questioning look.

'They're from England – sorry, Wales – and are here to talk about Ellen Kelly.'

A crease appeared between the boy's eyebrows.

'Because this lady is a genealogy investigator, working on behalf of a client, and this gentleman,' indicating Bob, 'is her husband. He's a Chief Inspector of Police in Wales. Marilyn will have to be careful this time.'

The boy's working eye opened wide in an expression of pleasure. He tried to speak, but only a grunt and a dribble of saliva came out, and the priest moved forward and wiped it away with a soft gesture, before running his hand down the boy's face. 'I think that maybe, finally, Will, we may get some answers. Truthful ones.'

The boy gave a small flick of his head and turned to Maggie with an intense look.

'The woman in that photograph – how old was she when it was taken?' Maggie asked.

'Around sixty,' Jimmy replied.

'Her name was not Ellen Dillon. Her real name was Honora Madigan, known to family and friends as Norrie. Norrie Madigan. She was wanted in Ireland for murder. She killed a land agent by the name of Seamus McMahon; slit his throat. She was due to go to Australia on a scheme to send out young girls, ostensibly for a better life, but in reality to become servants and to marry the convicts the British were sending there. Norrie set out but didn't arrive. She only reached Liverpool with two of her cousins, before she turned back, and went back to Dublin, where she met David Dillon. He helped her find two companions, probably members of the Molly Macguires, who walked with her back across Ireland to Kilrush, where she came from and where she found and murdered McMahon. Her alias – Ellen Margaret Dillon – she chose to honour her two cousins, Ellen O'Donnell and Margaret "Peg" Dillon. David and his wife Norah were planning to come to America. When Norrie returned to Dublin, she may have come across the army captain who had been hunting her in Kilrush was also there. For whatever reason, she decided she had to leave Ireland, so she became David's younger sister, Ellen Dillon, and sailed to America in March 1850.'

She stopped. She wasn't sure what reaction to expect but was thrown back in her seat when Jimmy Kelly laughed out loud, then stood and went to hug Will Kelly. The boy had tears in his eyes.

When Jimmy turned back to Maggie, his eyes were also glistening. 'Will knew something was wrong. He had been brought up on the legend of Ellen Kelly, but he and his mother, Marilyn didn't get along, although Marilyn still expected Will to take over from her eventually. He noticed some inconsistencies in her telling of the story. He started to investigate, quietly. He did a DNA test, found David Dillon and traced his descendants. They also did a DNA test, all three of them, and found there was no DNA relationship. He also found that David Dillon never had a younger sister.'

Maggie nodded. 'That's also been my finding.'

'That was as far as he got before his… accident. He challenged Marilyn with what he had found.' He paused and looked at Will, who gave his tiny nod. It sounds to me like there's a lot more to this story, Maggie. Are you willing to tell us all of it, right from the start? If you can, we'll tell you what we know, from our own investigation.'

'Do you have time now? It will take some time,' Maggie said.

'I have a couple of hours. Will is going to need his lunch soon.'

Will grunted again and waved a spindly arm at Jimmy.

'Will says lunch can wait. He wants to hear the story.'

'OK. I'll begin with my client – not his name or any details about him – but I'll tell you the story of the three sisters and their daughters, the three cousins, and what happened to each of them, in Ireland. Then, I'll be pleased to hear about what you know about Norrie Madigan here in America.'

She began with the story of the client, her discovery of his Irish roots and being able to trace them back to Clamhunger Row, in County Clare. She talked about information she had regarding Ellen O'Donnell in Australia, what happened to her and to Peg Dillon, although she didn't mention Joan and the letters. Finally, she explained that they were not really in New York on behalf of the client, but because Maggie and her fellow investigators wanted to know about Norrie Madigan. There, she was convinced, from the information she had uncovered, that there was more to the story, and she and Bob had come to find out.

'That's an amazing story,' Jimmy said when she had finished. 'But how did you find your way to us?'

'We were recommended to speak to you by a man at the museum. When I began to tell Norrie's story – I didn't mention her real name – he gave me what I thought was a strange sort of look and recommended that I come to speak to you. I saw he realised a familiar tale, but was not willing to discuss it with me, which I thought was rather odd.'

Jimmy nodded. 'My sister is well known in Manhattan, as is her story about Ellen Dillon, but it's also known that Marilyn has a temper and holds a grudge and that you shouldn't cross her.'

'What, right down to a person working in a museum? She has that much influence?'

'Uh huh. If the museum relies on city funding, Marilyn would be more than capable of finding a way to have it stopped.'

Maggie shook her head. 'I don't get it. The only reason she would do that is because she knows her version of the story is wrong.'

Jimmy slapped his hand hard on the arm of the chair, making Maggie jump. 'Exactly! She knows there was no such person as Ellen Dillon. And she also knows that the woman did even worse things than you've described, to establish her dynasty.'

'Such as?' Maggie asked.

'Will and I believe she killed two more men, in her quest to succeed here in America.'

'Time for you to tell me your stories,' Maggie said.

'Indeed, but first, let me get you all another drink.'

He left the room, leaving them with Will.

Bob went to sit next to Will and took his hand. 'I'm so sorry for what happened to you, Will,' he said gently. 'Was it deliberately done?'

A grunt and slight downward movement of the head said "yes".

'Did the police catch the person who did this to you?'

The lips parted slightly in a rictus of a smile.

Jimmy came back into the room, looked at Bob and frowned.

'He's told me this was a deliberate attack,' Bob said as Jimmy put the drinks on the table. 'But he didn't tell me who did it.'

'He won't tell you that. They were hired to beat him. I suspect it was meant to kill him.'

'I see,' Bob replied and returned to his seat.

'Um, I don't see. Is it relevant?' Maggie asked.

'Yes,' Bob said, taking her hand. 'The person who organised this beating was his mother, Marilyn Kelly.'

Maggie looked open mouthed at Bob, then over at Jimmy who nodded. 'How did you guess?'

'The look of contempt and disgust whenever you mentioned her name. Those are strong emotions, micro expressions, you don't realise you're doing it, but you are.'

'Time to tell us your stories,' Maggie said.

Chapter 28
New York 1852

Norrie had been working for Mr Mansard for eighteen months and was now well established as a dressmaker. The popularity of Mansard's had brought in a steady stream of new customers, including friends of Mrs Poole. She still lived with the Allen family but had the corner to herself and was able to pay enough rent for Paddy to decide they didn't need another tenant to share her space. Jacob Borowitz remained upstairs and was content, although Norrie noticed that he struggled for breath walking up the three flights of stairs.

David and Norah had found their own accommodation and Norah had delivered a baby girl but hadn't recovered well from the birth. These days she rarely saw them.

As the summer ended she noticed for a week or so that, as she walked to work from the Allen's home, a young policeman stood at the same spot each day, first nodding to her, then wishing her good morning, and then starting to walk with her.

'What makes you think I need your company?' she said, the first time he walked beside her.

'These areas can be dangerous, miss. You never know what's waiting around the next corner.'

'There's really no need to,' Norrie replied. 'People will talk.'

'Let them. My name is William Kelly. My family call me Billy.'

'I'll be calling you constable.'

'May I know your name?'

She thought for a moment, then decided there was no harm in it. 'I'm Ellen Dillon. I work as a seamstress and dressmaker for Mr Edward Mansard.'

'I know.'

Norrie stopped walking. 'How do you know?'

'My mother talks about Mr Mansard's new seamstress, who has replaced his wife.' He saw her face turn to thunder. 'I don't mean it like that,' he stammered. 'I mean, your reputation as a dressmaker is equalling that of Mrs Mansard. And she had a great reputation.'

His cheeks had turned bright red. Norrie took pity on him. 'Well, if that's all you meant, Mr Mansard is my employer and old enough to be my grandfather.'

'I apologise Miss Dillon.'

'So you should. Tell me about yourself, Constable Kelly.'

For the rest of their journey Billy told her that he was third generation Irish American, his grandparents having emigrated after the Act of Union in 1801, which formally made Ireland a part of the United Kingdom. 'He arrived here in 1803 with my grandmother and their five children. Grandpa thought the dissolution of the Irish parliament and being part of the UK and ruled over by them, despite having its own MPs in the British parliament, would mean nothing but trouble for the Irish and he was right. My father was born here in 1810. He married my mother, who's English, in 1831 and I was born in 1832, down in the Five Points, where my family lived until my father moved us out in 1845.'

'We are of an age, Billy Dillon. When did you decide to become a policeman?'

'Two years ago. I was afraid of being assigned to the Five Points, but lucky for me, my father made sure I stayed on the Lower East Side.'

'Your father is a man of influence, then?'

'He's a policeman, too. A Detective Sergeant. He began down in the Five Points, and he almost lost his life.'

'Mrs Allen has warned me to keep away from the Five Points, because of the gangs.'

'Indeed, you must not go near there. It's practically lawless, and run by Tammany Hall, which is totally corrupt, my father says.'

They had reached the shop on the corner of East 4th Street. 'I'll bid you good day here, Miss Dillon.' He looked at the shop window. 'Those are mighty fine dresses.'

'Thank you, constable.'

Norrie had persuaded Mr Mansard to give the outside a new coat of paint and had made dresses to be displayed in the window, along with matching hats and other accessories. A new name board had been made to go over the windows and "Mansard's Fine Outfitters" had been painted fresh on the door. She was now working on a plan to have Mr Mansard move out of the Lower East Side and into a premises on Broadway. It was a long-term plan, but she had hopes of succeeding, eventually.

'Good morning, Ellen. How are you today?'

'Well, thank you, Mr Mansard. I think I'll be here late tonight. Three dresses to finish and one of them that walking out dress for that friend of Mrs Poole. I want to make sure it's perfect, as she's collecting it tomorrow.'

He beamed at her, then let her through to the sewing room, where Beatrice, the apprentice awaited her.

They'd had to take on another girl, as the orders mounted up, following the success of Mrs Poole's dinner dress. Beatrice was neat, tidy, and clean, and eager to learn. She had nimble fingers and although she was limited to mainly sewing on buttons and other decorations, Norrie was showing her the basics of dress making.

Norrie would never agree to call her employer anything other than Mr Mansard, although he had encouraged her to call him Edward. She wanted no relationship of that kind with him. Norrie's plan was to have Mr Mansard think of her as a daughter, and as his natural successor. She knew he had two children, a son and a daughter, whom he never saw and who appeared to take no interest in Mr Mansard or his business. They hadn't even attended their mother's funeral.

She knew he was a lonely man who missed his beloved wife. She encouraged him to talk about Louisa Mansard, and she talked about how much she missed her family in Ireland, all of whom were dead. She told him that she particularly missed her father.

'He and me used to walk along the shore, before the hunger came. We talked and talked about this and that. He had nets and sometimes would catch a few fish, to supplement the potatoes. I loved him dearly.'

Gradually, Edward Mansard fell into a fatherly role. He advised her about Billy Kelly and the Kelly family, when he saw her and Billy together, said they were good people, untainted by the horrors of Tammany Hall and the Five Points.

Norrie also helped out Bridget Allen with clothes for the children. Bridget was more than happy to keep Norrie in the basement with the family, long after David and Norah departed. Not only did she pay good rent but provided the children's clothing free of charge and had even made a new dress for Bridget.

Despite her ongoing efforts, Norrie had never heard from her uncle, Edward Corcoran. Now she was established as Ellen Dillon, she decided this was probably for the best. She had thought that he would be vital to her survival in America, but now she was doing well enough for herself she no longer needed him and indeed, it would be dangerous for her to continue looking.

Her friendship with Billy Kelly continued throughout the autumn and over Christmas. He introduced her to his parents, and she took him to meet the Allens and Jacob Berkowitz, who had become her best friend. Norrie liked Billy well enough and felt that marriage to him would give her an additional layer of protection. They became an officially courting couple.

It was a day of mixed feelings at the Allen household when Norrie announced that she and Billy Kelly were to be married. Paddy and Bridget were overjoyed for her, but now would have to find another couple of tenants. Jacob Berkowitz would miss her greatly, too. They had had many fine discussions sitting on the stoop on a Sunday.

The wedding took place on a Saturday in March 1853 at the church of St Bridget, the service performed by the Pastor, Rev Thomas Mooney. The witnesses were Bridget Allen and Jacob Bercowitz, the latter being a Jew and therefore none too welcome, but Norrie insisted, and won. A small wedding breakfast took place at a local tavern and Billy and Norrie began their married life living with Billy's parents. The fact that no member of the Kelly family had been a witness was felt by Billy's mother to be an insult to the family, which didn't make a good start to Norrie and Maria sharing the same household. Billy had to make frequent interventions, usually managing to keep the peace.

At the same time, Norrie commenced a gentle introduction with Mr Mansard to the idea of moving the shop to Broadway. Given the volume of business Norrie's reputation had generated, they were about to hire another apprentice and would soon run out of room.

For ten months everything went according to plan. Norrie did not love Billy, but he was kind and generous, an adoring husband and she was able to announce that they could expect their first child early the following year.

Then, two events occurred within two weeks, that changed everything.

Chapter 29
New York 1854

Norrie and Billy's married life went well enough, despite the frequent altercations. Maria held onto her resentment of no Kelly family member being a witness at their wedding, besides being certain that no girl would ever be good enough for her eldest son. The couple had their own room in the Kelly house, but this had been achieved by making three of the younger boys sleep together in a small room, which they constantly complained about, and which led to fights.

Norrie was in the middle of yet another angry confrontation with Maria one evening in early December over Norrie's lack of cooking skills. She was tired and not minding her tongue, as Billy had begged her to do.

'My boy loves my cooking, so why shouldn't I prepare something specially for him? His job is hard, he needs to be well fed. Not that you have any idea of how to look after a man.'

'Because he's not a Mama's boy,' Norrie replied. 'When will you let him be his own man and eat what he wants to eat, when he wants to eat it. You'd like him tied to your apron strings forever. What's your plan for getting me out of the house this week?'

It would have escalated further, as they moved, hands on hips, closer into each other's face, when Billy arrived home, white faced. Norrie saw at once that something was wrong, but Maria got in first.

'What's happened?' Maria demanded. 'Is it your father?'

'No.' He turned to Norrie. 'Ellen, its Jacob Berkowitz. He's dead. A heart attack.'

She stared back at him. 'If it was a heart attack, so be it. But there's more to it, isn't there? You wouldn't look so shocked if there wasn't.'

Billy nodded. 'You know he worked down on the dockside, labouring?'

She nodded. 'He was too old and weak for that work.'

'He was a Jew and one of the Irish gangs, the Dead Dogs, had a gang master, who decided to make fun of Jacob, by making him carry sacks on his back until he collapsed from the strain. He just fell over and died. His mates, other members of the same gang, they laughed.' Billy's face had turned red now. 'They're bastards.'

'They did that to an old man? A defenceless old man?' Norrie said.

'He was just a Jew,' Maria remarked, turning away back to the stove.

Billy didn't challenge her.

'What's been done with his body?' Norrie asked.

The Jews have taken it. He'll be interred immediately. It's their way.'

'And the man who did this? Is he to be punished?'

'No, Ellen. All of the witnesses say there was no coercion. Others saw it but are too afraid of the gang master to speak out.'

'What's his name, this gangmaster?'

'O'Reilly. Jefferson O'Reilly.'

Maria Kelly spoke then, without turning around. 'Nothing to be done,' she said. 'No-one can lay a hand on Jeffy O'Reilly. Tammany will protect him.'

Not from me, Norrie thought.

**

She attended the funeral at the synagogue on Orchard Street the following day, sitting with the women. She didn't understand much of what was happening; much, she supposed, like Jacob Berkowitz must have felt at her wedding mass, but it didn't matter. It was her last opportunity to pay her respects to a man who had become her closest friend. She shed no tears. Tears were a waste of time.

The following day Norrie left work early, telling Mr Mansard that she wasn't feeling well because of her pregnancy. From the shop she walked down to the Five Points and the dock, and soon found Jefferson "Jeffy" O'Reilly. For two weeks she watched him whenever she could, learned his habits, where he drank, who he associated with, the brothels he visited.

On the fifteenth night, she was ready. She had discovered his only point of vulnerability, on the stairs up to his lodgings on the fifth floor of a filthy tenement. Tonight, it was raining and there was no moon. The darker the better. She waited on the third-floor landing. Here, she had observed, a widow lived with four children, and locked herself in her apartment at night.

O'Reilly said goodnight to his companions and made his way up the staircase where, no doubt, his wife was waiting in fear of her life, depending on what mood he was in. Tonight, he was in a good mood, whistling a well-known Irish tune. He stumbled several times. As he reached the third-floor landing, he saw a woman standing, perfectly still, in a black cloak and dark bonnet.

'Now who would you be, my pretty girl,' he muttered, groping his way towards her.

As he stretched out his arm, Norrie grabbed it, spun him around and pulled him to the floor. She stuffed a rag in his open mouth to keep him quiet and put a boot on his chest.

'Nemesis,' she said quietly. 'This is for Jacob Berkowitz.'

In her other hand she produced the knife, held back his head and before he could react, she slit his throat. As the blood splattered out, she waited a few seconds, staring into his dying eyes without a shred of remorse, before bending down to carve a "V" into his forehead. Then, she turned and walked quietly down the staircase, took a quick look into the street, pulled her cloak around her, tugged her bonnet down, and walked out into the rain.

It took her half an hour to reach home. Billy was out on a nightshift, as was his father. Only Maria was at home with the younger children, who were asleep. She managed to creep in. Luckily for her, Maria was asleep in the armchair in front of the kitchen fire. She crept up the stairs, hid the cloak and bonnet – both had been made especially for this night – which she would dispose of in the shop in the morning and got into bed, waiting for Billy's return.

The second time had been much easier than the first.

**

Billy arrived home two days later with the news that Jefferson O'Reilly had been killed and it looked like a gang killing.

'Good riddance,' Maria said. 'Does anyone know who done it?'

'No,' Billy replied, as Norrie sat quietly sewing by the fire. 'Just one witness who saw a woman in a black cloak and hat leaving the building shortly after O'Reilly had entered it. We haven't been able to trace her, but we don't think she was involved. Someone had carved the "V" of the Vermins gang into his forehead. Them and the Dogs are now at war, and with a bit of luck, they'll wipe each other out.'

'As long as they stay away from us,' Maria said.

Norrie smiled. The cloak and bonnet no longer existed, having been torn apart and put on the rag pile at the shop. Soon, they would go with the rag merchants, who collected weekly.

**

The following day at the shop Norrie and Mr Mansard discussed the death of O'Reilly in relation to Jacob's death. Jacob and Edward had been good friends for over twenty years and Edward Mansard had taken his friend's death badly.

'However it was done, I cannot blame the perpetrator,' Edward said. 'Jacob was a good man, a very good man. I will miss him.'

‘As will I, Mr Mansard. He was good to me. He taught me a great deal about the ways of the world here in America. I learned a lot of new words.’

Edward Mansard was amused. ‘What words, Ellen?’

‘Oh, I don’t know. Words like, constitution, reductive – I’m still not sure what that one means – and nemesis. There’s lots of others, but I can’t remember them now. Anyway, I must get on.’

He smiled at her, turned, and without a word, fell to the floor.

Norrie jumped up, ran to him, called to Beatrice to help her and between them they turned him over. His eyes were wide open. Norrie knew at once that he was dead, but she checked for breathing. There was none. She sent Beatrice to find Billy or any other policeman and to fetch a doctor.

Billy arrived, out of breath, ten minutes later. He looked at the body and shook his head. A few minutes later a doctor arrived and declared Edward Mansard to be dead from apoplexy.

‘But he’d seemed so well,’ Norrie said. In response to Billy’s questions, she told the story of their conversation, confirmed word for word by Beatrice. The doctor arranged for the body to be taken away and Billy took Norrie home. The shop was closed.

Three days later, after the funeral, a lawyer called on the Kellys, asking to speak with Norrie. Being a man of distinction in Maria’s eyes, she allowed Norrie to speak to him in the front parlour. Billy, who was about to begin a shift, accompanied them.

‘I’ll come straight to the point, Mrs Kelly. Mr Mansard has left you everything. The shop, and his considerable savings of a thousand dollars.’

For a few moments Norrie couldn’t speak. ‘Everything?’

‘Yes. He has been very clear about it. His will says that you have been the cause of his return to great success and for that you deserve to have the shop and the money to keep it going.’

'But what about his children?'

'He specifically states that they should have nothing. They are estranged from him, he hasn't seen them for many years. I don't even know how or where to contact them,' the lawyer said. 'There are a few papers to sign, if you please.'

As Billy looked on in shock, Norrie signed the papers, which transferred both the shop and the bank savings to her.

She gave the lawyer the details of her own savings account, with the Greenwich Savings Bank on Fifth Avenue. 'You can transfer the money,' she said.

'Are you sure this is lawful?' Billy asked. 'When the man has children.'

'I believe it is, Sir. However, I guess that if his children find out he's died and left them nothing, they may attempt to challenge the will.'

Bring it on, Norrie muttered.

'What was that my love?' Billy said.

'Nothing, Billy. I guess we'll just have to wait and see what happens. In the meantime, when it's decent to do so, I'll re-open the shop.'

My shop, she thought. Broadway, here I come.

**

It took a further month for the news of their father's death to reach Wayland and Sophia Mansard in Washington. They arrived in Manhattan three days later, vowing that no little Irish slut was going to take what was rightfully theirs.

Chapter 30
New York 1854

'You, woman, name!'

Norrie looked up from the counter where she had been frowning over the outstanding bill of a woman whose name was well known in Manhattan society and wondering how to approach the individual.

The speaker was a bull of a man, towering over her, with a large head, his hair covered by a stovepipe hat, a round red face, small fat lips and, as far as she could see, practically no neck. His gut protruded to the extent of straining the buttons of his waistcoat. He carried a wooden cane and wore gloves. The woman accompanying him was, by contrast, small, emaciated and white faced, with a long nose and the same small fat lips. She wore a black dress and bonnet. They both looked at Norrie with a stare that was both condescending and overbearing.

She had been anticipating trouble and here it was.

'Would you be speaking to me, Sir?'

'Who else is there to speak to?' he mimicked her Irish accent, gazing slowly around.

'You must be Mr Wayland Mansard, and Miss Sophia Mansard?'

'And you must be the Irish slut who has stolen our inheritance. Tell me, how did you coerce our father into leaving the shop and the money to you? Irish witchcraft, that's how.' He gave his sister a triumphant smile.

'Mr Mansard left the property to me because of the excellent work I've done for him, taken his name right back to the top of the popular couturiers of Manhattan, as it was when your mother was alive. And I will tell you sir, I am not to be insulted. If you wish to have a polite discussion, that's fine with me. If not, I must ask you to leave my premises.'

'Your premises? Our premises! It's you that'll be leaving. I am giving you notice that I and my sister will be challenging my father's Will.'

'Then you must do as you wish, Sir. Now, please leave. If you do not, I will call the police and have you arrested for threatening behaviour.'

'How dare you speak to me like that, you insolent slut. I will have you out of here, you hear me?'

Norrie called through to Beatrice, who had been hiding behind the curtain. 'Go find the constables and tell them I require their assistance to remove a rude and threatening person from my shop.' Beatrice ran from the premises. She was back in five minutes with Billy and his sergeant.

'Gentleman, this person has called me an Irish slut and accused me of acquiring this shop by false pretences. I have suggested he leave. I am happy to provide the name of my lawyer. It is my wish that he does not return here again.'

Billy's face turned red on hearing the insult, but Norrie scowled at him, a warning not to lose his temper. He nodded.

'Please come with us, Sir. Your presence is upsetting these ladies.'

Beatrice was now hiding behind Norrie.

'More Irish scum. I will see myself out. Do not lay a hand on me.' He turned back to Norrie. 'You will be hearing from me imminently. Come Sophia.'

A carriage had waited outside, and the brother and sister got in and gave orders to the driver, watched by Billy and the sergeant. When they were gone, Billy returned to the shop.

'There's going to be trouble. He has a lot of money.'

'I don't understand why he cares so much,' Norrie replied. 'He's had nothing to do with his father for the past ten years. He didn't even attend his own mother's funeral. He doesn't need the shop. What's the matter with him?'

'The sergeant told me what the problem is. Wayland Mansard is a "Know Nothing", and a bigwig in the organization at that.'

'Oh,' Norrie said. 'No wonder he hates me.'

'They're rabid against the Irish,' Billy replied. 'He'll be taking the insult bitterly, seeing himself a laughingstock in his organisation. The great Wayland Mansard, ousted from his father's business by an Irish girl.'

'The lawyer said I had a good case. Mr Mansard was of sound mind and his witnesses agreed. I don't see how those two can—'

'They have deep pockets, friends in high places and a vitriolic hatred of the Irish. He'll burn this shop down before he gives in to your ownership. We'll have to be careful, Ellen, very careful.'

Norrie said nothing. She needed to think, mainly of how to get rid of Wayland Mansard without appearing to be involved in any way.

**

As good as his word, Wayland Mansard's lawyer sent a letter to Norrie, challenging her ownership, accusing her of coercing Edward Mansard into leaving everything to her, and promising to drag her through every court in New York until the property was returned to the Mansards. It was daunting, but Norrie was forming a plan. She needed, however, to know more about the "Know Nothing" organisation. She went first to Bridget Allen.

'Oh, dear God, keep away from those people. They're crazy! And spiteful and nasty.'

'They're actually called "The Native America Party", and got some people elected,' Paddy added. 'Secretive, too. If anyone is asked if they're a member, they're supposed to say, "I know nothing." That's where the name comes from.'

'And they hate the Irish?'

'They hate Catholics. They believe the country is being overrun and immigration has to be stopped. They're

Protestants, all believing there's a conspiracy by the Pope and the Bishops to take over America.'

'That's mad,' Norrie said. 'Mr Berkowitz told me that the Indians are the native people of America. Everyone else is an immigrant.'

'That's true enough. But these people's ancestors came here up to two hundred years ago, from England, and set up settlements. They now call themselves the Founding Fathers, considering themselves to be the native Americans.'

'Well, to hell with them – sorry Bridget. We have as much right to be here as they do. They probably came with nothing. We come with nothing. There's no difference. And anyway, Mr Mansard told me his family came to America about one hundred years ago, so they weren't these so-called Founding Fathers.'

'I agree, many don't. It's a matter of degrees, far as I'm concerned,' Paddy said, puffing on his pipe. 'That Mansard man is going to give a speech in the Five Points later this week. Bound to cause trouble. Beware, Ellen, he may use you as an example of the thieving, deceiving Irish scum, as he calls us.'

Norrie sat up. 'When is the speech due to be made?'

'Friday, I believe. Now don't you go thinking about going anywhere near the Five Points. They're likely to string you up after he makes that speech. There's already unrest, with the Dogs talking about a revenge killing against the Vermins for what they done to Jeffy O'Reilly.'

Norrie pressed her lips together. She had to get away and think. She had resources now, ears on the ground, knowledge. She had come to realise that knowledge was the greatest weapon she could possess.

'Thanks, Paddy and Bridget. I'll be sure to keep well away. I'm real scared I won't be able to keep my shop. Wayland Mansard is going to go after my customers, spread vile lies about me.' She shook her head. 'I'll go now. Thanks for the warning.'

'Poor girl,' Bridget said to Norrie's departing back. 'With a baby due soon, this is tough on her, after all the hard work she's put in. I'll pray for her in church tonight.'

At the end of the street, at the crossroads, Norrie didn't carry straight on, but turned left and walked slowly to Mulberry Street where it intersected with Baxter. On the far corner a man stood, a cap pulled down to hide his eyes. His hands were pushed carelessly into his pockets, although Norrie knew that the right hand contained a vicious long bladed knife. He was known as Hunter. She crossed the street to where he stood, lounging, watching.

'When will it happen?' she asked.

'Friday, before Mansard's speech. They're hoping to stop it.'

'No. Let him speak first. He needs to show exactly what he is,' Norrie said. He's going to condemn the Irish, a real inflammatory piece of speechifying.'

The man raised his eyebrows. 'Not sure if I can make that happen.'

'Try. It's important he speak first. Where should he be led to?'

'Into the old mill,' Hunter replied.

He nodded. She handed over five dollars and walked on. The whole exchange had taken no more than one minute. She knew he would succeed. Time for the next part of her plan to destroy Wayland Mansard.

Chapter 31

'What evidence do you have that she committed those murders?' Maggie said. 'And the third one, that Mansard man, wasn't even murdered, well not as such, but definitely not by her.'

Jimmy Kelly sighed. 'We don't, that's the problem. But Will and I have examined each death closely for over a year and we're convinced we're right.'

Maggie sat thinking, shaking her head. Should she talk about the letters in Ireland? Not yet. She had promised Joan she wouldn't reveal what she knew, but she'd already told Jimmy and Will that there was some information in Ireland, although it didn't reveal anything new about Norrie, apart from her ownership of a shop, plus a husband and baby. Another thought struck her. She needed to speak to Mary Dillon.

'Jimmy, I don't think there's much more we can do here, at the moment. This is a lot to take in, for all of us. Why don't we take a break for today. I'd like to make a couple of phone calls, then come back tomorrow, if that's OK with you both?'

Jimmy looked at Will, then nodded. 'Fine with us. What time? I have an early service, then a couple of meetings. We have a homeless crisis here, at present. How about you join us for lunch tomorrow?'

Maggie looked at Bob, who nodded. 'I want to spend some time in the library here in Manhattan, although I think you may be as good a source as they are,' she smiled.

'One o'clock work for you? I can show you what papers we have.'

'Yes,' she replied, standing up. 'Thanks so much for meeting with us, and for the information. We'll see you tomorrow.'

'Before you go, let me show you our church. You know, Ellen, or Norrie, would have worshipped here. It's the first Catholic church to be built in Manhattan and it has some interesting features.'

He led them into the church and began to talk about its history. Bob, who was finding the heat and stuffiness nauseating, said, 'Would you mind if I go outside for a minute. It's too hot in here for me.'

'No problem,' Jimmy replied. 'sadly, we can't afford air conditioning. Maggie, let me show you the rest, if you can deal with the heat?'

'Certainly,' she replied, not wishing to offend the priest.

He led her over to a statue, next to an ornately carved panel. 'This is Saint Bridget, after whom our church is named.'

Maggie smiled politely. It wasn't a particularly well carved or interesting statue. Saint Bridget appeared to be looking towards the panel.

'I know she's not very beautiful,' Jimmy grinned, 'but she has a secret. He moved closer to the statue and reached behind it. Something clicked, and part of the panel slid back, revealing a staircase leading down. 'This is our crypt. I have no idea why it was built with the church, possibly to give refuge to any poor Irish man or woman running from the gang warfare around the time it was built. It's just a small room. We can't use it much, because it's damp. Some of the plaster is dropping off. But it's fun to know it's there. Would you like to see?'

'Yes, please,' Maggie replied enthusiastically. 'I love hidden places in old buildings.'

'Right, follow me. The steps are steep.'

He had turned a light on. In the few seconds it had taken to reach the bottom, the temperature had dropped about twenty degrees. They were in a small square space, facing a door. Jimmy flicked another switch and the door swung out. Maggie glanced inside.

'I see what you mean about the state of it. Any paperwork you stored down here would rot, rapidly. What a shame. Still, interesting, thank you, Jimmy.'

After exiting the stairs he flicked the hidden switch again. As the panel swung back into place, he sighed. 'It would be good to have it treated for damp, but we can't afford it, like so much else in this church.'

'But you love it,' Maggie said.

'It's our Irish history, built by Irish dock workers. Yes, I love it, all of it. Even the smell of damp whenever I'm forced to go down there.'

Maggie laughed. 'I'd better find Bob. Thank you for showing me around, Jimmy. It's a lovely church.'

Jimmy walked her to the front door, where Bob was waiting. After promising to see him again the following day, Bob and Maggie set off in the direction of Broadway.

'What are you thinking? I know that look?' Bob said, as they strolled along to the intersection of East 14th and Broadway.

'Norrie Madigan turned from a young, innocent girl into a murderer to get what she wanted. Marilyn Kelly must know that,' she said as they turned up Broadway and joined the crowds out in the sunshine. 'Does anyone in this city not have their ears plugged up?' she complained.

'This is the city of the mobile phone,' Bob replied. 'But they find a way of navigating around the crowds without bumping into anyone. Same as those bikes and scooters. Quite amazing, really.'

'Anyway, I don't know about you but I'm hungry. Shall we stop and eat?'

'Definitely,' he replied. 'Let's try one of these diners. They look fascinating.'

They had reached Union Square and found a small diner on one of the streets leading off. They decided to try something specifically new to them.

'I don't know what a New York Cheese Steak is,' Bob said. 'But when in Rome…' He ordered two.

'It's cool in here, thank goodness. It's getting humid outside.'

'Thunderstorm due,' Bob replied. 'What's bothering you?'

'It's about the story of what Norrie became, if it's true. The events in Ireland changed her. If she did kill those men, that's very sad, but who knows what people will do after they've been through the kind of trauma and horror that she'd seen. Not that I'm excusing it,' she said, seeing Bob's frown. 'It's just, I can't see that it's enough for Marilyn Kelly to have her own son almost beaten to death because of family history. For me, there's something off about that. I don't get it. She could have threatened him, disinherited him, called him a traitor to the family. She must have had the PR to handle the public side of it, too.'

'If he said it publicly, I bet a whole load of other genealogists would have jumped on it, which would, if they had come to the same conclusion, have been beyond embarrassing for her.'

Maggie shook her head. 'I see that, but I still think she could have found a way around it. You know what genealogists are like. You think you have something pinned down, then up jumps another fact to disprove what you thought you knew. No, I feel it in my gut, there's something else going on.'

Their food arrived. Fifteen minutes later, Bob sat back and rubbed his stomach. 'No taxis for the rest of the afternoon. I need to walk that off. It was very good.' He had eaten all of his own and half of Maggie's. She'd tried her best, but the portion was just too big.

'I agree. If we keep walking we'll reach Times Square. Then it's only about fifteen minutes back to the hotel. Walking helps me think. Do you want anything else?'

'No food, but a coffee would be good.'

'I'll have tea, if they do Earl Grey tea here. I'm going to send a message to Mary Dillon in Kilrush. I want her to visit Joan, to see if there's anything else.'

'Gut again?'

'Yep.'

'Let's walk and talk,' he said, checking his watch. 'It's almost three here, so eight in the evening in Kilrush. If Mary's working tomorrow, she'll see your message. You may get something back before we visit Jimmy again.'

They walked from Union Square slowly up Broadway, taking in the sights and sounds of a busy Manhattan afternoon, stopping to photograph the iconic landmarks: 42nd Street, Tin Pan Alley, until they reached Times Square, where they paused to take in the ever-moving billboards and watch the many acts taking place in the square.

'It's smaller than it looks on TV on New Year's Eve,' Maggie said. 'But lively.'

From there they crossed to 6th Avenue, up past the Radio City Music Hall and back to their hotel.

By the time they reached their room, Maggie was flagging. She showered and decided to take a short nap before dressing for dinner. Bob was back on the balcony with a beer.

'I was just thinking,' he said, 'before we meet up with Jimmy and Will tomorrow, we could go down early to Battery Park and take the boat out to the Statue of Liberty. Then, we could go to Ellis Island, to see the display about the immigrants arriving there. What do you think?'

'That should work,' Maggie replied. 'I can leave my visit to the library for the following day. I'm not sure how much I'll learn there, anyway. Jimmy is a better source of direct information.'

They had an early, quiet dinner and both slept well. When she woke at seven the next morning, she saw an email had arrived, from Mary Dillon.

Got your message. Went down to see Joan first thing this morning. At first, very wary, but when I explained everything to her, admitted there is another letter. Very personal and informative re. Norrie. She has given it to me to copy and send to you. I will transmit asap. I have promised her I will tell you that you are strictly forbidden to show it to anyone. That goes for me, too.'

Maggie wondered if she should wait for this second message to arrive. Bob persuaded her to have breakfast and think it over. As they sat at their usual seats in front of the window of the deli, he said, 'You'll be able to see it on your phone. Isn't it better to do something, rather than just sit in a hotel room, waiting for something that might not come for hours?

She wasn't sure, although she did want to keep to their plan, for Bob's sake. She agreed to go, so long as she was able to keep a close eye on her phone. And it was worth it, she thought afterwards, to see the iconic statue. The visit to Ellis Island also proved interesting, although Maggie knew that the earliest immigration centre, at Castle Garden, wasn't in place when Norrie had arrived.

After returning to Battery Park, they took the subway back uptown and walked across to the church, just before one in the afternoon. As they approached the church, Maggie's phone buzzed. The email from Mary had arrived with a copy of the letter attached.

They stopped on the street corner. Maggie opened it up and read both the message and the attachment. Wordlessly, she handed over the phone to Bob. When he had finished reading he said, 'Are you going to share this with Jimmy and Will?'

'I think so. Do you think we can trust Father Jimmy Kelly?'

'He's been pretty open with us so far; I think we can take a chance.'

Then let's go. This is going to shake the socks off them.'

Chapter 32
New York 1854

Norrie ran and ran and ran. Her belly and her back ached from the weight of the baby. Her legs buckled a couple of times, but she kept running. Lucky for her it was a dark night, no moon, few people on the streets.

She was triumphant. The plan had worked beautifully. Beatrice, in a heavy disguise had informed Wayland Mansard that there was a woman who had information about Ellen Kelly that would ensure he won his case. She wanted to meet him after his speech on Friday, at the old, deserted mill, where no-one would see them. The information was gold, he could be assured.

Mansard had delivered his speech at seven and, as expected, stirred up the crowd to a mighty roar against the Irish and all Catholics.

Norrie had secreted herself in the corner of a room in the mill, on a floor below where the revenge killing was to take place. Hunter had been as good as his word, informing the Dogs that the man who had killed Jeffy O'Reilly was going to be at the old mill for a secret meeting with Wayland Mansard. At eight thirty she heard the door open. A screaming man was hauled up the stairs. She heard the sounds of the man being held down, pinned to the floor and the laughing of men holding him. The screaming stopped abruptly. As soon as the last of the men left the building, she ran up to the landing where the body lay. The man wasn't quite dead, but close enough. Blood was flowing from somewhere behind his neck.

'You don't have long,' she said, kneeling over him. 'Is there anyone you want me to tell about who did this.'

The man tried but couldn't speak. She watched, as life slowly left his eyes. She had recognised him – Eddie Makepeace, one of the leaders of the Vermins. She didn't have long. She had brought a kitchen knife with her. She dipped it in his blood, and, using his finger, wrote the letters "Mans" on the floor next to his dead body. Then ran back down the stairs and hid in the room again, as Wayland Mansard entered on the ground floor and began to make his way up the stairs.

As he turned the corner on the floor below the murdered man, she crept out of the door, a brick in her hand. As soon as he passed the door, she jumped out and hit him on the side of the head. He fell like a sack of potatoes. Within a minute she had put the knife in his pocket, smeared a little blood on his hand and began to make her way down the stairs. She had reached the first-floor landing when the door opened below her, and a crowd of men streamed in. They were Vermins, shouting out for Eddie Makepeace.

Damn! Her timing was off. She didn't think they'd arrive so quickly. She'd managed through Hunter to put about the rumour that, after his speech, Mansard was going to a secret meeting with Makepeace at the mill. When Makepeace didn't return, the Vermins became suspicious and headed for the mill.

There was a door to her right, leading into one of the holding sheds in the mill. It was unoccupied, as she had discovered on a previous visit. Norrie had become a thorough planner. She slipped into the room and left the door an inch ajar.

Within seconds the gang members found Mansard, just regaining consciousness on the fourth floor. A few went up to the fifth floor and found Makepeace's body on the landing.

As much as she would have liked to stay to find out what would happen, she couldn't risk discovery, so as soon as all of the men were a few floors above, she crept down to the ground floor. There were more men waiting at the entrance.

Again, Norrie had prepared for this eventuality. There was a back entrance where once goods had been brought in from the docks. She made her way there, as silently as possible, blood pumping, exited the mill and crept through the streets back towards the Lower East Side.

There was a great hue and cry increasing in anger, but the farther she got away, the less she heard. Then, the sound of the whistles of a police vehicle making its way down to the Five Points.

Now, she ran. By the time she reached home, the house was dark and silent. She crept up the stairs, took off her cloak, put it in the cupboard with her bonnet, put on her nightdress and climbed into bed, but didn't sleep, instead praying that the idiots would make the wrong series of connections about the two deaths.

At six the following morning she heard Billy returning from his shift.

Norrie pretended to wake up. She yawned and stretched. 'This lump managed to give me a decent night last night. I needed a good sleep. How was your night? Quiet, I hope, my darlin'?'

He thumped down on the bed. 'No, not quiet. There's a riot in the Five Points. I have to go out again soon.'

But you've only just got home!' she protested. 'Surely they can do without you for a couple of hours.'

'It's bad.'

'Why, Billy?'

'You know Mansard was delivering his speech last night?'

'Of course I know. What happened?' She sat up now.

'Mansard proclaimed there should be a total ban on any more Irish entering America and no catholic should be allowed to take up public office. The Irish were incensed and went looking for Mansard. The rumour spread that he was at the old mill, plotting with Eddie Makepeace to have key members of the Irish community arrested and hanged. They headed for the old mill and found Mansard with a knife with blood on it, and Makepeace dead.

'That's terrible,' she said, then pretended to ponder for a few seconds.

Billy went on. 'Mansard was there, stunned but alive. So was Eddie Makepeace. His throat had been cut, and part of a word – "Mans" – had been written by him in his blood before he died.' He stopped, frowning. 'I don't understand how that could have happened.'

'Why not?' Norrie asked, a cold feeling creeping over her.'

'Because Eddie Makepeace couldn't read or write.'

She hadn't taken that into account. 'So what happened then?'

'That's when the Dogs arrived. They saw Mansard staggering out, with the knife in his hand. They went crazy. They didn't know right then it was Makepeace who was dead. They assumed it was one of theirs, who'd got there ahead of the mob. They were in a rage of blood.'

'They've handed him over to you, then?'

'No. They decided on their own justice. They lynched him. Mansard is dead. The Vermins were too late to stop it, and it was them who found Eddie Makepeace.' He frowned again. 'It doesn't make sense.'

Norrie's hands flew to cover her mouth. 'Oh, Billy, that's dreadful! As much as I hated the man I didn't wish him dead. I was prepared to fight him through the courts. This is going to start a gang war, isn't it?'

'Already has,' he said. 'Police from all districts have been called in, to try to keep them apart.'

'A curse on them all,' Norrie spat out.

'Don't say that,' Billy replied, putting his hand on her stomach. 'It'll upset the baby.' The gesture made her wince, but she didn't show it. She put her hand on top of his. 'You make sure you keep safe, Billy Kelly. I have to go off to meet Beatrice. You know she's leaving today?'

'Yes, that's bad for you. She was a good girl.'

'She was, but her family has decided on going to Philadelphia, to try for better luck there. They're taking the wagon from 42nd Street up to the station. I want to see her off. I'm going to give her ten dollars for herself and her family, to help them get started. Then, I have to see a couple of girls who've been recommended.'

Billy leaned over and kissed her. 'You're a good, decent, generous woman, Ellen Kelly. I love you.'

'And I love you. Now, go off, if you must. I'll see you later, God willing.'

As soon as he had gone, she lay back down on the bed. Mansard was dead. It was a perfect outcome, albeit she had made a mistake with the writing. That had been a step too far and, as it turned out, unnecessary. At least there would be no story to tell about Mansard meeting a woman to learn more about Ellen Kelly. She only had to ensure Beatrice's silence and the rest would be plain sailing. Except for Hunter, but she'd deal with him. She knew that Billy would continue to worry on the attempt to write the word "Mansard" in blood, for it had been assumed to be his name that Makepeace was trying to write. She wondered if Billy would tell his superiors about his doubts and suspicions. No matter, she would think of a story to cover her mistake. Mansard was dead and there was gang warfare in the Five Points. That would be enough to keep Billy busy for some time to come. She would find out every detail of whatever investigation took place, if any did. Knowledge was everything and her network of informants was growing by the day.

Back to business. After she'd seen Beatrice off, she would go to look at the shop on Broadway. It had living quarters above, and plenty of space for a sewing room to accommodate at least three girls.

**

The pain in her back increased during the day, but she took no notice. It was probably due to the running.

By the time Billy came home that evening, she was pacing up and down. He took one look at her and took her by the elbow to the settle in the kitchen.

She tried to shake him off. 'It's nothing, Billy. I'm not due for weeks yet. It's been a busy day, is all.'

Before she reached the settle, she stopped suddenly, as warm water gushed to her feet, and she screamed as the pains began.

A few hours later James Kelly was born; early, small, but robust enough. Norrie looked down, formed a happy expression and looked up at Billy, who was already besotted. She felt nothing.

'The start of the Kelly dynasty,' Billy said. 'And more to come.'

The only "more" that interested Norrie was the size of her property and money in the bank.

A week later she was back on her feet in the shop. She had agreed to feed the baby herself. Sophia Mansard had not bothered her, being, she said, too overwrought at her brother's death. Norrie heard that she had returned to Washington, vowing never to set foot in Manhattan again.

There was no further investigation into the strange events that occurred on the night of the death of Wayland Mansard and the riot that continued, on and off, for weeks.

A week after the birth of James she wrote to Father Jerome in Kilrush. She felt she had, at last, some good news to share. She told him about her luck in meeting Mr Berkowitz, her taking over the shop from kind Mr Mansard, her marriage to Billy and now the arrival of James. She asked for news of her cousins, how they were getting on in Australia.

It was a further six months before the reply came. She had asked Father Jerome to write to Mrs Ellen Kelly at the Broadway address where she and Billy now lived.

What he told her, Peg's death and Ellen's forced marriage to a convict, completed the transition of Norrie Madigan to Ellen Kelly, who had done bad things for what she believed to good reasons, a vengeful, angry woman, bent on her own rise, caring nothing about destroying whoever got in her way.

Yet, in her heart, she knew the terrible wrong she had done. She would never tell a living soul in America, but the part of her conscience that retained some former aspect of her good character, confessed all in a letter to Father Jerome. It ended with the instruction this was a written confession, as sacred as that in the confessional box itself, and she hoped he would give her absolution.

She never heard from him again.

Chapter 33

Jimmy welcomed them and led them through the sitting room into a sunroom, where lunch had been laid out. Will waited there.

'I've tried to keep the food simple, for Will's sake,' he said.

'Good,' Maggie replied, grinning at Will. 'Yesterday we both ate a New York Cheesesteak, or at least Bob did. I couldn't finish mine, so he ate what I left. He's going to have to run miles in Central Park to take off what he put on yesterday.'

Will grunted and nodded.

On the table was a selection of meats, cheeses and cooked fish, plus salad and a plate of bagels.

'This is perfect,' Maggie said. 'Jimmy, before we start, I have some news. Do you want to hear it now, or later?'

'Is it good news, or bad news?'

'Both,' Maggie replied.

'Then, after. I'll say a quick grace and we'll begin.' They chatted over lunch, keeping the conversation light and simple, as Jimmy had to help Will with his food.

'The Statue of Liberty and Ellis Island this morning? That was good going. What will you do when you leave here?'

'Not sure yet.'

'I think we're all done now. Shall we go through to the sitting room? I've prepared coffee.'

Once they were seated and ready, Maggie brought out her mobile phone.

'I sent a message yesterday to Ireland, to reach the person who has information from Australia; that's where my information came from, in letters from Ellen O'Donnell to a priest in Kilrush. I told you that some of the information referred to Norrie Madigan in America. I asked my contact to ask the owner of the letters if there were any more, because I suspected there might have been, and I was right. This morning, I've received a copy of the final letter sent by Norrie to a priest in Ireland. She must have asked for news of her cousins in Australia and was told the terrible stories about what happened to them. I'm going to read you the email from the owner of the letters, and the original letter received from Norrie Madigan in 1856.'

They all nodded. She began with the message from Joan included in Mary's email.

'Hello, Maggie, well you certainly know how to stir things up. New York, eh? I'm sorry that you went after Norrie's story. It's a bad one. I kept back the final letter from her to Father Jerome. When he received it he was already ill. He put it in a sealed envelope and apparently intended to burn it, then reply to her. But his illness progressed too rapidly, and he died before he could carry out either task. The letter remained in the envelope for a hundred and twenty-five years. It was then opened by my mother and as soon as she saw it, she tried to burn it, but I stopped her. I have kept it aside from the others, as something told me that one day, someone would come who needed this letter and the information it contains. Mary Dillon told me about what you're doing in New York. Now I know that someone is you. Please keep in mind that this letter was sent as a confession to a priest. It asks for absolution for horrors carried out. I leave it up to you to decide how you use it. Best wishes Joan. PS. I hope you'll come back to see me when you return from the United States.'

'If that letter is a confession to a priest, then I'm not comfortable about it being read out,' Jimmy said, shaking his head.

'I thought you might not be,' Maggie replied. 'But, as Will did the original research, perhaps I can give him the highlights. If you want to leave the room, we'll understand.'

'If it's just the highlights, I'll stay.'

'I'll keep it as brief as possible,' Maggie replied. 'Bear in mind that Father Jerome already knew that she had killed the land agent, Seamus McMahon, in Kilrush, because he had hidden her from the British soldiers. Now, she confesses that she killed two more men, and was responsible for the death of a third. The first was the killer of her friend and mentor, Jacob Berkowicz. The second was a man called Hunter, an informant. The person for whose death she was responsible was a man called Wayland Mansard. She set him up hoping to start a gang war for which Mansard would be blamed. She was shocked when the crowd took it upon themselves to hang Mansard. She had thought he would be tried for murder. She says she was sorry it happened, but in the end had no remorse about the man's death. She asks for absolution for all of these wrongs. My feeling is that she didn't get it. Not because Father Jerome would not have given it, but because he died before he could do anything about it. What would you have had her do, Jimmy?'

Jimmy didn't answer for a few minutes, as they all sat in silence waiting.

'I can't answer that,' he said finally. 'I know that Wayland Mansard was trying to take the shop away from her, and Will and I had already thought that she might be involved somehow in his death. If she had come to me, I guess I would have asked her to answer to the law for her sins. But if she didn't, there was nothing I could do. I am bound to never reveal what I hear, no matter what it might be.'

'But it does confirm that you and Will were right. Norrie, or Ellen Kelly, turned from a young, innocent Irish girl into a murderer. And we all think that Marilyn knows, right?'

Jimmy nodded.

'And that's why you think she had Will beaten?' Bob asked.

Jimmy looked puzzled. 'Yes. Why are you questioning me on this?'

Bob sat forward in his chair. 'Jimmy, I'm not questioning you, in the sense that I don't believe you. If you say Marilyn did this entirely on the basis of the lies she's been telling about her family history for years, then I believe you. You are a man of integrity and truth. However, from what you've described of your sister, I think she could have said mea culpa and pleaded innocence, said she had been deceived, but that she'd based her life on the morals she believed existed and were handed down to her. In other words, Jimmy, she has very good PR. Of course, some people would have sniggered, but anyone who's going to do that, will do it anyway. She could even have found a way to put a positive spin on it. Are you sure there wasn't more to it?'

Jimmy turned to Will, and they stared at each other. Maggie thought there was a bolt of electricity running between their eyes. Suddenly Will raised his hands and banged on the tray in front of him.

'Are you sure?' Jimmy asked in a low voice. 'Once this cat gets out of the bag, there's no shoving the damn thing back in.'

Will grunted and indicated his head in a way that Maggie knew meant "yes".

Jimmy put his head down and closed his eyes. His lips moved without words. Maggie thought he might be praying. He looked up.

'What I am about to tell you takes us into uncharted territory and could harm me and Will, well, probably not Will, the harm's already done there. There is something else. There are more people involved. Maggie, when you told me about the letter being a confession, I knew I couldn't read it. I'm now about to ask you to act like a priest. What I am about to tell you goes no further. Can you promise me that?'

Maggie also looked down and closed her eyes, then up again.

'I cannot give you a one hundred percent 'yes' or 'no' on that, Jimmy. It depends very much on what you're about to say. If it affects us, meaning Bob and me, or Maze Investigations, or my client, then it's a "no". I'm sorry.'

'In that case, I can tell you only part of the story.'

'Fair enough.'

'I am speaking partly on behalf of Will when I tell you this. It's about not only Marilyn's business, but her ambitions. She's married to – no, I have to go further back. Have you seen a family history chart of the Kelly family?'

'Not yet,' Maggie replied.

'That's where I need to start. Norrie, or Ellen as we know her, married Billy Kelly. He was a policeman and the son of William and Maria Kelly. They were of Irish descent, but American born. Billy and Ellen had three children, three boys – James, William and Michael.'

Maggie said, 'She named her first son after her father, James Madigan and her third son after Michael O'Donnell, Ellen's brother, the toddler she stole away from the Workhouse in Kilrush.'

'If she did, then that was an act of remembrance, and perhaps of penance,' Jimmy said.

'Sorry I interrupted, Jimmy. Please carry on.'

'She moved the family to Broadway; her shop became very successful and after a couple of years she had a further five girls working for her. Her work began to appeal more and more to the upper classes of New York society. By all accounts she was a gifted seamstress. Then, the worst happened. The American War of Independence began, in 1861, when the South seceded from the Union. President Lincoln called for men to join the army. Billy naturally thought it was his duty to fight for his country. He signed up and was killed at the battle of Gettysburg on 3rd July 1863.'

'Did she care?' Maggie asked.

'That's a brutal question,' Jimmy replied. 'But you're right, I don't think she cared too much. She had three children already and hadn't seen him for almost two years. After he died she changed the name of the shop to Kelly's Emporium and began to add to her lines of sales. Women's accessories, that kind of thing.

'Then, she had a massive stroke of luck, if it was luck. It was now the 1870s. She was asked to make a walking out dress for Catherine Vanderbilt, the youngest daughter of Cornelius Vanderbilt. You know the name?'

'Of course,' Bob replied. 'That must have been quite something for her.'

'Yes, Bob. She put everything she had into that dress, made to the exacting requirements of Miss Vanderbilt, who, it's said, was highly delighted. She must have been, because she came back for another dress. She recommended Mrs Kelly's establishment to her friends. It was enough to start the social climb Ellen desired so much. She was able to move the shop again after another year, this time further up Broadway, to the more desirable end, closer to Macy's. Then she took a huge risk – she borrowed money and put it all into a new building, a new Kelly's Emporium. It was based on The Marble Palace, which was one of the most fashionable stores of the day. She had plate glass windows installed, where she could make a full display of her dresses. By the 1880s James had joined her and he proved to be an insightful businessman. Apparently, Ellen wanted to challenge Macy's, but James insisted she stick to what she was good at – clothes for middle and upper middle-class ladies. He also insisted she keep the store a medium size, not allow it to become a department store. The area was known as "Ladies Mile". Ellen took his advice and it worked. She was known to be exclusive. Catherine Vanderbilt remained a loyal customer. Ellen produced her finest work to fill her window. Some ladies were seen by appointment only. Ellen grew very rich and began to serve the needs of women of the highest echelons of Manhattan society.

'She handed over control of the store to James when she was in her sixties. He already had his son working for him as his natural heir – another boy who'd inherited his father's talent for business. This son, William, wanted to expand into another store in New York, but his father, although he liked the idea of expansion, had a vision for Kelly's Emporium. He decided they should open two more exclusive ladies' stores, in Boston and Philadelphia.

'Ellen died in 1905, at the age of seventy-six. She had never re-married. She left the business to James and legacies to her other sons, William and Michael. William became a doctor, Michael a lawyer. The stores thrived throughout the next three generations, surviving the crash of 1929. Sadly, a family tragedy occurred, in 1944. William Kelly, who had taken over from his father James, joined the army and was sent over to Europe. He died on the beaches of Normandy. He had only married in 1938. His children were aged just six and four. The person who took over until they grew was William's brother, Stanley. Stanley was no businessman. He was a fool who liked money, women and gambling. He almost ruined the business, by trying to turn the New York shop into a downgraded department store, which was a disaster and almost bankrupted the family.

'By the 1960s William's children managed to get back control. They were Louisa and James. James was particularly ruthless. He made sure Stanley was removed not just from the business but from the family. He did not tolerate failure, in any sense. He was the most ruthless, unforgiving, cold man I have ever met. He was my father. And Marilyn's father. The family had remained Catholic. I had been somewhat wild in my youth, first the Merchant Marines then the boxing. But I knew what I really wanted was to be a priest. My father wanted me to take over the business. I refused so he cast me out, like an unwanted dog.' He stopped and held up a hand. 'Please, don't feel sorry for me. I was glad to be out. I had found who I was and who I wanted to be, and I couldn't be happier. Father turned to Marilyn, who's younger than I. She sucked it all up. She's almost a clone of our father, in both looks and temperament. And Marilyn not only finally brought the business back to where it had been before Stanley got his hands on it, she achieved what no other Kelly had done before her – she married into American society and old money. Her husband is Anderson Bradford. Have you heard of him?'

Maggie and Bob both shook their heads.

'Probably just as well. She married Anderson for his name, not for his money, because he doesn't have any. He married her for her money. They live here in New York, on Fifth Avenue, with a house in Martha's Vineyard, and another in Tuscany. They have two children, Will here, and Corey. Here's the part you'll be interested in.'

He paused and took a long gulp of water.

'Covid restrictions took their toll on Marilyn's business. She'd diversified, but all of her businesses took a hit, as they were commercial, and customer focussed. As of a year ago, financially things weren't looking good. People – women – weren't buying like they used to. The ultra-rich, of course, they hadn't been affected, but Marilyn hadn't quite gotten back to that level. She had to look for another source of income. I've told you Marilyn is ruthless. She's also looking to increase her power base and has turned her eye to politics. She has some good supporters, especially in the Irish community, and she has Anderson and his old money contacts. However, an election war chest is a big space to fill. About six or eight months ago, she put out feelers to – what shall I call it – a community of less moral people. She had feedback from one source, who enquired if she would be willing to get into importing – "goods"'.

Maggie began to shuffle in her chair.

'Is something wrong?' Jimmy asked her.

She shook her head. 'No, carry on. I presume when you say "goods" you're referring to people?'

'Yes, I'm ashamed to say. I help to look after a lot of undocumented people and other immigrants here. Some of them have paid a lot of money to gangs to get into America.'

'Is Marilyn part of such a gang?' Bob sat forward and asked, 'because if she were, I would have to do something with this information. I'm a policeman. I can't be a priest.'

'No, Bob. She's not part of a gang. Marilyn would never sully herself. She has a "business" partner,' Jimmy said, accompanying the "business" with air quotes. 'Just one person, as far as I know.'

He looked at Will again, who gave his nod.

'Will had already challenged Marilyn with her lies about the family history, but she laughed because she knew he didn't have sufficient proof, which we now have. But, he knew she was up to something unconnected with the family retail business, so he followed her to a meeting with the business partner, in Boston. Unfortunately, the partner had a security guard that Will didn't see. Will had managed to overhear some of their discussion but was caught. Marilyn was furious, but the partner just smiled and said, "leave this to me, Will and I will have a nice chat. I'll make sure he won't speak about what he heard".'

A tear fell from Will's eye as Jimmy spoke.

'The business partner did this to you Will?' Bob asked.

A grunt.

'He was supposed to die, I think,' Jimmy said in a shaky voice.

Maggie sat up straight and took a deep breath. 'Will, would you be prepared to describe this person to us?'

'Don't ask if you can go to the police with the information!' Jimmy interjected. 'We don't know who we can trust. It could do more harm than good, to all of us.'

He was interrupted by Will banging his hand on his tray table.

Jimmy turned to him. 'You want to tell them?'

Will nodded.

'Let me,' Bob said. 'Will, I'm going to ask you only 'yes' and 'no' questions, OK? I want you to tap once for yes and twice for no. Can you do that?'

With a slight upturn of his top lip, Will banged once on the table.

'Right, let's start. Is this person a woman or a man?

Will pursed his lips.

'Sorry. Is it a woman?'

Two taps.

'A man, then. Did you see enough of this man to identify him again?'

One tap

Was he black or white? Sorry, was he a Black man?'

Two taps.

'A white man. Young?'

Two taps.

'Middle aged?'

One tap

'American?'

Two taps.

Bob frowned. 'Did you recognise his accent?'

Instead of a tap, Will waved his arm at Bob and managed to hold out one shaky finger, pointing directly at Bob.

'You mean, a British accent?'

One tap.

'Did you hear your mother call him by name?'

One tap.

'OK. I'm going to go through the alphabet, and you stop me when you hear the first letter of his first name.'

Will hesitated.

'Is something wrong Will?'

Three taps.

'That means there's more to it,' Jimmy said.

Bob began to go slowly through the alphabet. Will stopped him on the letter "H".

Bob began the alphabet again, Will stopping him next on an "E", then on an "N".

Maggie felt a tingle in her fingers.

'Bob, please, I have to ask Will something.'

Bob moved out of the way.

Maggie knelt in front of Will. 'Will,' her mouth was dry. 'Was his first name Henry?'

One tap.

'Is he around Bob's height, dresses in a three-piece suit? Dark hair and blue eyes?'

One determined tap.

Maggie's heart rate had speeded up. She could feel the pounding in her chest and the shaking in her hands. She sat back.

'What's wrong?' Bob asked.

She gave him a piercing look. 'Think, Bob. Who does that description fit?'

For a second Bob looked puzzled, then shook his head rapidly from side to side. 'Co-incidence,' he said. 'Lots of British men look like that.'

Maggie turned back to Will.

'Do you know this man's full name, Will?'

The boy hesitated. He stared at her. His breathing had quickened.

Jimmy jumped up. 'Enough,' he said. 'He's traumatised. Leave it.'

'Will, is this man called Sir Henry Camberwell?'

A small hesitation then – one tap.

'Oh my God,' she whispered, and stumbled as she tried to get up. Bob leapt forward and took her elbow. 'How can this be possible?'

'What is this?' Jimmy demanded, kneeling to hold Will's shaking hand. 'Do you know this man already?'

'Yes,' Maggie replied. 'Jimmy, you know it's said that if there were to be a nuclear explosion, little would survive, apart from the cockroaches?'

'I've heard that said, yes.'

'Henry Camberwell is a human cockroach. He has a supposed business of importing antiques and ancient objects. What he actually imports is girls, young girls, some as young as ten, for brothels and for the vilest uses you can think of. He runs an underground operation on the dark web, where these children can be bought and sold. That's who your sister is now in league with.'

Jimmy said nothing, just knelt, looking stunned.

'Will,' Bob said, 'is this the man?' He had pulled up a picture of Henry Camberwell, a rare picture as Camberwell kept away from cameras, but Bob had found this photo from a previous case and put the phone in front of Will.

Will grunted and looked at Jimmy.

'This is bad, very bad,' Maggie said. 'We bested him on a case last year. He hates us.' She paused for a moment. 'We need re-enforcements.'

'And I need to contact Will Sharpe, a policeman, of sorts. We worked with him on the case Maggie just spoke about. He runs a task force dealing with human trafficking, and he's been after Camberwell for years,' Bob said. 'But I'll call him later. Make your call first.'

Jimmy brought a chair across to sit beside Will, who was still shaking, as Maggie went into the sunroom. When she returned after five minutes, she nodded at Bob.

'She'll get on a flight as soon as possible,' she said to Bob. Then to Jimmy, 'I just called the one person Camberwell will take great care around, my colleague, Zelah Trevear. She's the wife, or widow rather, of the artist Martin Fitzgerald. She has excellent contacts here.'

'If she can help, that's good, but why is he bothered about her?'

'Sit down,' Maggie said. 'We talked about trust. Put your priest's hat on. I'm going to "confess" what my friend Zelah can do. Will, that goes for you, too. Bob already knows.'

Fifteen minutes later, Maggie and Bob left Jimmy and Will, all still shaken and Jimmy especially flummoxed and sceptical, despite Maggie's insistence that it was really true, and that Zelah never used her "gifts" to do harm.

'This is about to get even more interesting,' he said as he closed the door on them.

They'd been walking in silence for about ten minutes, when Maggie realised she'd left her sun hat behind.

'I'll just run back and get it; wait here, Bob.'

As she reached the house, the front door was open. She pushed it and looked inside. There was no sign of Jimmy, but she could hear the sound of Will's lift on its way upstairs. She was about to shout out, when she heard Jimmy's voice coming from the summer room. The door was slightly ajar. He was on the phone. Maggie stopped for a moment and was about to call out his name to catch his attention, when she heard one sentence.

'They know about Camberwell.'

For a second, she froze, then took a few steps back, to the entrance to the living room, and knocked loudly on the door, calling out, 'Jimmy, are you here?'

The priest rushed out from the summer room, pushing his phone into his pocket. 'Maggie, is something wrong?'

'Not at all. I've left my hat here, is all. I'm not sure where I put it.'

He looked around, his face red, his eyes flicking in her direction as he looked for the hat. Maggie put on a cheerful smile.

'Here it is. Fell down beside your chair.' He handed it to her.

'Thank goodness,' she said. 'Are you OK, Jimmy? You look a bit disconcerted.'

He smiled back. 'What you've just told me would disconcert anyone.'

'Will you be OK?'

'Of course. Thank you for asking me.'

'Right, I've left Bob at the street corner.'

She turned and walked as slowly as possible, turning to wave as he closed the front door. Then, she ran.

What's the matter?' Bob asked as she practically ran into him.

'We've just made a terrible mistake,' she said.

Chapter 34
New York 1905

Norrie knew she was dying. She had powered through, ignoring the pains and the debilitating lack of energy, against the advice of James, William and Michael and their wives and her grandchildren. She was Ellen Kelly. She didn't give in to pain or discomfort. She was determined to die on her feet, so kept going until she collapsed in her office in the store.

A doctor was called, and she was carried to her house and put to bed, protesting, but knowing she wouldn't get out of the bed again.

She had lived to see in a new century. She had five stores in five cities. Kelly's Emporium was a well-known and respected brand. She had many acquaintances – no real friends, she had left those behind in Liverpool – but her reputation was good. No hint of her past had ever escaped.

There were just days left. She found herself floating in and out of – what? Not sleep or consciousness, but a kind of dream state, where she was back in Kilrush, with her parents and her brothers and sisters, and with Ellen and Peg. Whenever she thought of them, she felt anger churning, starting in her gut, and spreading out to take over her body, making her shake and cry out. What had those girls done to deserve such terrible endings? She closed her eyes as the blackness consumed her. Whatever she had done, it was no worse than the British government, who had allowed the Irish to starve to death. She had heard of one senior minister, who had said the hunger was an Act of God and must not be interfered with. She hoped to meet him in hell.

Hell. That was where she was going, but for the sake of her family she allowed a priest to be called. He arrived, ready to graciously give her the sacrament. She asked to be left alone with him. She intended to make a confession, knowing she would receive no absolution, no forgiveness; because she wasn't sorry for what she'd done, all those years ago.

'My child,' he began.

She stopped him there. 'Father, I want to make a confession. There are things I haven't talked about for years, some things I've never talked about. Your job is to listen, then decide what you want to do.'

'Of course, Ellen,' he replied soothingly. 'Your confession will never be repeated by me.'

'Right then, let's start.'

He sat beside her, smiling. The smile soon disappeared.

'Forgive me Father, for I have sinned. To begin with, my name isn't Ellen Kelly, nor was it Ellen Dillon. My name was – is – Honora Madigan, Norrie to my friends and family. I changed it because I killed a man.'

She saw him shudder and felt happy. She'd tell this man of God exactly who she was, what she had done, and what she thought of his God.

'Tell me Father, have you ever seen the body of a dead woman with a dead baby at her breast, her nipple bitten off by a child that desperate for food, when the mother had nothing to give, so they both died, in a field, at the side of the road, probably left to rot there, whilst landlords and their masters took the best produce, sold it at profit and ate well themselves, ignoring the countless number of bodies lying dead in homes and fields and Workhouses. Have you?'

The priest shook his head.

'Well that's just the start. I'm going to tell you everything about what happened to me and my family, and what I did about it. And about what I've done in this country to make sure that my children would never have the slightest idea about what hunger means, what it does to people.'

For the next twenty minutes she took him through a vivid picture of scenes of unimaginable horror, a graphic description of the deaths of every member of her family, including the clubbing to death of her grandfather whilst soldiers looked idly on. How she'd made money for what remained of her family and friends by selling her body to soldiers, but too late to save her father.

'Do you know what a rotten potato looks like, father?'

The priest shook his head, no longer able to speak.

'Let me give you a picture. You pick it up and it's covered in what looks like scabs, it's soft in your hands. You pull the potato apart and the inside is purple and black and rotten. It squelches in your hand, and it stinks. I won't ask you to imagine that smell. Just know it's worse than any human or animal decay you've ever come across. Try to think about thousands of acres across a whole country, all in the same state. Now imagine that's your food, your only food, that was supposed to get you through the winter. Then the landlord comes for his rent, and you don't have any money, because you've sold everything you have to buy what little food there is available. Imagine now you have no furniture, no clothing apart from the rags you stand up in, and it's freezing cold. There's nothing to make a fire with, because everyone else is starving and freezing and the wood's all gone, the trees stripped bare.' She paused, having run out of breath in her passion.

'Now imagine three years of that. People dying in their thousands, hundreds of thousands, homeless, diseased, hopeless. Whole families. Now tell me that was God's will.'

The priest remained silent.

'Here's what I did.' She took him through her murder of Seamus McMahon, her escape from Dublin to America. How she killed three men, in order to save herself, as she saw it.

The priest looked as if he had finally found the bottom end of the pit of despair.

'Do you regret any of this, Ellen? Do you want absolution? To receive it you must ask pardon of God.' He knew what the answer was going to be, and it came immediately.

'Not a single regret, Father, and when I am to be judged by your God, I shall tell him of his cruelty towards the Irish people. You can go now. Leave me to die in peace.'

The priest left, passing by the group of puzzled children and grandchildren waiting outside the bedroom, not speaking to or even acknowledging them.

They entered the bedroom together.

'Is everything OK Ma?' James asked.

'Couldn't be better,' Norrie said. 'I shall soon be dancing outside those heavenly gates.'

'We'll miss you, grandma,' cried the youngest grandchild, Jane, James' daughter and so far the only girl any of her boys had produced.

'I'll be just fine. Leave me please, all of you. I'd like to sleep.'

For the next two days she moved in and out of sleep before falling into a coma. She died the following day.

Her grandson had been the last person to be with her before she closed her eyes for the last time. He was holding her hand, when she suddenly opened them, looked fiercely into the distance and said, 'Madigan, Clamhunger Row.' Then she died.

In the following days, James, when he heard her last words, assumed this person must have been a friend and searched for the name but found nothing. No-one called Madigan appeared at the funeral, although the family did try to trace him or her out of respect for Ellen. James had never come across anyone called Madigan and soon forgot the name. Nor could they find Clamhunger Row anywhere in the USA.

He told his son, another William, about Grandma Ellen's final words. William wasn't particularly interested in finding out who Madigan might have been, but he told his son James, who passed the story on to Jimmy and Marilyn, from whom it reached the ears of William Kelly V, Jimmy's nephew Will, who, at the age of seventeen, was intrigued, and decided to investigate, and was the first person to think of looking outside America, or so he thought.

Chapter 35

Bob and Maggie went into the first small diner they could find, and sat at a table at the back, well away from other occupied tables, so they wouldn't be overheard and, in the unlikely but possible chance that if Jimmy Kelly went out walking, he wouldn't be able to see them from the door.

They ordered coffees. 'Did he give any indication of who he was talking to?' Bob asked.

Maggie slowly shook her head. 'I only heard the one sentence before I backed off and knocked to let him know I was there. He was flushed when he came to the door. I think I pulled it off.'

The coffees arrived.

'Bob, what do we do now?' Before he could answer her phone buzzed and she pulled it out of her pocket.

'It's Zelah,' she said. 'She's at Heathrow tonight for a seven o'clock flight tomorrow morning, UK time. She'll be with us here at the hotel around ten tomorrow morning, allowing for traffic from the airport. You don't look pleased. Should I not have asked her to come?'

'It's not that,' Bob said. 'He knows you must have overheard something.'

'What? How could he possibly know?'

'You didn't notice the cameras? I didn't think to mention them, but there's one at each entrance to and from the church, and to the house, plus one in the hallway. If he suspects you might have heard anything, he'll just have to make a quick check and he'll see you entering the living room, then going back out again. Maggie, I really do need to call Will Sharpe now.'

'Yes, you must. What are we going to do next?'

'Back to the hotel,' Bob said. 'I'll phone Will Sharpe in London. Have you been in touch with your client lately?'

'No, I was planning to send him a quick email this evening.'

'You can check if he's related to anyone called Kelly in the US.' He put his hand out and took hers. 'I'm afraid this is going to spoil our holiday.'

'It was meant to be a sightseeing and a research trip,' she said, with an ironic smile. 'This is more than I expected, but that's what happens to us, isn't it. Come on, let's get back.'

'We haven't reached Broadway yet. Why don't we walk up Fifth Avenue? We can see some interesting sights on the way. It'll take at least an hour.'

'And give us time to think,' Maggie replied, 'although at the moment I have no plan.'

'The plan will arrive with Zelah, I have no doubt about that,' Bob said as they left the café.

They walked up Fifth Avenue and took a detour off to Forty Second Street, for Bob to see the hallway of the Grand Central Station, which had been on his bucket list for many years.

'If things were different,' he said, 'I'd like to spend some time here, it's just amazing, but we have to get back.'

Maggie felt sad and guilty. He had paid for part of this trip, in the expectation of some sightseeing as well as some research. She was spoiling it. Now her work had pushed aside everything else, as usual. They returned to Fifth Avenue and began to walk back towards the hotel, when she suddenly stopped. 'No. We are not going to let this ruin everything. Come on.'

A bewildered Bob followed her as she turned a corner and marched off, turning a few more corners until she stopped and said, 'Over there.' They were almost at the entrance to the Top of the Rock, the observation deck on top of the Rockefeller Centre, famous for its views of New York. An elevator would take them up to the 71st floor.

'This may turn out to be the last day of sightseeing we have. We're going up.'

Maggie wasn't keen on lifts or elevators as they were known here, and the forty seconds of high-speed ascent in the elevator with its glass roof and flashing lights that highlighted the stretch of tunnel so high above them with flashing red and purple lights, was a bareknuckle ride for her. It was with much relief, when they arrived at the top, that she was able to walk with some dignity out of the lift – although she felt like running – and climb the last short set of stairs. Bob, on the other hand, loved every minute.

There was a slight breeze blowing at the top and the view was spectacular.

'We might not have time to get up the Empire State Building, but at least we have a wonderful view of it, and the rest of New York, and whatever those parts are,' she said, pointing in different directions.

They spent twenty minutes looking around taking photos of the views and strolling around the top deck, before buying a few gifts in the shop, then descended back down through the tunnel of lights, throughout which Maggie clung onto Bob's shirt sleeve.

Back on the ground, they made their way through the crowds back to Fifth Avenue, walking quickly past the infamous and rather ugly and ostentatious, Maggie thought, Trump Tower.

Back at the hotel they went straight to their room, showered, changed, and sat out on the balcony.

'I have to phone Will Sharpe now,' Bob said. 'Holiday over, I think.'

'Sorry, Bob.'

'Don't apologise, darlin'. You expected to research a story. Neither of us could have anticipated this outcome. I'll go inside to get him on the phone.'

He returned five minutes later.

'That was quick,' Maggie said.

'He didn't say much, until I mentioned Zelah being on her way. Then he groaned.'

'I presume he said we are not to get involved.'

'As you would expect. He's going to phone a contact in New York. That was it, really. He said to enjoy our holiday.'

'Huh. As if. He knows we won't take any notice of him saying not to get involved.'

'I expect so. Let's wait for Zelah to arrive tomorrow morning. It's already six. We can eat in the restaurant here, if you like.'

'OK,' Maggie replied. 'Make the reservation for eight o'clock.

Bob made the reservation, then picked up a book he had bought at the Tenement Museum. Maggie opened her Kindle and tried to read, but she couldn't concentrate. She had managed to distract herself on the walk back, but now the full force of Jimmy Kelly's betrayal hit her like a kick to the gut. She had had enough of Henry Camberwell. She thought she had probably seen the last of him the previous year when they had cheated him out of his expectation of making a fortune from a rare stolen ancient Chinese vase. The man really was a cockroach. There was just no getting rid of him.

**

They were prepared and ready when Zelah knocked on their door a few minutes before ten the following morning.'

'Hello, both. Are you ready to breakfast and plan?'

'Naturally. How was your flight?'

'It didn't crash and half an hour early. What more is there to say?'

'Let's go and eat,' Bob said, keeping the smirk off his face.

Down in the breakfast room they were shown to a table with four seats.

'You can take away the fourth chair,' Bob said to the waiter attending them.

'No, leave it there, please,' said a voice from behind the waiter. 'Not for the whole meal, though. I won't be staying.'

The waiter turned around, to reveal a man in an immaculate three-piece suit and perfect grooming.

'Will Sharpe,' Bob said, holding out a hand. 'That was quick, seeing as I only phoned you late last night.'

'What did you travel by, supersonic jet?' Zelah growled.

'I've been here a week,' he replied, taking no notice of Zelah and sitting down on the fourth chair. 'And you are interfering with a plan that's been long in the making to halt both Marilyn Kelly and Sir Henry Camberwell. You've dumped yourselves right into the middle of it, causing chaos, as usual.'

'How were we supposed to know—' Maggie began but he raised his hand.

'You weren't, I acknowledge that. But now, you do know. And I would thank you to retire quietly and get out of my way.'

'Stuff that,' Zelah replied. 'We are here, I have come over specially and we three are going to an event at the National Arts Museum and Gallery tonight, to which a special friend has invited me. Maggie and Bob are coming with me, as my friend is looking forward to meeting them, well at least to meeting Maggie anyway. Sorry Bob, you'll just be a hanger-on, but a welcome one.'

'I'll look at the exhibits and eat the food,' Bob replied with a grin. 'There will be food?'

'Lots of it,' Zelah said. 'Prepared and served by New York's finest fine dining company.' She turned to look with a dagger gaze at Will Sharpe. 'And even you won't be able to stop us.'

'You think?' he replied, sitting back and folding his arms.

'I know,' Zelah replied. She took out a pen, wrote a name down on her napkin and pushed it over to him.

His eyebrows shot up and he gave her a penetrating gaze. 'Is this a joke?'

'Nope.'

'If you so much as put a foot out of line, that prevents us from catching Camberwell in the act, you will deeply regret it. I've spent years getting someone inside his organisation and now I have, if you screw it up, I'll destroy you.'

'That sounds nasty,' Maggie said to Zelah.

'Threatening,' Zelah replied. 'I don't know why he thinks we would screw it up. All we're doing is attending a social event.'

Will Sharpe looked at Maggie. 'You are attending one of New York's premier social events of the year. You will be completely out of place.'

'No, they won't,' Zelah snapped back. 'I'll make sure of that. Now please go away. We want to enjoy our breakfast.'

Will Sharpe jumped up. He went to say something, bit his lip, and turned and marched away in his shiny shoes.

'Zelah, now he's gone, what have we gotten ourselves into?'

The waiter came up to check they were ready to place an order. Zelah sent him away with an order for champagne and told him to come back in ten minutes.

'Tonight, Marilyn Kelly, whose soiree this is, is planning to announce her intention of a run at a political position. The great and the good of New York will be there, plus all of the wealthy and influential in the Irish community, including the Chief of Police and the Archbishop. My friend is the guest of honour. She's invited me because I've just sold her one of Martin's paintings and Marilyn believes that makes me a target for her war chest.'

'Hang on,' Bob said. 'Are you saying you just sold a painting to Marilyn Kelly?'

'No, to my friend. Her name is Julianne Millar.'

Bob spat out his champagne. 'Are you talking about—?'

'Keep your voice down,' Zelah hissed. 'Yes, that Julianne Millar. The wife of the Vice President.'

'We're going to meet the wife of the Vice President of the United States?' Maggie could barely get the words out. 'I don't have a dress.'

'You will have by this time tonight, and an evening suit for Bob. Don't look so worried. The plan is all in hand.'

Chapter 36

Before dinner the previous evening, Maggie had made the call to Mike and Jay, who were still in Devon for another two days before making their way down to Cornwall for a few more days.

'Might as well take advantage of this beautiful weather and scenery,' Mike said. We've found the village where Jay's family lived and we've traced one descendent, a lady who now lives in Bude, just over the border into Cornwall. We're going to stay there for a day or so, then go to look at some grand stately homes.'

'I'm so pleased you're having a good time,' Maggie said. 'Is there any more news from your Australian contact, or any of the American ones?'

'We've sent out a lot of messages,' he replied. 'A few have answered. We've told them we're in England and that we're waiting until we get back home, when we'll have so much more time to get to know them.'

'Have you had any responses from any O'Donnells?' Maggie asked, hesitated, then went on, 'and was there a Kelly?'

'Yes to both,' he replied. 'I can't think where the Kelly connection comes from,' he said. Must be through a marriage. It' a very small amount of DNA, about 12 centimorgans, so it goes a long way back.'

'I may have an answer for you on that, but I'll let you get on with Devon and Cornwall first.'

'Jay wants to take us down to a place called Helford,' he said. 'She's read about it.'

'It won't disappoint,' Maggie replied. 'It's a beautiful, tiny village on the estuary of the Helford River. Have fun.'

'We will. Speak to you when we're both back.'

‘He has a Kelly in his Ancestry list,’ Maggie said to Bob.

‘Did you tell him who that is?’

‘No, they’re having a really good time in the West Country, so I said we’d wait until we both returned home. I’ll give him the shock when he’s back in his own place. I’m surprised there are any at all, but I can work it out when we’re home.’

‘Which is in two days,’ he replied. ‘After whatever comes tomorrow.’

**

In the wildest of her wild dreams, or imagination, Maggie was in no way prepared for what began when she was whisked away after breakfast in a private car and taken to a store on Fifth Avenue, where a personal shopper, Skyvella, met her.

The woman took an appraising look at her, then walked around her, clapped her hands and started to walk off. ‘Come, Maggie. We’ll start with a dress and shoes, then a massage, then hair, then makeup.’

‘Stop right there,’ Maggie said. ‘I can’t afford this.’

‘All taken care of, courtesy of Mrs Fitzgerald,’ the woman chirped. She saw Maggie’s grimace. ‘Look, it’ll be fun. Come on, let’s get going.’

Maggie would never before have dared entering this kind of shop, the kind where there are no price tags, the “if you need to ask the price, you can’t afford it” kind of shop.

After two hours of trying on dresses, dress and jacket combos, and gowns, all of which Maggie rejected, the enthusiastic Skyvella was decidedly less enthusiastic. Finally, the woman assigned to assist them, with the more sober name of Eloise, suggested she had a few more garments that Skyvella had initially told her not to bother with, but now Maggie insisted on seeing. Eloise brought one out and Maggie loved it on first sight. It was a dress and jacket combo, the dress in white silk chiffon with a ruffle overlay, heavily patterned in gentle gold thread, based on what Maggie thought was a series of delicate medieval designs. It fell to just below her knees at the front, and to calf level in swishing folds at the back. Accompanying it was a soft white blazer with the same patterns embroidered around the neck to below the bust line, where it followed a thin line to the back.

She tried it on. It fitted perfectly. She swirled in front of the surround mirrors a couple of times. 'This one,' she said firmly to the pouting Skyvella. 'Just tell me if it will work for the occasion.'

'I think it's a little too strong,' Skyvella said. 'You'll stand out, I'll say that.'

Maggie turned to the assistant. 'Eloise, what's your opinion.' She told her where she was going.

'I think it will be perfect,' Eloise replied, but I would make a few alterations, if I may suggest?'

'Of course you may.'

'Then I suggest we remove the ruffle from the top of the dress, to make it simpler, and we take up the back. It should remain long and flowing, but I think, a couple of inches shorter at the back.'

'Can you do it in time?'

'No problem, ma'am. We can have it sent to your hotel,' Eloise smiled. 'I have a great idea for matching shoes.'

'Whatever, as long as they don't have six-inch spiky heels.'

'No ma'am, nothing like that.'

Skyvella looked like she was about to cry.

**

Following the massage, Skyvella informed Maggie that a hairdresser and make-up artiste were booked for four o'clock at the hotel. Maggie told her to cancel them both.

Skyvella gave a stiff nod, then left her, without saying goodbye.

Back at the hotel, an evening dress suit had arrived for Bob.

'I hate these,' he said. 'Black tie do's.'

'You'll look beautiful,' Maggie replied with a grin. 'Women will be all over you, with that suit and your Welsh accent. Welsh is very popular in Manhattan, so the assistant in the dress shop told me. Very sexy.'

'Only if you're a thirty something with exceptional good looks, and a film star body,' he grumped.

'I think a mid-fifties, shaved head, handsome man with a good figure, only slightly running to fat, will go down very well.'

He harumphed, and blushed.

'I'm going to sort out my hair and make-up, if I can remember how.'

'Good luck.'

She poked out a tongue at him and went into the bathroom. Half an hour later a package arrived. Maggie poked her head around the bathroom door. 'Ah, that would be my outfit.'

It was a huge box, which, to her relief, consisted of a great deal of tissue paper. Bob handed it in to her.

Fifteen minutes later, he was about to shout to her that they were going to be late for the car that was due to pick them up at five, when she emerged from the bathroom.

'What do you think?' she asked anxiously.

Bob didn't speak.

'Is it too much? Oh God, I can't go if it's too much. I've overdone it, haven't I—'

He put a finger to his lips. 'If I didn't know it was you, I wouldn't have recognised you. You look absolutely beautiful,' he said as he gazed at her. 'And no, it isn't overdone. It's perfect. Come on, let's go.'

They made their way down to the foyer just as the limousine arrived. Hotel guests watched them walk across to the door with admiring glances, whispering to each other. Maggie held Bob's hand in such a firm grip that he muttered she was cutting off the circulation to his fingers.

They reached the venue in half an hour, right on time, most of it having been spent in stationary traffic. The entrance had been cleared fifty yards back on each side, but their car was allowed to drop them at the door. They were to wait there for Zelah and her 'friend', who would be arriving in five minutes. Maggie stood, nervously shuffling on the pavement, as a crowd behind a rope line looked at them, pointing, commenting, and whispering, watched by men with blank faces, in matching dark suits.

'If this is what it's like to be famous, I definitely prefer anonymity,' she whispered to Bob who didn't have time to reply as a cavalcade of cars turned the corner at the top of the street and pulled up in front of them. Words were exchanged between the blank-faced men and others unseen. The driver of the car at the centre of the cavalcade opened the back door of a limo. Out stepped a woman, tall and elegant, in a black pant suit embroidered in gold. She wore short heels. Behind her, Zelah emerged from the car. She was dressed in an outfit that Maggie recognised, a dress and jacket combo, long and tightly fitted, well suited to Zelah's hourglass figure, and wearing the ubiquitous six-inch heels studded with diamonds. She wore her usual diamond jewellery in her swept-up hair. She walked over to Maggie and Bob and brought them forward to introduce them to Julianne Millar.

'I've been looking forward to meeting you,' Julianne Millar said. 'I've heard so much about both of you from Zelah.' She leaned in and whispered, 'We all have an important job to do tonight,' giving Maggie a slight, knowing nod.

The Vice President's wife then walked off to pass along the receiving line, where she was met with smiles and compliments. She replied with a sweet smile to all of them.

'Well, don't we just look like the kids who won the prize in the "who can smarten up best" competition,' Zelah said as they began to walk forward. 'Love the outfit. I couldn't tell from Skyvella's feedback if it had worked out OK or not.'

'Let's say she got me to the right shop. After that, she was surplus to requirements.'

Zelah raised an eyebrow. 'It worked out well enough. If I didn't know it was you, I wouldn't have recognised you. I like the hair and makeup. It's understated but effective. Who did it?'

'I did it myself, Zelah.' Zelah laughed.

They had reached the receiving line. 'Brace yourselves,' Zelah said. 'The fun is about to begin.'

'Something's about to begin,' Bob muttered, 'but it's not fun.'

Chapter 37

Within a few seconds Maggie reached Marilyn Kelly; the woman she had heard so much about. She hadn't been sure what to expect, someone tall, well-built perhaps, with an air of belligerency. Marilyn Kelly was none of those things. She was around five feet three inches tall, with jet black hair that had been dressed off her face. She wore a black organza dress with a smart blazer, an Alexander McQueen that Maggie had rejected for herself earlier, beautiful though it was, but not the right look for her. Marilyn's jewellery consisted of rubies around her neck, and on her ears and fingers, which Maggie thought brought a jarring rather than graceful look to the elegant outfit.

'Maggie Gilbert,' she said in a soft, husky voice, holding out a hand for a barely touched finger shake. 'I've heard a lot about you.'

'And I about you,' Maggie replied. Neither of them smiled.

Maggie hadn't looked ahead before she stopped at the next person. She was horrified to find herself standing in front of Father James Kelly. He held out his hand. She didn't take it. He smiled condescendingly. 'You win some, you lose some,' he said, his tone smug.

She moved along, courtesy of Bob taking her elbow and pushing her forward to be introduced to Marilyn Kelly's husband, Anderson Bradford, who had a vacant look, a vacuous smile, and nothing to say.

The final person in the line was a young man, or rather a boy, of about seventeen or eighteen years, slightly red faced, pulling occasionally at the collar of his dress shirt. This must be Corey Kelly. Maggie shook his hand and walked on. She and Bob joined Zelah, who was standing behind Julianne Millar.

The Vice President's wife turned her head around. 'She's a real nasty piece of work. I hope they get her soon,' then turned back again to give her gracious smile to the next person trying to take her attention.

After five minutes, when there seemed to be no further guest requiring a special greeting, the party, led by Marilyn Kelly and Julianne Millar, moved into the main area of the art museum. It was already full of people chatting in groups and pairs. The volume diminished when Marilyn and her guest of honour entered, then began again as Marilyn and Julianne split into two parties to work the room.

'Camberwell's not here,' Maggie whispered to Bob and Zelah, who had stayed back and together.

'He'll turn up,' Zelah said. 'Just wait a—'

She stopped dead as Sir Henry Camberwell entered the room. He looked carefully around, saw Marilyn with other guests, then halted momentarily as he spotted Zelah, Maggie, and Bob. With barely a noticeable hesitation he made his way over to them.

Accepting a glass of champagne from a passing waiter, he said, 'I didn't know they allowed ragtag and bobtail in.'

'I didn't know they allowed cockroaches in,' Maggie snapped back.

Camberwell sneered. 'Sticks and stones, Mrs Gilbert, sticks and stones. I must find our patron and thank her for the invitation. I'll leave you to your fatuously uninteresting conversation.'

As he walked away Marilyn caught sight of him and went up to greet him, drawing him towards a small group of men.

'Gentlemen,' she said in her most unctuous voice, 'I'd like you to meet my latest business partner, Sir Henry Camberwell, soon to be elevated to the House of Lords in England. Henry deals in antiques and items of rare ancient provenance. He and I are going to look at bringing his business to America.'

The group immediately began to question Henry Camberwell, who gave them his full, smooth, attention.

Maggie gritted her teeth and Zelah's face was bright red. Only Bob appeared calm. He stopped a waiter passing with a tray of canapes. 'These look delicious,' he said, taking two. 'Why don't you try some, you two?' The waiter moved the tray in their direction but they each shook their head.

'I don't know how you can eat this woman's food,' Maggie hissed at him.

'I can eat her food, drink her ridiculously overpriced champagne and do everything I can to see her arrested. The food won't be quite as good where she's going.' He went to say something more, but stopped and cocked his head to one side and nodded.

'What are you… are you wearing an earpiece?' Maggie whispered.

'Shush and smile,' he whispered back, as Julianne Millar approached them again. 'Zelah, can I borrow you for a minute or two? I know you don't like it, but the President of the National Bank is a great fan of Martin's and he'd like to talk to you about Martin's painting on the wall over there.' She indicated a landscape hanging on a wall at the far end of the room.

'Of course, Julie,' Zelah said. 'And for your sake I shall be gracious and kind.' Julianne Millar laughed and led Zelah away. After Zelah had spent ten minutes in front of the canvas, she moved away.

'Let's go take a look,' Maggie said. They wandered across the room to the painting, which took up the whole of the wall.

'He certainly liked to paint big,' Maggie said. 'This is magnificent. It reminds me of what Kilrush would be like on a stormy day. Hang on,' she moved closer. 'Bob, this is Kilrush. I recognise the pier. Zelah never told me he had painted it.' She looked at the description underneath. It said, "West Coast of Ireland, A Storm by Martin Fitzgerald".

'It's breathtaking,' Bob said. 'This close up, you think you could almost be hit by one of those waves. He must have been a very special man.'

'Zelah says he was just rather shy, comfortable at home, didn't like people too much. He wouldn't have liked this fuss.'

A man approached them and introduced himself as the Director of the Gallery. 'It's wonderful, isn't it. Quite scary, I think. It's on loan, from his widow, Mrs Zelah Fitzgerald. I saw you chatting to her earlier. Do you know her well?'

'Yes, Maggie replied. 'She and I work together on genealogy projects.'

'Oh. You're Maggie Gilbert.'

'Yes, I am, and this is my partner, Bob Pugh,' she looked around for Bob, but he had moved away, his head again cocked slightly to one side. 'He's a policeman, in Wales.'

'We have plenty of those here tonight, but not from Wales,' he replied, laughing at his own joke. 'Ah, Mrs Kelly is about to call us to attention. Nice to have met you.' He hurried away to stake his spot as close as possible to Marilyn while Maggie strolled casually over to Bob, depositing her champagne glass on a table containing an art sculpture of half of a giant bee.

'Looks better with the empty glass,' she muttered as she reached Bob. 'What's going on?'

'Not sure, yet, but there's a lot of excitement. Something is going down tonight. Will Sharpe says to keep an eye on Camberwell.'

Maggie glanced over. He was surrounded by a group of men and women who appeared to be hanging on his every word. 'He's not up to much at the moment, just entertaining the crowd with tales of some stolen ancient treasure, I expect. Maybe I should tell the story of the Chinese vase.'

'Don't even think about winding him up,' Bob warned, 'not tonight.'

They could see that Marilyn was arranging her family on the small dais, along with the museum director. She then turned to Julianne Millar, who was shaking her head, politely but firmly. No way was the VP's wife going to give the slightest of hints that she would even for a moment consider endorsing Marilyn Kelly. Zelah was looking on, amused, when Marilyn Kelly approached her. This Maggie had to hear.

'I would greatly appreciate your support, Mrs Fitzgerald. I am a great admirer of your late husband's work and I know that you yourself are of Irish descent. Don't you have an estate in Ireland?'

'I do, Marilyn, but the answer's still no. And besides, Julianne is about to leave. You'd better get a move on with your speech. By the way, Henry Camberwell is a cockroach. If he hasn't told you of our previous encounters, then he should have done so. I won, by the way. Every time.' She gave Marilyn a wolfish grin and began to walk towards Maggie, when she was stopped by the museum director, who had heard her talk to Marilyn and was frowning and speaking in a low voice.

Maggie, worried that Zelah might make a scene if the man harangued her further, had almost caught Zelah's attention, when she was stopped by a hand on her arm, as someone approached her from behind. Assuming it was Bob she turned her head. It was Jimmy Kelly, smirking at her.

'My sister is about to make her announcement. Doesn't matter what your friend does now, it's too late. Nice try, though.'

Behind him, she could see Henry Camberwell approaching, with a smile of condescension on his handsome face. It was too much. Maggie snapped and before she could stop herself, or Bob, who was also on his way over, could stop her, she raised her hand and gave Jimmy Kelly a loud slap across the face, that echoed across the room and momentarily stopped all conversation.

'You hypocrite, you stinking rat,' she hissed at him. 'How could you be part of this, doing what you do, knowing what you know?'

Jimmy rubbed the imprint of fingers on his cheek and smiled at her. 'I do believe you're about to be thrown out.'

Marilyn Kelly was speaking with two security guards and pointing in her direction. They walked over to her and took an elbow each. 'You need to go, ma'am. Please come quietly.'

Marilyn had mounted the dais and made some comment that Maggie didn't hear but that made everyone laugh.

She looked around for Bob but couldn't see him in the crowd. What she did see was Zelah approach Marilyn and crook a finger. Marilyn got down from the podium and Zelah whispered something to her that made her blanche. Next thing, Julianne Millar and her entourage were on their way out, to Marilyn's dismay. She returned to her position in front of the microphone, cleared her throat and announced an unspecified incident, something to do with Mrs Millar's family, a personal matter that meant that Mrs Millar had to leave, and how sorry she was about that. She was leaving with all best wishes for success to Marilyn in her endeavours. Maggie was willing to bet every penny she had that Julianne Millar had said no such thing, but she was being led away.

The audience was back with Marilyn, looking excited, awaiting the big announcement. There was nothing Maggie could do. She had ruined everything, had allowed her temper and disgust with Jimmy Kelly to overcome her common sense and had made a fool of herself. She was ashamed now. She had let go of her professionalism and embarrassed herself and Bob. Where was Bob? Her escort finally let go of her elbows when they reached the pavement outside. Julianne Millar's convoy had departed. She was alone now, except for the scowling guards. She presumed that Zelah had gone, too.

As a tear run down her cheek, she turned at the sound of footsteps approaching from behind. Bob, at last. He put an arm around her shoulders. 'Don't worry about it. I just stayed for a few minutes to hear what Marilyn Kelly said. She hasn't made her announcement about running for public office. She's just announced a major charity appeal for an organisation that helps children trafficked into the country for the purposes of prostitution and worse. The audience looked nonplussed. Not what they were expecting.'

'Back to the hotel for us, I suppose,' she said looking around. 'How are we supposed to get there?'

'Not the hotel,' Bob said. 'Come on. We're walking. It's not far.'

'It's too far in these shoes,' Maggie protested. Bob ignored her and walked off up the street. She had no choice but to follow him. He was tense, she felt that. Perhaps he was going to wait until they reached the hotel before shouting at her. She deserved it. She ran to catch up with him. At the corner he turned left.

'Our hotel's the other way,' she said in a small voice.

'We're not going to the hotel.' He walked towards a van parked a hundred yards along the street. As they reached it, the side door slid back and a sardonic English voice said, 'Get in, quickly.' Will Sharpe. That explained Bob's earpiece.

Without looking at Maggie he said, 'Thanks to your theatrics, we've lost the feed. Bob, could you hear anything?'

'Not much.' Will Sharpe leaned into the main computer screen that showed an animated discussion between two men on the pavement outside the main entrance – Henry Camberwell and Jimmy Kelly. 'That's better,' he said. 'Now we can hear. 'They're talking about only just managing to get the girls out before the container was breached. Kelly says there must be someone on the inside. Camberwell is furious. He'd arranged for the container. Now, they need somewhere to put them, where we can't find them.' Jimmy Kelly smiled, leaned in and whispered to Camberwell.

'Damn,' Will Sharpe said. 'Kelly has just said, "no-one will know; they'll never find it". But he hasn't said where "it" would be.' He banged his hand on the computer frame. 'Damnation!' He glared at Maggie.

'You screwed up,' said a tall, well-built Black man sitting next to Will Sharpe. 'We almost had them. This is the first time there's been direct evidence of Camberwell's involvement, and we've lost them. Thanks to you, Mrs Gilbert.'

Bob went to speak, but Maggie put up a hand to stop him. She had been deep in thought, watching the playback of herself on another screen, seeing Jimmy Kelly approach her. 'He deliberately wound me up,' she said thinking hard. 'Why would he do that? In the middle of his sister's big night, he took the attention away from her and caused the VP's wife to leave.' She was frowning.

'Does it matter?' the man asked.

'Who are you?' she demanded.

'He's my counterpart in the United States,' Will Sharpe replied. 'This is John Wilkes.' The man didn't smile or acknowledge the introduction.

'We'll keep looking,' Will Sharpe said. 'They can't have disappeared into thin air.'

'Where are Jimmy Kelly and Henry Camberwell now?' Maggie asked.

'They left as soon as Marilyn Kelly made her speech.'

'You're following them?'

'No, we thought we'd just have an early night,' John Wilkes replied. 'Of course we're following them. They're heading for the church, but we've already searched it. There's no-one there.'

'What about Will Kelly? He can't go far in his wheelchair.'

'There was no-one there, I told you. You can both go now.'

'We're not going anywhere,' Maggie said. 'I know exactly where they are. And without Bob and me, you'll never find "it"'.

Bob looked at her, puzzled, then the answer hit him too. He turned to Will Sharpe. 'We've probably got an hour, no more. We need a breach plan, fast.'

Chapter 38

'Just a minute,' Maggie said. Her brain was whirring. She stared at the wall of the van, over the heads of Sharpe and Wilkes. It could be a trap. Perhaps Jimmy Kelly had anticipated this possibility, seen several moves ahead, considered potential outcomes like moves on a chessboard. Yet, why take the time to show her? The answer hit her, shockingly.

She brought her eyes down to Will Sharpe and John Wilkes. 'Jimmy Kelly's your man on the inside,' she said. 'Am I right? You knew what they were discussing on the pavement, which means a hidden microphone. It can't be Camberwell, so it must be Jimmy.' Neither man spoke. There was silence in the van for several seconds, as Sharpe and Wilkes stared at each other. Then, Will Sharpe nodded.

Maggie slapped her hand to her forehead. 'I hit him. Really hard. Half the room saw it.'

John Wilkes grinned. 'That actually didn't do us any harm. Increased his cred with Camberwell, and probably Marilyn.'

'He won't thank me for it,' she said. 'We need to get going. The church has a crypt. Few people know about it. It was included in the building to hide fugitives from the law, following the terrible gang warfare that went on in the 1840s. Bob didn't see it, but I did. The entrance is hidden, so any rampaging gangs couldn't possibly find anyone hiding there.'

'Hold on,' Will Sharpe said. 'There's no "we". Tell us where it is. You aren't coming. It's too dangerous for civilians. Tell us how to get in.'

'No.'

Will Sharpe stood up, as did John Wilkes. 'We have no time to mess about. Tell me where the entrance is, or I'll have you arrested.'

'Good luck with that,' Bob said. 'And don't look at me, I don't know how to open it. He showed Maggie, and he did that for a reason, when I wasn't there.'

'We don't have time for this,' Wilkes said to Will Sharpe. 'Let her come with us.' He turned to Bob and Maggie. 'Every man there will be armed. Once they're in the crypt, their instruction will be to preserve life but if they believe anyone is getting in the way, they'll shoot.'

Maggie shuddered. 'I'll show you where it is and how to get in, but I won't go down. On the way over I can describe the layout.'

Wilkes nodded and the van began to move. Maggie and Bob sat in two spare seats. The screens still showed the reception, where small groups were whispering together.

'Where's Marilyn?' Maggie said. 'I've been watching those screens. I can't pick her out.'

'Find her,' Wilkes said tersely to the operator who had sat silently staring at his screens throughout the exchanges. He switched from screen to screen, for two minutes, then said to Wilkes, 'Sir, she isn't there. Her husband and son are there, but not Ms Kelly.'

'She'll be on her way to the church,' Maggie said. 'Someone must have warned her there was trouble. She'll be panicking and in need of a way out of this.'

The van lurched around a corner, throwing them all sideways, then stopped with screeching brakes.

'We're here,' Will Sharpe said.

Wilkes spoke into the microphone, checking that his breach team was in place. He listened and frowned.

'They've neutralised two guards, one outside, one inside.' He turned to Maggie and Bob. 'Is there CCTV in the crypt?'

'I don't think so,' Bob said. 'There's a camera at the entrance to the church, but as far as I'm aware the feed goes to the priest's house. Maggie, did you notice anything in the crypt?'

'No,' she replied. 'I didn't actually go into the crypt; I only saw the room from the outside. From what Jimmy said, it's just bare stone walls.'

'We're going inside. Detective Chief Inspector, I can authorise arms for you. Do you wish to be armed?'

Bob nodded. 'I'm certified and trained.'

'I know.' Wilkes handed him a heavy-looking pistol. Maggie shuddered, as Bob checked and quickly familiarised himself with the gun. His expression was grim and intense. This was the first time she had seen him like this and prayed it would be the last.

They crept into the church. A man in full armoured gear was waiting for them. He spoke in a low voice to Wilkes. 'Far as I can tell, Sir, they don't know we're here. We've checked the feeds in the priest's house. There's no camera in the crypt. We just need to know where it is and how to access it.'

All faces turned to Maggie, who bent down and took her shoes off, to their puzzlement.

'Clicking heels,' she said. 'There are two switches, one at the top that leads to the stairs, and one at the bottom to open the door to the crypt. It swings outwards.' She turned to stare intensely at Wilkes. 'Whatever you do, those little girls will be terrified and traumatised. Don't hurt them.'

'Get us to the bottom of the stairs,' he replied curtly. 'We'll take it from there.'

Maggie took them down the right-hand side of the pews and crept down to where the tall statue of St Bridget stood, one arm pointing out. She reached behind it, found and flicked the switch Jimmy had shown her, and a panel slid silently aside, revealing the steep set of steps.

'We'll take it from here,' Wilkes said. 'Just tell me where the second switch is, and how the door opens.

'It looks like a plain panel,' she whispered, 'you can barely make out the outlines.' She showed them approximately where the door was. And keep your voice down. It's just a thin panel. They may be able to hear you.'

Wilkes nodded.

'It's best I show you, then I'll get out of the way. The door opens outwards, it swings back.' Wilkes nodded again and Maggie led them down the steep stairwell, lit only by the beam of Wilkes' torch. She had to hold up the hem of her dress to stop herself slipping on it.

When they reached the bottom, she felt around the bracket on the wall, as she had seen Jimmy do, and located the switch. She silently took Wilkes' hand and moved it to the switch. He nodded and indicated to her to get back up the stairs. 'And go back outside,' he whispered.

Behind Wilkes were half a dozen armed men, intent on what was coming, not looking at the woman in the gauze dress creeping past them.

At the end of the line, she passed Bob. She squeezed his arm and they nodded at each other. She turned at the top of the staircase and could just make out the armed men standing against the wall, one either side of the door. She didn't go outside, but stood next to the statue, barely breathing, gripping it's pointed hand, her eyes closed. It didn't take long.

There was a sudden crash, a scream of "armed police", and "surrender your weapons". Then, mayhem.

Smoke came pouring up the stairs, with shouting and screaming, much of it young voices. Then, footsteps running up the stairs, followed by a shot. The footsteps stopped and a man fell out of the entrance, his chest covered in blood. Maggie glanced at his face; not one of Wilkes' men. This man had no body armour.

Standing in the dark church, lit only by votive candles here and there, Maggie's legs began to shake. The yelling and shouting were lessening. Footsteps came up the stairs and Maggie squeezed herself behind the statue, shaking.

'Maggie? Where are you?' Bob's voice. She extricated herself from the statue's back and ran to him.

'I knew you wouldn't go outside,' he said, hugging her so tightly she could hardly breathe. 'It's over. It's all OK. No-one hurt, except the one gang member who tried to get away.'

More footsteps came up the stairs. Will Sharpe appeared, saw Maggie and rolled his eyes. He was followed by Wilkes.

'The situation is contained,' Wilkes said as Sharpe went back down. 'Child services is outside. We're about to bring the children up.' He spoke briefly into a radio and suddenly the church was full of people with blankets, paramedics, and police.

Some of the people went down into the crypt and began to bring the girls out. There were twelve, all tiny, crying, and shaking.

'They were going for children this time,' Wilkes spat out. 'I reckon the oldest of these girls is no more than ten. We have your friend Camberwell. He's not talking right now, but he will. We'll wait until the children have been taken away, then we'll bring him out. There were three smugglers with him. We'll bring them up first, keep Camberwell until last.'

Maggie and Bob watched as the procession came up the stairs after the children were out of the church. The gang members, angry and frustrated, handcuffed and chained, then more of the armed men.

The church began to empty. 'Who's still down there?' Maggie asked.

'Camberwell, Will Sharpe and two armed officers, plus Jimmy Kelly,' Wilkes replied.

'I'd like to go down,' Maggie said.

'Absolutely not,' Wilkes replied. 'I don't want you compromising or contaminating anything. We'll need our forensic team in there. No-one talks to Camberwell, not me, not you. We'll get him and Father Kelly down to the station. You'll be needed, too.'

Maggie sighed. 'OK, I understand. I wanted to apologise to Jimmy for hitting him.'

Wilkes grinned. 'He'll forgive you. You can wait until we have the church completely secured. Then we can bring them up.'

It took another fifteen minutes. Maggie and Bob didn't move. They heard the sound of more footsteps on the stairs. Will Sharpe came up first, followed by Henry Camberwell in handcuffs, then Jimmy Kelly, then the armed guards.

Camberwell stopped when he saw Maggie and Bob. 'Bitch,' he said as he passed her.

Jimmy stopped in front of Maggie. 'I can still feel it,' he said, putting his hand to his cheek. 'But thank you. It helped this cockroach believe one hundred percent in me.'

Maggie grinned. She followed them into the church porch. John Wilkes told them to wait and went outside to check the path was clear to the transport waiting for Camberwell.

'Don't anyone move.' The voice was low and menacing. They all froze. A side door, which was slightly ajar, was pushed open and Marilyn Kelly appeared, a gun in her hand.

'Put it down,' she said to the armed guards, who looked at Will Sharpe. Sharpe nodded and the guards laid their semi-automatic rifles on the floor.

'You too,' she said to Will Sharpe, who took his gun from its holster and put it on the ground. 'I'm taking these two,' she said, nodding at Henry and her brother. 'It's I who will have vengeance for their misdeeds.'

'You can't kill them,' Maggie shouted.

'My game, my rules,' Marilyn replied. She nodded at Camberwell and Jimmy. 'Move,' she said.

'No,' Jimmy replied. 'Not this time, Marilyn.'

'Then he'll take the blame alone,' she said and turned the gun on Camberwell. Before anyone could stop him, Jimmy Kelly leapt forward in front of Camberwell, and fell to his knees, looking questioningly at her, blood pouring from his side.

Maggie screamed and ran to him as he fell. Marilyn was momentarily distracted, and, in that moment, Bob pulled out the gun he had been given, leapt at Camberwell, who had been eyeing the side door, and put it to his head. 'Mrs Kelly, put your weapon down,' he said quietly.

'English policeman,' she replied with a smile, and turned her weapon on Maggie.

'What do we have here?' An instantly recognisable voice came from the entrance to the church as Zelah Trevear stepped into the porch.

'You!' Marilyn said. Camberwell groaned, as Zelah snapped her fingers, and the gun jumped out of Marilyn's hand, letting off an aimless shot up into the air. Will Sharpe rushed over, knocked Marilyn down and put one knee on her back. Marilyn Kelly turned her head and looked up at Zelah in confusion. Zelah grinned and shrugged. 'Butterfingers,' she said, looking down at Marilyn.

John Wilkes came flying back into the church porch. 'What the fuck happened here?'

Jimmy Kelly groaned and looked up at Maggie. 'I didn't believe you. You were telling the truth about her, but I didn't believe you. If I hadn't seen it, I would never have believed it,' he whispered.

'Stop talking,' Maggie ordered, as paramedics rushed in, and she was forced back.

'Just in time, as usual,' Zelah said to no-one in particular. 'Aren't we having a lovely time.'

'At least this time you've been useful,' Will Sharpe said as he marched Marilyn out and into a waiting police car.

'Good holiday?' John Wilkes said to Zelah.

'You can't imagine.'

Chapter 39

The rest of the night was chaotic and, in Maggie's opinion, like something out of an American crime drama. She and Bob, and Zelah had been questioned and re-questioned until Maggie felt as if the inside of her brain had been stripped to a raw carcass.

They were eventually allowed to go back to their hotel at six in the morning.

'My beautiful dress is ruined,' Maggie said to a silent Bob. He hadn't spoken much since the gun was taken from him. 'Did you hear what I said? I had plans for this dress.'

'Sorry, miles away,' he replied. 'I'm going to take a shower.'

When he came out twenty minutes later, Maggie was sitting in bed waiting for him. 'You hate them don't you: guns.'

He nodded.

'Would you have shot Camberwell, if Zelah hadn't appeared?'

He stood at the end of the bed, looking at her. 'I can't answer that question. Marilyn Kelly was pointing her gun at you. I just want to go home, get back to my South Wales crims. Some of them must be back from the Costa del Sol by now.'

'We're going tomorrow night. Let's get some sleep, then decide what we want to do.'

'There's going to be more questioning, some later, but probably mostly after we get back.'

'I want news of Jimmy Kelly, before we go anywhere. And I want to know who's looking after Will.'

Bob's phone rang. He listened without speaking for a few minutes, then said "thankyou" and ended the call.

'That was Will Sharpe. Jimmy's come through surgery. It was touch and go. Marilyn is claiming she was trying to be the heroine, save everyone from the evil people smugglers. She tried to have you, me and Zelah incriminated for being in cahoots with Camberwell. Jimmy surviving has put paid to that. He's going to testify against her.'

'And against Camberwell?'

'Yes.'

'At last. Can we be sure he doesn't find a way out of this one?'

'You were right, Jimmy was wired. Everything said down in the crypt is on record. It will finish Camberwell. Unfortunately, Marilyn's name wasn't mentioned.'

Maggie fell back on her pillow. 'Jimmy has to give evidence against his sister.'

'It'll be his word against hers. We may have to testify too. Will isn't sure yet.'

'If I can, I'd like to see Jimmy before we leave.'

Bob got into bed beside her. 'This has been quite a ride,' he said, and yawned.

He was asleep almost immediately. Maggie understood how he was feeling. He was trained to use a lethal weapon and had on a few occasions been in a position where he'd had to carry one. He had never been in the position of having to make the choice of whether or not to shoot another human being. And he had himself been shot, some years before.

She was beginning to feel sleepy herself, now. She put an arm around him and in his sleep, he took hold of her hand.

Before she closed her eyes, she ran through the plan that she was forming, and smiled.

**

Maggie awoke first, followed ten minutes later by Bob.

'What time is it?'

'It's half past one in the afternoon. I've called the hospital. Jimmy is doing well. He's out of the intensive care ward. They say he's been lucky, but he can't have visitors today. Maybe tomorrow. Will is being looked after by ladies from the parish who are doing shifts to make sure he's OK. Bob, I'd like to go to see him.'

'Of course. Do you mind if I don't come with you. I'd just like to stay here today.'

'No problem, she replied. 'How long would you like me to stay away?'

He went to speak, but she put up a hand to stop him. 'This has upset you, horribly. You need time to yourself to process it. I'll be a couple of hours. I might even take Zelah with me.'

'That might be too much for him.'

'Don't be sarcastic. Zelah removed the gun from Marilyn, in her own, very special way.'

He smiled. 'I think I'll sleep again,' and turned away from her, his face buried in the pillow.

Showered and dressed, she went to find Zelah, who was already up and hammering away on her laptop.

'You won't be able to use this story for months,' Maggie said. 'The police won't allow it.'

'I know that. I'm not stupid.'

'Never said you were,' Maggie replied. 'No offence meant,' she added, picking up a sandwich from a tray sitting on the table.

'I want to make a call. Do you mind?'

Zelah waved a hand, which Maggie interpreted as "go ahead".

Her call was answered immediately. 'Maggie! How are you? How's New York? Have you found out anything interesting about Norrie Madigan?'

'I'm fine, thanks. New York is very hot, and I have a long story to tell you. And yes, we've found out something very interesting about Norrie Madigan. Mike, from your "cousins" list, could you take a quick look at the person called Kelly?'

'Certainly. Just a moment.' There were a few seconds silence, during which Maggie could hear the sound of a laptop starting. 'Uh, yes, got him.' Maggie closed her eyes. 'Can you tell me more about the individual?

'Sure. It appears to be a young man, living in New York. It's a very low connection, just ten centimorgans. His name is—'

'William Kelly,' Maggie said.

'Yes, it is. How do you know? Have you come across him?'

'I have, or rather we have, Bob and I. Mike, I have a story to tell you, but it's a long story and I'd rather tell you in person. What are your plans after Devon?'

'Actually we've moved on to Cornwall. We're staying in a very nice little seaside town called Fowey. Do you know it?'

'I do. I have a friend living there.'

'Jay and I are thinking we'll go from here to Ireland. I want to see County Clare and Kilrush.'

'That's great news, Mike, because that's exactly what I was going to propose. How about you and me, and Bob and Zelah meet up there? We're leaving here tomorrow night, back Friday morning. We could meet in Kilrush at the weekend.'

'Works for me, and I know Jay will agree. I'm intrigued about this news. Can you tell me anything?'

'Better in person, if you can hang on for a few days.'

'OK, if I must. By the way, Nick has been extra helpful. He's tracked down our DNA relative in Australia. And I've had a reply. The person sounds cautious, but at least they've replied.'

'I'm so pleased you have a response. In our experience, about seventy percent of people don't bother to respond.'

'Maggie, thank you for everything you've done for me.'

'I haven't finished yet. Now, we must get going. Zelah and I have a visit to make. We'll see you in Kilrush on Saturday. Shall we say lunchtime, in the town centre?'

'Fine. See you there. I'm looking forward to hearing this story.'

'Who am I going to meet?' Zelah said, looking up from her laptop.

'The client, Mike Walker. The person who started all this off.'

'Can I make a suggestion?' Zelah asked.

'Hit me with it.'

'You and I change our return flight and fly direct to Dublin. We can still be there Friday morning, stay overnight at Rosscarbery, then drive over to Kilrush on Saturday morning.'

'Hmm. Would be easier, but I'll have to talk to Bob.'

'Of course.' Zelah stood up and went to sit on the settee next to Maggie. 'How's he doing?' He didn't look great in the cab coming back from the police HQ.'

'He doesn't like guns. He was shot, remember, which was traumatic enough.'

'And he had a decision to make, a split-second decision, to decide who might live and who might die. That's tough for anyone. No matter how many years as a policeman, that must have been horrifying for him.'

'Thank you for understanding that Zelah. He's staying here whilst we go to visit Will Kelly.'

'We?'

'Yes. You're coming with me. He'll want to meet you. I told Jimmy about you. Will was there. Jimmy was, as you would expect, totally sceptical. He's not anymore, by the way. But Will looked – gripped. He didn't dismiss the idea. You'll make his day by just turning up.'

'No party tricks,' Zelah warned.

'Absolutely not,' Maggie replied, crossing her fingers behind her back.

Chapter 40

The visit to Will Kelly was a great success. When they arrived, they had received a frosty reception from the woman on shift. 'You're the one who got our Father James into this,' she said. 'I don't think the boy will want to see you.'

'His name is Will, and I can assure you, he'll want to see us.'

The woman stepped into the sitting room, then quickly returned. 'You can see him, but you'd better be quick.'

As they entered Will waved his arms and hands together in a clapping gesture. Maggie hugged him, introduced Zelah and they both sat on the settee.

'You know what's happened?' Maggie began.

One tap.

'Did you know right from the start?'

One tap.

'Your uncle Jimmy is an incredibly brave man. But, your mother is going to fight back, did you know that?'

Two taps.

'Unfortunately, she is. Will, would you be willing to testify in court, against her? It's a big ask.'

One very loud bang.

'Good boy. Don't let anyone put you off. Your mother might say horrible things about you.'

A shrug accompanied by a look that Maggie interpreted as defiance.

'I have a question to ask you about your genealogy search. You found Norrie Madigan, didn't you?'

A downward movement of the chin.

'You were right, one hundred percent. I think I may have also found another relative, living here in Manhattan. He's descended from one of the three cousins, not Norrie but a girl called Ellen O'Donnell, who was sent to Australia, on the Earl Grey scheme. Do you know about that scheme?'

Another nod.

'This man is our client, descended from Ellen's brother Michael. It's a very small fraction of DNA, just ten centimorgans, but DNA is funny stuff. I'd like to check your results to see if you have him on your list. Is that OK?'

Will's arm waved towards a desk in the corner, where a laptop sat. Maggie went to get it. 'Is there a password, Will?'

Two taps.

She opened it up, found Ancestry. 'I'm going to look at your cousins list, on your mother's side. Let's do a search.'

It came up immediately. A "distant cousin" called Michael Walker.

'Amazing.' Maggie showed Zelah. 'He's here.' She turned her head to Will. 'Our client is a relative. I believe he's a good man. When he gets back to Manhattan, I'm sure he'll want to come to meet you and Jimmy. Will that be OK with you?'

A grunt and a slight upturn of the lips.

'Alternative family,' she said. She looked at her watch. 'Time to go. Bob sends his regards. He's very tired and stressed.'

Will was listening, but now looking at Zelah.

Zelah stood up. 'Definitely time to go.'

She turned to the door, which quite suddenly flew open. She walked to it, looked theatrically around, then turned back to Will. 'How odd,' she said. 'No-one there,' and walked back to Maggie. The door crashed shut again and its lock clicked. 'Fancy that,' she said, in a puzzled voice, looking at Will, then grinning.

For a second, he looked back at her, then a tear appeared in his eye. She walked up to him, took a napkin and wiped it away. 'Don't ever tell anyone you saw that,' she said, with a twinkle. He put out his hand, and she high fived it.

A banging on the door began, and Maggie walked to unlock it.

'Did you lock that door?' the minder woman said in an accusing voice.

'That was me,' Zelah said. 'To keep a nosy busybody out.' She winked at Will, who was shaking, saliva running down his mouth.

'Now look what you've done!' the woman said, oblivious to the fact that Will was laughing.

'We were just going,' Zelah said meekly. 'Goodbye Will. Good to have met you.'

Maggie gave him a hug and whispered, 'Jimmy will be home soon. He'll tell you exactly what she did. He's not quite so sceptical now.'

**

Back at the hotel, Bob was up and dressed.

'How are you,' Maggie asked casually, and described the visit.

He shook his head. 'Better,' he said, putting his arms around her waist. 'By the way, someone came to collect the dress and jacket. She thought it could be brought back to look like new. I don't understand why you'd want it, after what happened.'

'I have a plan. But first, I need to tell you about an idea of Zelah's.'

She explained about Ireland for herself and Zelah, leaving him to head home and get to work on Friday morning, as per the original plan.

'No,' he said firmly. 'I'm coming with you. I know he's your client and has no idea of who I am, but I don't feel ready to leave you on your own yet.' He stood back. 'Wilkes is arranging around the clock security for Jimmy.'

Maggie went to ask why, as the reason hit her. 'Marilyn. She'd kill him if she could. You think she'd go for us, too?'

'I do,' Bob replied. 'Besides, just before you came back my Super called, wanting to know why she's been receiving early morning transatlantic phone calls from the FBI singing my praises. When I told her the whole story, she told me to stay off until next week. I'm coming with you to Ireland. It'll be good to see Zelah's place there, and meet the boys, and the dreaded Mischa again.'

'Fine with me,' she replied. 'Better than fine. After we've met with Mike Walker, Zelah will drive us back via Fishguard. We'll be home on Sunday.'

'And the hospital called. Jimmy is asking for you. He's making remarkable progress. Do you want to go for a quick visit before dinner?'

'Absolutely, Bob. Let's go now. I'll let Zelah know.'

Zelah didn't want to go with them. 'He's asking for you, not me. Plenty of time for me to meet him on a later visit. I have to come back to New York in a couple of months. The Museum wants to talk to me about a loan of more of Martin's landscapes, for a dedicated exhibition. Go see the man. He wants to thank you.'

'I think he'll want to thank you, too.'

'Then he can be a guest of honour at the exhibition when it opens, and I can meet him properly next month. Shoo!'

Maggie laughed and set off with Bob. Zelah and Jimmy were going to meet sooner than either of them knew. Another part of Maggie's plan, which was coming along nicely.

**

The visit to Jimmy Kelly was quick, but emotional. To get to his room in the hospital they had to go through layers of security checks.

'More men with guns,' she muttered to Bob when they finally reached the floor for Jimmy's private room.

'And women,' Bob said, nodding at the formidable female police officer standing outside Jimmy's door. John Wilkes had accompanied them, to make it easier to reach the room.

Jimmy tried to sit up when he saw them but couldn't quite make it.

'Lie down and rest,' Maggie said. 'After a slap on the face like I gave you, a man needs time to recover.'

Jimmy laughed, winced, and allowed his head to rest back on the bed. 'That I can get over. Henry gave me a nod of approval when you did that. I must say, Mrs Gilbert, you pack one hell of a punch. Bob, watch yourself.'

'I have no intention of ever getting that close to one of her admonitions,' Bob said. 'It was a cracker, though, wasn't it?'

Jimmy laughed again, then his face became serious. 'I knew you were the right person to tell as soon as I met you. I knew you'd work it out if it ever became necessary.'

'Yeh, I'm clever like that,' she said, grinning at him. 'They say you won't be long getting out of here. Zelah and I went to see Will earlier. He's doing fine but misses you. Zelah made him laugh.'

'I want to meet her, too. I bet her "abilities" are as close as anyone will ever get to Satan.'

'Henry Camberwell thinks so,' Maggie replied. 'She doesn't often go for the jugular, hardly ever, in fact. Like I told you, she only ever uses her gifts – that's what I prefer to call them – for good and necessary reasons. But when she does, it's awesome. Times Square's New Year fireworks have nothing on her.' She smiled, but there was anxiety in the smile and Jimmy saw it. He took her hand, which had been resting on the bed. 'Don't worry, Maggie. My priestly gut tells me that she will only ever act to the full extent of her ability in extremis. I shouldn't have said "Satan". I'm sorry. For me, it's what my religion tells me is only possible in the works of the devil, but now I know that's wrong. I have to look at it in a different way, not as bad, just – different.'

'I hope you can do that,' Maggie replied. She shook herself. 'Anyway, there's something I want to ask you, just between the two of us. Bob, would you give Jimmy and me a couple of minutes?'

Bob stood up. 'You're plotting something. I know that look.'

'Then clear off,' she said. 'You'll be finding out soon enough.'

**

'He's doing well, physically,' Bob said in the cab ride back to the hotel. 'Not sure about mentally, though. I noticed he looked away into space a couple of times. Like I did, at first.'

He yawned. 'Is Zelah joining us for dinner?'

'No idea,' Maggie replied. She sent a quick text, which was answered immediately. 'No, she says she's too tired. She's changed our flights and booked a ferry for Sunday morning.'

'I'll join you when you speak to your client if you like,' Bob said. 'It's going to be a lot for him to take in.'

'Yes, thank you. Just the two of us for dinner, then. I'll tell you why I wanted that private chat to Jimmy.'

'I think I can guess,' Bob replied.

'How well you know me.'

He leaned over and kissed her. 'And looking forward to getting to know the future Mrs Pugh all over again.'

Chapter 41

Mike Walker stood at the end of the former Clamhunger Row, looking out over the Atlantic towards Scattery Island. He had been standing there for almost half an hour, when Maggie decided to join him.

'Beautiful, isn't it, in a rugged kind of way,' she said.

He nodded.

'It will all sink in, Mike, eventually.'

The tall, silver-haired man turned his head slowly to look at her. 'You think so?'

'I do. With researching your family history, there's always the chance you'll find something shocking, something you don't like and may not want to talk about, yet. Or, never.'

'I can deal with most of it.' He paused and scowled. 'I met Marilyn Kelly on a number of occasions, socially and professionally. I never took to her.'

'Just as well,' Maggie replied.

Mike's scowl disappeared. 'I'll be following the trial with extra interest, now.'

'Mike, are you disappointed with the outcome of this search?'

'Absolutely not. I feel a terrible sense of injustice about what happened to Ellen. And the fact that there's nothing I can do about it. It's weighing down on me. It's sad about Peg Dillon. But for Norrie Madigan I feel only contempt.'

'I think what she did here in Kilrush changed her,' Maggie said. 'I understand her anger. What was done to the people here was horrifying, and that it was done by a fellow Irishman makes it even worse, for me anyway. I get that she wanted to punish Seamus McMahon. If she had stopped there, maybe there could be forgiveness. But it changed her, in the worst possible way. But don't forget, she took Michael

O'Donnell from the Workhouse here, took him to Dublin, to a new life. You still have a number of O'Donnell descendants to look up back home. Remember it was Norrie's story that led us to the exposing of Marilyn Kelly who, by the way, has gained freedom on bail. The cost must have been exorbitant, but she's out. Apparently, she has to wear an ankle bracelet and can't go beyond the boundary of her estate. That's something.'

Mike gave a snort of disgust. 'It's all about who you know.'

'Her brother will give evidence against her. He and Will are being kept safe until the trial. She'll go down.'

'And the other man, Camberwell?'

'He's pleading not guilty, which seems crazy to me, but that's Henry Camberwell. He probably thinks he has enough friends in high places who'll help him out of his predicament. He was anticipating a peerage. There's no chance of that now. He'll be shocked at how those friends run like poachers from a gamekeeper when he tries to call in favours. The only thing he might have to offer is someone higher up the chain, but Bob says that so far, he hasn't tried that one. Or the names of the people to whom he supplied the children. I suppose he could do a deal there, but if those include dangerous people, which is also possible, then he won't ever be safe. No, we've seen the last of Sir Henry Camberwell. And good riddance.' She paused for a moment. 'What will you and Jay do next?'

'We're going to Dublin. Your Nick has been helpful in trying to track down some of the names on my list of "cousins", who might trace back to Michael O'Donnell. I'd like to find some of them, if I can. And Nick will help with those in the US, so we'll stay in Ireland for a while, then go home. After that, I'm thinking about Australia. But I'll have to take my time cultivating that cousin. There's reticence, for which I'd like to discover the reason.'

'Ellen O'Donnell went out there on the Earl Grey scheme. Some of the girls were given a choice, others weren't. I think it began with good intentions but wasn't thought through and no-one took the time to properly administrate it. I don't suppose they cared enough; it was just a way to get rid of indigent Irish orphan girls. It became a mess.'

'I'm going to find out more about the scheme. It'll be important to know as much as I can before I contact my Australian cousin.' He paused, then said, 'Maggie, I can't thank you enough. This has changed me, especially knowing Michael O'Donnell's story, and what happened here in Ireland, the famine, the deaths, the emigration. It decimated this country and the English Government just let it happen.'

'There were some who tried,' Maggie replied. 'But not enough.'

'I like Joan,' Michael said. 'She wants me to have the letters, as Michael and Ellen's last direct relative. But I have children and they have children. Who knows what might happen when we carry on researching? I think they should go to a museum. What do you think?'

'I believe they should be in a museum. I do wonder about the Norrie Madigan letter, though. I've asked Bob and he's going to check, but could it be evidence of Marilyn Kelly's lies?'

'Is there proof that she knew Ellen Kelly was really Norrie Madigan?' Mike asked.

'Only with the evidence of her son, Will. He wants to testify. He had the argument with her about Norrie Madigan and he says she knew for sure, but there's no direct evidence as far as I know. It would finally destroy her reputation if it could be proved she knew all along. The more important factor is whether or not it goes towards proving she was complicit in Will's beating. Bob thinks it's circumstantial at best, unless Camberwell gives her up.'

'There's time enough to decide. Have you told John Wilkes about the letter?'

'Not yet,' Maggie replied. 'I need to tell Joan first. She might refuse to give it up to anyone, you and I included, if she thinks it will get out into the wider public.'

They stood for a further five minutes, looking at the waves crashing onto the beach in front of them.

'I'll head back to the cottage. Joan has prepared a special tea for us. Look at those clouds. Don't be too long here. Storm coming,' Maggie said.

'In many ways,' Mike replied.

As she turned to go, Mike took hold of Maggie's arm. 'Maggie, I've something I want to say. When I began this journey, it was for a hobby, something interesting to do in my retirement. Now, I feel emotional, angry, sad, for people I didn't even know existed. Is that crazy?'

'Mike, you'd be amazed at how normal it is. We have something in us that was given to us by our ancestors. Whatever it is, centimorgans, whatever, it's a connection. Once it's made, it can't be broken. We don't know what they were like. We don't even have photographs going that far back,' she waved at the houses on the Row. 'But we have a picture, pictures, in our mind of what they might have been like, how they looked, what they talked about, and how they lived their lives. You'll never lose that. I have a plaque above my desk with a poem that talks about being the person chosen by our ancestors to guard and cherish their memory. I'll send you a copy.'

'Thank you,' he whispered and turned back to the raging sea.

Chapter 42
Two Months Later

Maggie and Bob were married on the second Sunday in September. The weather didn't let them down.

On the morning of their departure from New York, Bob had organised a ride around Central Park in one of the decorated horse-drawn carriages. It had been a fine day. Maggie and Bob chatted casually for the first ten minutes until Zelah said, 'Enough. Tell me why we're here and what's really going on.'

'Easy enough,' Maggie said. 'Bob and I are getting married, probably early September, when the fuss has died down. Before you say anything, it's not going to be a big affair. Just people we care about. I told Alice and Jack last night.'

'Alice OK with it?' Zelah asked.

'She's delighted,' Maggie replied. 'She's come around.'

'Which comes as a great relief to me,' Bob added. 'I was worried that when the point came where the celebrant says: "If there is any person here who knows of any reason why…" etc, etc, Alice would jump up.'

Maggie laughed. 'She likes you now. Take the win.'

'I'm delighted for you both,' Zelah said, leaning forward and giving Maggie a hug. 'Where, when and who?'

'You and Nick, obviously, and Rick if he'll travel over, plus Mischa and the boys. Then, Stella, Max and Flora. I'll invite my sister, but I don't think she'll come.'

'That woman knows how to hold a grudge,' Zelah muttered.

Maggie shrugged. 'Her girls will come. That's good enough for me. Bob has a few friends he wants to invite. Miles the ex-coroner and his wife, his old sergeant, who's retired to Spain but will come back, as Bob's asked him to be his best man. And I want to have Joan from Moy. I'm hoping Mary Dillon will come with her. And Jimmy Kelly to perform the ceremony, to which he's already agreed; and Will, which might pose a challenge. And Mike Walker and his wife Jay. I'm hoping they'll help Jimmy with Will. John McRoberts from Liverpool and his dad, and Trys Wyn Davies from Fallough House and his mother. It'll be interesting to find out if Jacka and Helen are still as friendly as they were when we found John's policeman ancestor. And, of course, the steroid kid, and his mother. By the time we add a few neighbours and special friends, like Belle Harrington in Cornwall, that'll be enough people.

'The steroid kid, eh? Perhaps I should start calling him Gerry, now he's about to become part of my family.' Zelah said. 'I've forgiven him and, more importantly, so has Mischa. She's almost reconciled with her mother, too. We just don't mention Kennet Quinn.'

'Fine with me. You're the one who gave him the nickname and he seems to be done with the drugs now. That's it for people. The "where" is in the garden. When – I'm not sure yet. There's quite a lot to organise, but we have two months. I'm sure we can do it.'

It had been quite a task to find a way to get Will across the Atlantic. Standard airlines wouldn't take him. In the end, Zelah had hired a private plane. Jimmy had, naturally, objected to the cost, but Zelah wouldn't hear of it. 'Don't think you're going to get this again, apart from getting home. Make the most of it. The crew will look after you both.' Jimmy tried to thank her, but she waved him away.

'She can afford it,' Maggie said. 'I've told her it's her contribution to the wedding. She was outraged when we told her you might not get here.'

Now it was September and the big day had arrived. Everyone they invited had accepted, and were all sitting in anticipation, waiting for Maggie's arrival. Bob had decided to dress casually, which for him meant a dark suit, a dark shirt and no tie.

At three o'clock in the afternoon, Maggie walked down the steps of the garden decking to the flower covered arch, that Alice and Jack, with the help and advice of Matthew and Max, plus suggestions from Zelah, had put up at the end of the garden.

Maggie took everyone's breath away. She was wearing the New York dress, now brought back to its full beauty, with a white and gold bolero top specially designed for the occasion, by Eloise from the Fifth Avenue Shop. The gold embroidery shone in the sun and the dress itself seemed to float, as did Maggie.

She was accompanied by Jack and Alice. Zelah and Nick were ready to act as the witnesses.

Waiting for them, to perform the ceremony, was Jimmy Kelly. Will Kelly sat at the side, the rings sitting on a gold cushion on his tray.

Jimmy beamed as she reached him. Bob looked as relaxed and contented as Maggie had ever seen him. What she didn't know was that two plain clothes officers were at the opposite side of the canal and two were out front. Their job: to ensure that the witnesses in the trial of Henry Camberwell and Marilyn Kelly came to no harm.

The ceremony began. Jimmy made a short speech in the middle; funny, happy, with no hint of what had gone before. Then he pronounced them man and wife.

The rest of the day was filled with eating, drinking champagne, chatting and, in the evening, dancing in the small marquee, lit with fairy lights that Jack and Max had arranged, with Max acting as DJ. They had also bought dozens of lights for the garden, which lit up as evening drew in.

It was a bittersweet occasion for Nick. The following day, Max would be leaving for Birmingham to begin his training as a paramedic. He sat at a table, holding a sleeping Flora, watching his son.

‘He’ll be back for breaks, probably with piles of washing and in need of a good meal,’ Stella said.

‘I know. It’s just…’

She smiled at him. ‘You aren’t losing him again, because that’s what you’re thinking, isn’t it?’

He nodded. ‘But I’m glad he’s found his purpose.’

At midnight Bob and Maggie decided they’d had enough. They said goodnight to everyone and disappeared up to their room, having urged everyone to eat and drink as much as they liked. The following day most of them would be leaving; some they would meet again, others not so often, but these were all special people with whom they would never lose touch.

Maggie took off her shoes with a sigh of relief. ‘I’ve been wanting to do that all day. I notice you divested yourself of your jacket as soon as the ceremony was over.’

He grinned. ‘That was for the dancing.’

‘Yes, I never knew you had such mobile hips.’

‘Really? I think you do.’

Her cheeks flushed briefly. ‘Anyway, alone at last,’ Maggie said. ‘Now you can tell me what’s been at the back of your mind all day. Don’t think I didn’t notice the occasional flash of a suit behind the trees on the other side of the canal.’

‘It isn’t over,’ he said, sitting next to her.

‘I know,’ she replied, putting her head on his shoulder. ‘Is there more news?’

‘Yes. They’re talking about doing a deal with Camberwell, if he gives up his clients.’

Maggie jumped up. ‘You don’t mean he’ll be let off?’

‘That’s what he’s trying for, but no, he’ll do jail time.’

She sat down again. ‘I’m not going to think about him or Marilyn. This has been our day and it’s been wonderful. For the next couple of days I’ll see everyone off home, then, it’s back to business as usual. I expect Nick has a couple of cases lined up.’

‘What, no honeymoon period?’

‘Isn’t that what we had in New York? I liked Manhattan.’

'I liked it too, and one day we'll go back and explore more. However, Nick's line up of cases can wait. We're going away for a week.'

'Are we? Do I get a say in this?' Maggie asked.

'No. We're taking the camper van over to Ireland. We're going to explore the west coast.'

'When?'

'After our guests have gone. Nick's happy to hold the fort. And Zelah. We'll be back before Jack goes off to University.'

'As you know, Robert, I would normally object to you deciding without consulting me. But, this time, I'll go with it.'

'Good. For the next couple of days we relax. No work for either of us.'

'Works for me. And when we get home, I'm sure Nick will have plenty for me to do.'

'It was ever thus Mrs Pugh. I'm sure another brick wall will be waiting for you.'

'And plenty of crims for you, all back from the Costa del Sol, and ready for your particular attention.'

He smiled, switched off the bedroom lights, as the music played on in the garden, quieter and softer now, love songs and gentle rhythms, until the sun came up and the house was finally silent.

Research and Bibliography

I always knew about the famine in Ireland, but I didn't realise how little I knew until I began to write this book.

The first unknown fact, for me, was the Early Grey scheme, to send young Irish orphan girls off to Australia for the purposes of marriage and servitude. These girls were aged from 14 – 18. They were supposed to volunteer, but many had no choice.

I chose three fictional characters from County Clare, three young female cousins. As the book progressed and I went deeper into each of their stories, the book took an unexpected turn, with one of the characters going instead to America!

However he basis of the story remains the horror of the great famine in Ireland and its far-flung consequences. I had never truly understood or appreciated its extent and monstrosity, with over one million dead and one million leaving the country. I cannot say any more here. I remain speechless and horrified at what I discovered. I only hope I have done Ireland justice in my writing. As for the history itself, others have recorded it far better than I ever could.

These are the books that I used during my research.

"Tracing Your Irish Ancestors"
John Grenham

"Ireland's Great Famine: Interdisciplinary Perspectives"
Cormac Ó Gráda

"Annals of the Famine in Ireland in 1847, 1848 and 1849"
Asenath Nicholson

"Sable Wings Over the Lane"
Ciarán Ó Murchadha

"The Great Irish Potato Famine"
James S Donnelly Jnr

"The Workhouses of Ireland: The Fate of Ireland's Poor"

John O'Connor

"The Lost Children – A Study of Charity Children in Ireland 1700 – 1900"
Joseph Robins

"Oceans of Consolation: Personal Accounts of Irish Migration to Australia"
David Fitzpatrick

"The Hunger: The Diary of Phyllis McCormack, Ireland 1845 – 1847"
Carol Drinkwater

"The Irish Bridget: Irish Immigrant Women in Domestic Service in America, 1840 – 1930"
Margaret Lynch-Brennan

"The Irish Way: Becoming American in the Multiethnic City"
James R Barrett

"97 Orchard: An Edible History of Five Immigrant Families in One New York Tenement"
Jane Ziegalman

Thanks and Acknowledgements

As I always say at this point, the end point of any and every book is the product of many people, not just me as the writer.

Therefore, I owe a huge debt of gratitude to my first readers, Rose and to Carol McCullough in Australia. Carol checked the Australian portion to the novel, to ensure my historical accuracy. In the United States my cousin, Joanne Dillon checked out many historical issues for me in the history of the USA. Joanne and I are DNA cousins. We haven't managed to work out where we meet up on our respective trees yet, but we've been trying for three years now, and it was great to meet up with her when I visited New York and Manhattan earlier this year to research the US portion of this novel.

I must also thank the lovely people of Kilrush, many of whom and met and chatted to during my visit there.

I am not technically adept, so I need what is now my lovely team, to turn my manuscript into a 'proper' book.

The cover is created by Alison Morgan, of Ali-Cat Designs. Ali has created all of my covers for both series.

The book is copy edited and proof read by Rose and by Ellen Morrow. Between them they ensure that not only is my grammar and punctuation as it should be but also that characters, places and dates are consistent. This time, in one particular section of the book I got the time zones the wrong way round. Well spotted Ellen, and much re-writing needed.

As always, my family continues to encourage me, to keep going. Tea and sympathy is abundant, and much needed.

Thank You for Reading This Book!

If you have enjoyed it, please leave feedback on Amazon and/or Goodreads. If there's anything I've missed, or if you have questions about any aspect of it, please leave a message on my website: www.mkjonesauthor.com

In addition to the website I have a dedicated Facebook page, plus Instagram and Threads. You'll find them all under mkjonesauthor.

And if you can't wait to catch up with the stories of other cases the Maze Investigations team tackle between the books, I send out a regular newsletter, each containing a "Maze Report". These are available when you sign up for the newsletter on my website. You will immediately receive two as a thanks for signing up:

'The Missing Air Raid Warden 1941'

And

'Murder in the Family 1840s'

Have You Tried My New Series?

It's called 'The Curiosity Club of St Foy".

There are two books in the series so far, with the third in production. The first two are available at Amazon, in both Kindle and paperback versions.

This is the first in the series:

Printed in Great Britain
by Amazon

31323540R10166